"Menocal's looking for you, Bobby." He spoke quietly, trying not to patronize her, thinking, after all, there were things she would send him away for saying. "The other day at my place—he missed you by a few minutes."

"I'm safe here," she replied impatiently.

"Nobody's safe here!" Jack exclaimed, willing himself not to grip her shoulders. "Don't you understand? There's no *front line* in this war. And *you're* not safe anywhere in Cuba." He started to pace in front of the fireplace, trying to use up some of his nervous energy. "He's gotta be watching the airports. Look, I know a guy who's got boats. He can—"

"Boats?" she asked, bewildered. "What are you saying?"

His voice dropped to an urgent whisper. "I'm saying you need to get out of Cuba. Now."

ROBERT REDFORD   LENA OLIN

HAVANA

A SYDNEY POLLACK FILM

UNIVERSAL PICTURES PRESENTS A MIRAGE PRODUCTION

ROBERT REDFORD LENA OLIN "HAVANA" ALAN ARKIN

MUSIC BY DAVE GRUSIN COSTUME DESIGNER BERNIE POLLACK

EDITED BY FREDRIC STEINKAMP AND WILLIAM STEINKAMP PRODUCTION DESIGNER TERENCE MARSH

DIRECTOR OF PHOTOGRAPHY OWEN ROIZMAN, A.S.C. EXECUTIVE PRODUCER RONALD L. SCHWARY

STORY BY JUDITH RASCOE SCREENPLAY BY JUDITH RASCOE AND DAVID RAYFIEL

PRODUCED BY SYDNEY POLLACK AND RICHARD ROTH

DIRECTED BY SYDNEY POLLACK

A UNIVERSAL RELEASE

HAVANA

A novel by
Paul Monette

Based on a screenplay
by Judith Rascoe and David Rayfiel

Story by
Judith Rascoe

ARROW BOOKS

Arrow Books Limited
20 Vauxhall Bridge Road, London SW1V 2SA

An imprint of Random Century Group

London Melbourne Sydney Auckland Johannesburg
and agencies throughout the world

First published in Great Britain in 1991
by Arrow Books

Manufactured in the United States of America

ISBN 0 09 984340 4

In Memory of my Mother
1923–1990
brave lady

This belief is called "maturity of chances," and I wish I had a dollar for every gambler it has busted. It is sheer nonsense, and here is why: The dice have no memory.

—NICK THE GREEK

THE TROPICAL MOONLIGHT, banana yellow, was dashed to smithereens on the softly rolling waves. Here in the mid-Caribbean, a faint sweetness always rode the breeze, a mix of lemon blossoms and burned sugar. The perfumed air proved you were never far from an island. They were flung across this southern water like so many emeralds squandered in the sun, and always the promise that the next island would truly be unspoiled and virgin, fit for Robinson Crusoe.

Yet this particular ocean lane, overnight from Key West to Havana, was busy as a highway. The big-bellied ferry boat lumbering through the soft swell, churning a wake that glowed like snow in the moonlight, made the passage twice a day. *Suzi,* she was called, a hooker's name, stenciled in rusting letters on either side of her bow. *Suzi* had none of the airs of a four-masted schooner, the tall ships that had plied these waters like a dream since the days of Columbus. The vast, creaking ferry boat had no time for the romance of the sea. It moved like an ox, plowing the waves. The only thing on its mind was getting there.

From somewhere inside, cheap music floated out over the decks, gaudy and yet sentimental—a cha-cha version of "Jingle Bells." It was only a week short of Christmas, and the ferry was full of tourists looking for something a little more exotic than turkey and pumpkin pie. And lots of Cubans going home for the holidays, a Christmas Mass in a tiny parish church at the edge of a cane field. The ship's band segued to "Rudolph the Red-Nosed Reindeer," without a break in the cha-cha rhythm.

Suzi's voyage hadn't changed in thirty years, back and forth from Key West to Havana. But the island it was heading for was not the same at all, this Christmas of 1958. Under that yellow tropical moon, Cuba sprawled like a sleeping giant, twitching restlessly. On a hundred hills stood solitary soldiers, cradling machine guns in their arms. Deep in the jungle, a guerrilla's hand worked at the dial on a radio transmitter. He mumbled under his breath, as if the monkeys perched above him in the trees were spies.

In Havana, a mansion fit for a president glittered with a party that would go all night. Tuxedos and Paris ballgowns. Ropes and ropes of pearls. Ceiling fans moved the humid air, as elegant colonels in starched and braided uniforms mingled among the dazzling guests. The buffet table groaned with delicacies shipped in from New York and Miami.

Nobody here had anything to do with the man running frantically up the street, just a few blocks away, pursued by an olive-green car with tinted windows. No one at the party would even hear the burst of gunfire as the terrified man was riddled with bullets and slumped in the gutter, lifeless. In Havana in 1958 the first order of business was not to spoil the party. You learned not to hear the gunfire. You learned how to drown it out with laughter.

And so the ferry swayed its way across the moonlit water, heading for a lush and tropic land that still looked like a travel poster—half jungle and half casino. And ready to explode.

In the ship's lounge a small combo was playing, shifting lightheartedly from cha-cha to samba and back again. On the smoky circle of dance floor, a jostling crowd of Cuban and American couples mixed easily, charging the place with a party atmosphere, as if it was already New Year's Eve. They were two and three deep at the bar, ordering rounds of rum and Coke and negronis. The evening dresses weren't from Paris, but some of the women were sleekly gorgeous, ravishing as any models. For them the bar on the *Suzi* was like a practice run before the big casinos of Havana.

In the midst of the crowd, commanding a ringside table by the dance floor, was an American tourist family right out of a Norman Rockwell painting. The grinning father, sweat streaming down his cheeks, sported a Harry Truman aloha shirt, and his pink blond wife wore a bright green sundress. Four children, two of them toddlers, whined around them, the youngest nodding to sleep on his father's shoulder. The table was heaped with dolls and teddy bears. They all looked exhausted and yet grimly determined to enjoy every minute of their vacation.

And down below, in the bowels of the ship, a hundred cars were lined up in tight rows, big Chryslers and Caddies cheek by jowl with battered pickup trucks. Two large men with powerful flashlights inched from vehicle to vehicle, illuminating license plates from Florida, New York, Nevada. Methodically the two men inspected, stopping here and there to lift a hood or tap a fender.

A big-shouldered Buick with ducktail fins sported yellow Cuban plates. One of the men crouched down and slid under the chassis, shining his light around the axles. Nothing there. He grunted with impatience.

Up in the captain's quarters, behind the wheelhouse, Captain Potts, the skipper of the *Suzi,* rolled a fat cigar from one side of his mouth to the other. His eyes were sharp and glittering, as if he were studying a course through enemy waters. In fact, he was staring at a poker hand. At that moment he could have cared less if the *Suzi* was about to run aground. Let the first mate take care of all that. *This* was serious business.

"Check," said Potts around his cigar. He looked up with an impassive smile, as serene as if he commanded the *Queen Mary*.

Across the table a pair of rugged but manicured hands were motionless for a moment. One hand held a smoldering

Pall Mall with a half-inch ash. The other held a fan of five cards, lightly, without any tension at all. An elegant voice said very precisely, "Raise you ten."

Captain Potts could scarcely conceal his satisfaction. His own hands quivered, and his cards seemed sticky. "Ten and raise you twenty," he retorted coolly.

Back to the man with the Pall Mall, who lifted the cigarette now and gave it a languorous puff. The face was gruffly handsome, but there was a sort of arrogant indifference about his rugged good looks. He had the sun-blond hair of an athlete, the steel-blue eyes of a marksman. A sharp dresser—too sharp for some tastes. Beige silk jacket, black matte shirt, the checkerboard tie almost too flashy. It was the fastidiousness that kept it all in check, an insistence on top quality peculiar to those who've known lean times.

Jack Weil gave the captain a slow smile. In certain lights that face could look as if it had done a lot of hard living, but the smile was always ready, boyish and cocky and very seductive. At first sight some people figured Jack Weil to be a landed duke, with fifty generations in his blood. Other people pegged him as a mercenary, a soldier of fortune, even a spy. But it was very hard to see through that smile. The serious thoughts of Jack Weil were nobody's business.

"You guys know something I don't?" observed Jack, enjoying himself immensely. He looked casually around the table, from the captain to Billy the dealer, then to the red-faced Haitian, Pierre. "Raise you twenty-five," he said, almost like an apology.

Potts's eyes flickered. He stared hard at his sweaty cards again, disconcerted. Billy, who'd already folded, looked at him with a sort of pity. Then, suddenly, a loud knocking on the door. "Who the hell . . . ?" the captain boomed with furious agitation. "Come in," he barked, as if it was a dare.

It was Gomez, the second mate, agitated and spooked. "Sorry, Captain," he said, "but the bar boy, he saw a couple guys down in the hull, breakin' into the cars—"

"Wait a minute," Potts snarled in reply. Then turned to Jack, "What was your bet, pal?"

4

Jack's smile broadened perceptibly. His hand with the cards never moved, and he never looked down at it. "I said I'll see you and raise you fifty."

Gomez looked as if he would burst. "Captain, I told 'em they can't do that. But they say they're SIM, and so . . .'' The second mate shrugged, nothing further to say. SIM— Batista's secret police, what they called the Cuban SS— SIM guys did what they wanted.

Potts acted like he didn't hear. He looked over nervously at the cards in Jack's hand, as if they'd been dealt from a different deck. "Fifty?" he repeated hollowly.

"Take your time, Captain," Jack drawled, turning his lazy smile on Gomez.

Potts had had it. "Chrissake," he growled. "I'll call."

He dropped his hand on the table, the cards slightly curled from the tension of his grip. Full house: kings over nines. Potts gave a bark of laughter as the other men around the table murmured their applause. All but Jack. As Potts reached out for the kitty, three or four hundred dollars in the pile, Jack laid down the fan of his cards effortlessly. Four deuces.

Angrily Potts stood up from the table, backing off the gamblers who'd been watching the showdown with Weil. For a moment his face was so twisted with rage, it looked as if he might grab for a weapon. But Jack Weil never wavered, quietly gathering in his winnings and neatly stacking the bills in a pile. "I'll be right back," the captain growled curtly, shoving the second mate's shoulder and following him out.

Pierre the Haitian reached for the rum on the captain's desk. "What the hell is SIM?" he asked.

The Cubans in the room looked at him as if he were the last innocent man. Then one of them said tonelessly, "Military intelligence."

"They got no jurisdiction here," Billy observed stubbornly as he shuffled the cards. "This is an American ship. Ain't that right, Jack?"

Jack Weil hardly seemed to hear the question as he continued to neaten his pile of winnings. Then he spoke softly, more to himself than to Billy. "I wouldn't know anything about it," he said. "One thing I like about poker, there's no politics." He turned his slow smile on Billy. "Just me and the cards. Nobody has to salute the flag."

Potts stood by the boomerang bar in the ship's lounge, head held high, looking for once like an officer, even if the ship he commanded was a rusty tub. "Registered in Miami, gentlemen," he announced proudly. "And as far as you're concerned, we're standing on American soil!"

A dress-white admiral couldn't have said it better. Yet the two men he was addressing, hulking before him in mob suits and dark glasses, were utterly bored and indifferent. These were the goons with the flashlights who'd been nosing around in the hull. The sneers they sported were just short of laughing right in the captain's face.

"Car deck's off limits except to the crew," Potts continued gruffly. "Unless you can show me some kind of search warrant, I'm reporting you to the U.S. embassy as soon as we get to Havana."

The two men glanced at each other. Then the taller one did the honors, drawing a wallet from the inside pocket of his suit and flipping it open. Gomez was right. In cold black-and-white the ID revealed its bearer to be a lieutenant of the Cuban secret police. Batista's gestapo.

"There are arms on this ship, Captain," declared the SIM agent coldly. "Maybe we can save you the trouble of a full search in port. That could take days—right, Edouardo?" He grinned icily at his companion.

Potts stood his ground. "Have you *found* arms on this ship?" he demanded.

The one called Edouardo pulled a white handkerchief from his pocket. Unwrapping it, he revealed a pistol. "In the glove compartment of one of your cars, señor," he said, the last word mocking, refusing to call him Captain.

The tall one opened a greasy notebook and showed an entry to Potts, a license number. He shrugged. "So you see,

Captain, we have the evidence. We may have to detain your fine ship in Havana."

"For one pistol!" Potts was apoplectic. "You can't do that."

The passengers were now beginning to cluster around the bar, drawn by the commotion. The cha-cha combo fell silent as the dancers dispersed from the floor. The gamblers from the captain's cabin had slipped in through the wheelhouse door, Jack Weil among them. Everyone watched the captain in his face-off with the agent, whose cold superiority indicated he could do exactly what he pleased.

Everyone but Jack. His squinting eyes scanned the crowd instead, carefully examining each passenger. The SIM agent issued his formal challenge to the captain, "We've been advised there is contraband on board this ship." And Jack's gaze moved from face to face, cagy as a blackjack dealer, trying to figure out who owned the pistol.

He suddenly locked eyes with a portly, middle-aged man at the end of the bar, a Cuban in a rumpled business suit. The man was clearly terrified. Now, as he squirmed in the steely tension of Jack Weil's pitiless stare, he looked as if he'd jump right out of his skin. Coolly and instantaneously, Jack appraised his frightened prey: the gold watch, the Italian shoes. Then he turned abruptly on his heel and marched over to the captain and the pair of agents.

"It's mine," said Jack Weil calmly, smiling as if he still held four deuces.

"This is your car?" demanded the taller agent, holding out his ratty notebook.

Jack peered down at the scrawl of numbers, then shook his head. "I'm afraid you copied the wrong plate, amigo. But that's definitely my gun. Is there a problem? 'Cause I got a permit right here." He reached into his jacket pocket, ready to pull out his billfold.

The SIM agent slapped his notebook closed, irritated at the mix-up. He drew himself up pugnaciously and addressed the gambler. "It is prohibited to bring weapons of any kind into Cuba, señor. There is no such thing as a permit."

Jack glanced nervously at the crowd around them, as if he were embarrassed. The captain, who'd just lost three hands in a row to Jack, struggled not to grin with relief. The rumpled businessman at the end of the bar looked totally confused. "Excuse me," Jack offered apologetically, "can we talk about this outside?" Then to Potts, "Sorry about all the fuss, Captain. I'm sure I can clear up this whole misunderstanding."

Graciously, suave as a duke, Jack nodded his head to the two SIM agents. Somehow he managed to make both men feel very, very important. They moved to either side of the gambler and walked with him toward the double doors to the main deck. As the three slipped out, the combo scrambled to play again, a "Frosty the Snowman" samba. The relief in the lounge was palpable as the dancers moved once again onto the floor.

And at the other end of the boomerang bar, a woman sat in the shadows under a crepe paper palm. She was stunningly attractive in a white silk blouse and shantung skirt, sultry and sloe-eyed, her full lips cherry red with rouge. Her flawless features smoldered with passion, and yet there was something distant there, detached from the tinsel and cheap music of the ship's lounge. She might have been sitting on the veranda of a vast plantation. Perhaps she was thirty, and yet there was something older in her eyes. Nobody would have called her innocent.

She tossed the shivering mane of her hair, auburn shot with gold, and lifted her sweating glass from the bar. She took a desultory sip of iced coffee. She didn't seem at all worried that it would keep her awake. Maybe she was just a rich lady from Palm Beach, a couple of divorces behind her, headed for an amusing weekend with friends in Havana. Her looks were too much of a shield for anyone to know for sure what the story was.

She hadn't missed a moment of the exchange between Jack and the Cuban agents. From the moment the three men left the lounge, the look in her green-gold eyes grew ever so slightly anxious, but you would have had to be staring deep to see it.

"Mrs. Duran?"

Startled, the woman turned. A man in his fifties was leaning toward her with an amiable smile. His Brooks Brothers summer blazer was slightly seedy, and yet he exuded the relaxed breeding of Exeter and Yale. "Marion Chigwell," he said, introducing himself with a purr of self-deprecation. "We met the last time I was in Havana. At Nettie Greenfield's?" He grinned hopefully.

"Of course," said Bobby Duran vaguely, remembering nothing of the sort. "Hello," she added lamely, and yet there was nothing cold or aloof about her. She was a woman cursed with too much kindness, without the skill of cutting people dead.

"I'm writing an article," said Chigwell proudly, "for *Gourmet* magazine. Cuisine of the Caribbean." He rolled his eyes at the ceiling, as if even he found the whole thing silly. There was something oppressively overbearing in his fawning good cheer.

"Really?" she replied distractedly.

"Yes, and I was wondering—" He was eager as a golden retriever. "I understand your mother-in-law has the best cook in Cuba." His oily talent for ingratiation was running full throttle.

Bobby looked gravely at him. "What will happen to that man?" she asked, as if she'd heard nothing he said. And when he looked bewildered, she added impatiently, "The one who owned the gun."

Chigwell made a blustering sound as he tried to switch gears. "Well, I expect they're probably giving him a very hard time," he said, laughing idiotically. "Never pays to have too much to do with the secret police. Can I buy you a drink?"

Bobby Duran slipped off the bar stool. "Excuse me," she said, not impolitely, and managed to move around Marion Chigwell without brushing up against him, though the space was tight. She crossed the smoky dance floor toward the double doors that led out on deck, her movements languid and easy, unhurried. She betrayed neither anxiety nor tension, which proved what a good actress she was. To look at her, she was just another beautiful woman, pure and simple.

On the aft deck of the ferry, beside a coiled mound of anchor chain, Jack Weil faced the two SIM agents as they bent to examine his papers. The tall one squinted at his passport while Edouardo held his Cuban visa up to the light, making sure it hadn't been forged. Jack seemed almost amused by their earnest officiousness. He certainly didn't look worried. He slouched with his hands in his jacket pockets, softly kicking the toe of one shoe against the rusty chain.

"Is no joke, my friend," observed the tall one, taking the visa from his partner and slipping it back in Jack's passport. "Is a very serious offense, to smuggle a gun in. If you were a Cuban citizen, you would go to jail for many years."

"I see no permit," declared Edouardo, jutting his chin pugnaciously.

Jack smiled. "Maybe I got it here," he murmured smoothly, reaching a hand to his inside jacket pocket. Instantly Edouardo had drawn his gun, pointing it at the gambler's skull. Unruffled, Jack made a pacifying gesture, then withdrew his hand, clutching a roll of bills. "Maybe I need a new permit," he said.

Calmly he peeled off several bills, one hundred dollars in twenties. He held it out to the taller agent, who took the bribe without batting an eye, giving over Jack's passport in return. "Now that I'm legal," Jack declared dryly, "can I please have my gun back?"

The agent slipped the pistol out of his pocket, grinning as he held it out. Jack reached for it. Then, with a lightning flick, the agent tossed it over the rail. "Sorry, señor," he said, "we are no longer issuing permits."

With a sniff of superiority he walked away, followed by

Edouardo. Jack smiled after them, seemingly unperturbed, even with a certain appreciation of their style. He took a deep breath of the balmy ocean breeze, then turned and headed back for the lounge. For a man so alert, blessed with a radar honed by a thousand dangerous games, it was surprising that he didn't notice the figure in the shadow of the Number 4 lifeboat. The luminous white silk blouse should have given her away.

But he passed within a few feet of her, unseeing. The night breeze blew her perfume the other way. Jack grabbed the half-moon handles of the double doors and pulled them open, reentering the lounge as suavely as if it was a casino at Monte Carlo.

He paused just inside and lit a cigarette. The dance floor was crowded, three or four couples half in the bag trying to pull together a straggling conga line. The American tourist family slumped against one another at their ringside table, more asleep than awake. It was beginning to look like an all-night dance marathon, as if these jostling couples had to get the partying out of their systems before they reached Havana. A low-level desperation seemed to keep them going, more urgent than the cha-cha beat of the *Suzi*'s third-rate combo.

Jack crossed to the boomerang bar and ordered himself an *anejo*. He didn't bother to look around, appearing quite content to be left alone. The men he'd been gambling with in the captain's quarters had either run out of cash or luck. No one approached him to start another game.

And after a long moment the lounge doors swung open again, and Bobby Duran slipped in. If she was aware of the men who watched her move around the dance floor to the bar, she didn't show it. A woman of her ilk was accustomed to being stared at, after all. She only noticed the one who didn't appear to see her.

She skirted around to the far end of the bar, resuming her place beneath the crepe-paper palm. Now she was sitting directly opposite Jack Weil, who stirred his drink idly and read the labels on the line of rum bottles under the bar mirror. Bobby turned to the slightly disheveled figure beside her, who happened to be scribbling in a notebook. "So," she drawled, "tell me about your article."

Marion Chigwell looked up, startled, his face flushing red with delight to see that she had returned. He scooped the shaggy hair out of his eyes and made a sort of bow, panting again just like a retriever. He snatched his tall glass from the bar and eagerly offered it. "See if you like this," he blurted enthusiastically.

Delicately she took the glass, raised it to her lips, and sipped, barely a drop. She shook her hair and laughed, at herself as much as anything. "I'm crazy about it," she said, returning the glass to Chigwell with a small bow of her own.

"A pinch of ground coffee!" exclaimed the journalist. Then, grandly, he snapped his fingers to summon the hulking bartender. "Another for the lady, *por favor*."

She laughed again, the kind of sound that would have driven certain men crazy just to make her happy. Her eyes kept glancing across the bar at the gambler, but she never stared. The dancing was growing more raucous, the conga line swelling to fifteen or twenty. Suddenly Jack Weil pushed his stool back and darted a look toward the band. The rumpled businessman with the gold watch and the lizard shoes shrank from the laser intensity of Jack's gaze.

Jack gave him a barely perceptible nod and then headed directly for the bathrooms.

"How often do you get back to the States?" asked Chigwell, bending closer to Bobby. Yet there was no sexual tension here, nothing for her to recoil from. The man was only fawning.

"Not very often," she replied vaguely, her eyes on the door of the men's room where the gambler had disappeared. A moment later the businessman followed him, casting a nervous glance around the lounge as he went. Then the bartender set the tall drink in front of Bobby Duran, and she looked at it with a faint curl of distaste at the corner of her mouth.

"Just to go shopping, huh?" Chigwell asked brightly.

She blinked at him as if she'd never seen him before, then gave him a blank nod. She seemed like a woman who'd spent her life fleeing from such banalities.

And across the way in the men's room the gambler moved methodically from stall to stall, batting open the doors to make sure the place was empty. By the sinks stood the Cuban, shuffling nervously, not sure exactly what he was getting into. "Sir, I'm very grateful, of course," he began as Jack Weil turned to face him. "But may I ask why—"

"Three hundred," said the gambler curtly.

"I beg your pardon," retorted the other, sticking to a measured tone of elaborate formality. They were both of them gentlemen, surely.

Jack held up three fingers, giving a mischievous wink. Charming as ever, but no room for bullshit.

"Fuck," retorted the Cuban, abandoning all gentility now. "That's a lot of money, señor."

"Make that four."

The Cuban went beet red. "You just said three!"

Jack Weil made a clucking sound, heavy with disappointment. "My friend, I'm afraid you're beginning to sound ungrateful."

"Three fifty," pleaded the Cuban.

The gambler shook his head. "I'm afraid we're up to five now, amigo."

The wilted Cuban looked as if he would burst with exasperation. His hands shook as he reached out to Jack, trying to make the price stop going up. Then the door to the men's room swung open, and Edouardo the agent came clumping in, heading for one of the urinals. The Cuban went white at the sight of him and made a frantic gesture of surrender to Jack.

"Okay," he whispered pleadingly. "Okay, okay." Like a man caving in to water torture. He all but clutched at the gambler's jacket as Jack nodded briskly and led the way out. The Cuban's terror was real. The last thing he wanted in all the world was to be left alone in a squalid room with a SIM agent.

As they came out into the smoky lounge, the Cuban shoved a slew of bills into Jack's hand. The gambler stuffed the money into his pocket without even counting. "Nice doing business with you, pal," said Jack, and began to amble away.

"Wait a minute," protested the Cuban. "Where's my gun?"

Jack snapped his fingers. "Oh, didn't I tell you about that? The SIM goons fed it to the fish. Better luck next time, huh?"

Across the dance floor, at the far end of the bar, Bobby Duran went taut at the sight of Jack Weil. Her eyes blazed with intensity. The slow-witted WASP beside her continued to chatter amiably, not picking up on her mood swing. "Why don't you tell me what the secret is?" he asked in a tone of high drama.

"The secret?" Bobby repeated softly. "Of course. It's not parsley at all. He does it with fresh cilantro."

Chigwell gave a small gasp of delight, bending to scribble the secret down with furious concentration. He was as happy as if he'd uncovered a scandal that would bring governments tumbling down. Once more Bobby stood up from the stool beside him. "Would you excuse me again," she said pleasantly, and by now she had managed to charm him so, he wouldn't have dreamed of protesting.

Weil was standing idly at the edge of the dance floor, looking more than a little self-satisfied. He hadn't lost a single hand in the captain's cabin, and now he'd pocketed the extra bonus of the gun transaction. A very good night. He didn't even notice the elegant woman floating toward him from the bar. All of a sudden she was standing in front of him, raising her arms and trying to be very, very casual. "Dance, sailor?" she asked, almost teasing.

For a split second his face lost all expression, as if he couldn't quite believe he hadn't noticed her yet. He wasn't accustomed to being thrown by beautiful women—by *any* woman. But what he saw right away was that her casual smile was forced, and she couldn't sustain it. In fact, he had the most curious intuition that underneath the smile all she wanted to do was cry. In the next moment he glided an arm around her, and they were dancing.

"You seem so surprised," she said with an airy toss of her head. "Don't women ever ask you to dance?"

"The ones who do," Jack replied, "find it a lot easier than you did."

His eyes, fixed on her face, were as blue as the sea around a desert island. She turned her head away from the nakedness of his gaze, but her body was quick under his hand—she was a wonderful dancer. The samba hissed all around them, beckoning them like a hot Havana nightclub. They swayed and dipped, in perfect sync. Nothing had to be said right now, and yet she murmured softly against his shoulder.

"What?" he asked, bending an ear close to the thrill of her lips.

"I said . . . all that fuss over one little gun."

"Oh." He seemed to need to shift gears, as if they had gotten too close too fast. She wanted some small talk. "They said they got a tip."

"Is that the end of it, do you think?"

He could feel the tension in her shoulder blades, tight beneath the sensuous ripple of the white silk blouse. He could hear the pleading in her voice, and it made him feel curiously helpless. "The end of what?"

"The searching," she replied with a shiver of anxiety. It was as if there was someone searching for her.

Gently he lifted her chin so she couldn't look away. "Probably not," he said. "Why? You bringing in something you shouldn't?"

Her eyes flickered briefly like a trapped animal's. Then she shrugged indifferently, affecting the terminal boredom of a Palm Beach wife. "Just some perfume."

Jack chuckled. "I don't think you got anything to worry about. You can only smuggle that in the *other* way." He meant that Havana was a free port and Florida a duty port. His laughter seemed to indicate that she would make a lousy smuggler. "Smells real dangerous, though," he added, bending his head to the curve of her neck and drinking her in.

They swayed again silently, just a beat slower than the music, their pace unhurried. The other couples moving around them seemed to be dancing to some other music, cheaper somehow. She drew in her breath to speak, but then hesitated. He wanted to fold her deeper into his arms and tell her it was all right, she could trust him. And yet he waited, keeping his own slight distance, perhaps because he didn't quite believe the part about the trust.

Finally she spoke, haltingly. "It wasn't your gun, was it?"

Now he could see it coming, what she wanted from him. Abruptly he stopped dancing, so that the two of them were suddenly still in the midst of the swaying couples. She looked at him questioningly. His gaze had turned hard, a gambler who knew when to fold. "You'll have to excuse me, miss," he said, his courtliness unfailing, despite his wish to bolt. "I've got some friends waiting," he added, nodding vaguely toward the bar. He made a move to walk her off the dance floor.

She stood her ground and said with a certain defiance, "Five hundred dollars."

He looked at her and waited a beat before he answered. "No thanks," he replied, but he shouldn't have waited.

Her eyes flared with passion. "I haven't even told you what—"

"Let me guess," said Jack, cutting her off. "When we get to Havana, you're supposed to drive your car off the boat. Only it's developed a slight problem—too much weight on the axles." She was dead silent, stopped cold. "And for some reason," Jack went on, "you've got the idea that I'm some kind of mechanic. Isn't that right?"

She couldn't bear to keep looking into his eyes. She cast her own aside, looking bitterly toward the jaunty combo.

He took a firm grip on her arm and led her off the dance floor. She went without protest, a desolate slump to her shoulders. But instead of leading her back to the bar, he moved them toward the double doors and out on deck. As the doors closed behind them she stiffened. There was fight in her still, and a fierce pride.

He let her go and gently shook his head. "You can't be doing this for a living," he observed dryly. "You're too lousy at it." She looked out over the ship's rail, wrapping her arms about her, ignoring the sarcasm. His brows furrowed as he struggled to get a fix on her. Tentatively he asked, "Do people know you in Havana?"

"I live there," Bobby Duran replied carefully. "Listen, I'll pay whatever it takes. Eight hundred dollars." Then, as if the deal was already struck, she opened the buff-colored shoulder bag and drew out a ring of keys. She held them out toward him, a look of defiance in the set of her mouth. It was almost a dare.

He looked at her for a long moment, the cool silver of the moonlight casting its glow on the tumble of her hair. The night breeze was sweet with her lily perfume. She looked as if she could wait all night for him to decide. And he found himself saying in spite of himself, "You got the registration?"

She rooted through her bag and drew out an envelope thick with papers. She passed it over along with the keys. Jack hefted them in his hand, as if trying to weigh how far he was going to take this thing. He was a man who wasn't used to surprising himself: it was the other guy who usually got surprised. He tucked the envelope in the breast pocket of his sport jacket and dropped the keys in his pants, fishing out his own keys. He shook these in his fist like a pair of dice, smiling at Bobby, then opened his palm and let her take them.

"Why am I doing this?" he asked playfully, but not really as if he expected an answer.

She'd already pulled out a billfold and was counting out hundreds from one hand to the other. Implicitly her answer seemed to be that he was doing it for the money, pure and simple. Maybe so. She certainly didn't give off any air of disapproval as to his motives. Perhaps in her own way she was glad to strike a simple deal, because in Havana nothing was simple anymore.

When she had counted out eight bills, she folded them neatly in half and moved to hand over the money. Jack cocked his head and grinned, as if she would never learn. "The way it works," he declared, "is half now, half later. That way I'm less likely to run away with your . . . perfume."

Serious as a child, determined to get the rules straight, she took back four of the bills and stuffed them in her purse. Gravely she offered Jack the rest, and he took it with a sober nod, somehow not wanting to laugh at her anymore because it rattled her.

"The Lido," he said quietly.

She looked confused, and even more beautiful. "I beg your pardon?"

"That's where I'll take your car."

"Of course." She shook her hair and lifted her chin, affecting a pose that worked in the moonlight. "Why don't we say we'll meet at the casino at ten, for . . ." Her voice faltered.

"The payoff," Jack replied with a short nod, as courtly as Chigwell.

"Good night then." She smiled, relieved it was over. As she turned toward the double doors again the breeze lifted the curl at her shoulder, blowing back her hair to reveal a bloodred ruby drop earring swaying against her long neck. Jack let her cover the three paces to the doors and reach for the handle before he spoke. He seemed to want it this way, to call her back at the last second.

"You planning to tell me what kind of car?" he asked. "Or should I try them all?"

She had already opened the door—half in, half out. "A white Town and Country," she said, the smoke billowing round her as it tumbled out of the lounge, making her look like a sea nymph lost in mist.

"Mine's a green Cadillac. Convertible."

Bobby Duran permitted herself a moment of small revenge. Her tongue flicked out and grazed her upper lip. "Naturally," she observed with brisk irony, a brief playful smile lighting up her face. And then she retreated into the lounge, letting the door swing shut behind her.

Jack Weil crossed in her wake and peered through the porthole window in the door. The honey of her perfume still permeated the night air. He watched her move around the dance floor, heading once more for the bar. The dogged Chigwell stood up from his stool, wagging to welcome her back.

Jack's eyes moved restlessly, surveying the tawdry room. He saw the Cuban businessman, dancing close with a woman who was spilling out of her strapless dress. He saw Billy the dealer, swaying drunk by the door to the wheelhouse. In the corner he saw the two SIM agents, opaque behind their dark glasses, standing sullen on either side of a post.

But Jack didn't care about any of them. He was looking for something quite specific as he coolly examined the passengers one by one. He was just like the eye of fate, scanning them all without any judgment. And then he smiled, his gaze settling on the gaudy tourist family slumped around the ringside table, way past their bedtime. The Harry Truman shirt and the pink blond wife and the brood of kids with their stuffed toys. Just what he was looking for.

Except for that smile of satisfaction, you couldn't have said what the gambler was thinking. From here on in he was very busy, much too busy to think. He made his way midship and disappeared through a door marked CREW ONLY. He descended a spiral stair to the vast hold where the cars were parked. He retrieved a flashlight from the Caddy and made his methodical rounds till he found the white Town and Country.

He unlocked the driver's door and climbed in. Slowly he shone the beam around, settling at last on the passenger's door. He crawled over and pried at the door panel. It came away easily in his hand, making him sneer audibly at how obvious the work was here. In the hollow behind the door panel were several bundles wrapped in oilcloth, bound with electrical tape.

Jack heaved himself out of Bobby's car and started roaming again, swinging his flashlight back and forth as he went up the line. All of a sudden he froze the light on a battered, wood-sided station wagon. He moved to examine it closer. The dusty windows were plastered with vacation stickers from the Luray Caverns to Mount Rushmore. Bending to shine the light in, Jack saw a baby's rattle lying on the back floor, surrounded by a chaos of toys and puzzles and children's clothes. He moved around to the back window, which was open a bare crack. Just enough for him to slip a hand in and release the back gate.

There was a nice hollow well under the rear floor, where the spare was stowed. Jack grinned with satisfaction, a man whose luck was holding nicely, who'd already had four-of-a-kind tonight. He still had a lot of work to do, transferring the bundles from the Town and Country, but he didn't seem worried in the least. Though he'd protested as much to Bobby, it turned out he really was a terrific mechanic.

Yet as he threaded his way back to her car, smiling to himself, you still couldn't have said what he was thinking. Of course it didn't do for a man to think too much, not in the middle of a poker hand. One thing was sure: He was getting his hands dirty for once. Grime from the station wagon, grease from the bundles in Bobby's car. And yet he continued to smile as if the whole deal was an elaborate joke, something he'd gotten into for the hell of it.

As if it meant nothing personal at all.

II

THE MORNING SUN was already steaming yellow as the *Suzi* lumbered into the port of chaos called Havana. The teeming docks were choked with trade, some of it even legal: rusty trucks spewing exhaust, donkey carts, and jitney cabs honking their way along the garbage-strewn quays. Crowds of people pushed every which way—sailors and old wizened fishermen, officials of every stripe, pirates and confidence men, and always on the fringe a few desperate types, looking for any way out.

Bracketing the port were the ancient fortifications of another age, massive stone walls that jutted out into the water, once the perch of conquistadores. The scabrous buildings that huddled in the lee of those walls had been crawling with rats for centuries, and still they were open for business, always a new breed of merchant. Rising behind the brute structures on the docks were the Spanish streets of the eighteenth century, peeling stucco and cast-iron balconies looking down on narrow cobbled streets. Life was cheap and brutal here, and yet the tourists still managed to find it quaint and charming.

In turn, the crooked streets of the Spanish port led uphill to the central city, grandiose with boulevards lined in decadent rococo. Here was the gilded age of Havana, Louis-Napoleon French, a courtesan in a ballgown and powdered wig, fanning herself in the tropical heat. Yet above even this Havana rose something even grander—the sprawling, big-shouldered hotels that looked straight out of Miami, scraping the humid Gulf Stream clouds.

A city of a million now, still commanding the shimmering Caribbean. Yet terrifying somehow, with its brutal contrast of delirious wealth and delirious poverty. Beggars and Cadillacs roamed the streets, jostling and striking sparks. The threat of explosion was everywhere. And nobody knew anymore which was the real Havana—the port as old as Columbus, the colonial outpost, the high-rise megalopolis. No one could hold it together anymore, so all the power was up for grabs.

The *Suzi* chugged through oil-slicked water, skirting a Dominican tanker that was off-loading arms. Stevedores stripped to their underpants hauled crates of ammunition up the pier to a line of idling trucks. Every few feet along the way, soldiers bearing machine guns watched the stevedores grimly, in case the half-naked workers should palm a single bullet. All the firepower was for the generalísimo and his army, not a drop to be wasted.

Just beyond the tanker, the *Suzi* socked into her ferry slip, churning against it like a bronco in a pen. On the wide asphalt of the dock the bleary morning crowd of passengers waited, ready to sail on the day-trip back to Key West. A long line of cars snaked between sawhorse barriers, waiting to replace the vehicles that would emerge when the ramp clanged open from the hull. On every side the dock was thick with police and customs officials, armed with carbines and pistols rather than machine guns, but just as ugly and pugnacious as the army on the adjacent pier. People got shoved around. Paranoia was the order of the day.

Inside the *Suzi*'s hull, on the automobile deck, a pair of loudspeakers drowned one another out, braying in English and Spanish. Jack Weil, looking none the worse for having no sleep, made his way through rows of American cars bristling with chrome and tail fins. He reached the white Town and Country and slipped into the driver's seat, never once turning his head to the right, where Bobby waited a few cars over in the green Cadillac. She kept her eyes straight ahead, both hands gripping the steering wheel.

The steel ramp yawned open like a drawbridge, and the first car headed off the ship and into the customs enclosure. Immediately it was surrounded by a squad of inspectors, one of them ordering the Cuban driver out of the car, waving his carbine. The line began to form behind, inching out of the ship, and the wave of inspectors strutted along, scribbling license-plate numbers and barking them into their walkie-talkies.

Two hundred yards away across the port, where the harbor road curved up past the old stone ramparts of the fort, a young man with a feeble mustache and spectacles stood looking down as the cars emerged from the *Suzi.* The young man paced nervously, watching the line move forward through the battery of customs men. Then he suddenly squinted. A green Cadillac convertible waited in line, Bobby Duran at the wheel. She tossed her luxuriant hair and slipped on a pair of dark glasses, leaning back as if she were bored.

"That's not the car," the young man exclaimed, slamming the flat of his hand on the hood of a rusty Buick parked on the curb beside him. Tomas, he was called. His compatriot, who had been lazing half-asleep in the Buick, perked up sharply and followed Tomas's pointing finger. "What the fuck's she doing in a Caddy?"

Ricardo swung open the door of the Buick and stepped out next to his friend, who continued to swear a blue streak. Ricardo was sleeker, more of a dandy than the scholarly Tomas. His hair was slicked back in a ducktail, and he sported the open-necked shirt of a gigolo. He was far too young for the gun that lumped under the shirt at his waist. Tensely he studied the green Cadillac as the customs men moved up to question Bobby Duran.

As Tomas kicked the Buick's front tire in frustration Ricardo put two fingers to his lips and let out a piercing whistle. Fifty yards up the road, a bearded man who was eating a guava beside his Vespa shot to attention. He tossed the husk of the fruit and leaped on his scooter, lurching along the cobbled roadway till he came up next to the two men beside the Buick.

"Find Arturo," Ricardo barked. "Tell him something must've happened. She's in the wrong car."

The man on the Vespa nodded, stiff as a salute, and veered in a sharp U-turn, speeding away from the harbor. Ricardo and Tomas were still riveted on the Caddy, watching helplessly as an inspector bent to question Bobby. Then just as suddenly it was over, and the starched inspector was waving her through. She pulled out in front of several other cars still being detained and made her way into the maelstrom of traffic.

"There it is!" shouted Tomas, grabbing his friend and gesticulating.

For now the Town and Country had emerged from the *Suzi*'s hold, a blond stranger at the wheel. Already the Cadillac was disappearing into the honking mob. Ricardo looked from one car to the other, struggling to decide which way to go. Then he snapped at Tomas, "We'll stay with her!" And the two men clambered back in the Buick and roared off downhill into the choking congestion of the port.

On the ferry dock the car directly in front of the Town and Country was waved through without even being stopped, perhaps a lucky relative of one of the inspectors. A customs man in a brown uniform beckoned Jack forward, then signaled him to stop. His partner with the walkie-talkie immediately began to move around the vehicle, barking the license-plate number and running a hand up under the fenders. The brown suit with his clipboard approached the driver's side and held out his hand for the papers, which Jack obligingly handed him.

The inspector glanced through the documents, then said, "Please get out of the car, señor."

Jack, obliging again, betrayed no anxiety as he stood facing the customs man on the asphalt. He didn't even bat an eye as the partner opened the passenger's door and checked the glove compartment. Or a moment later, when the official noticed the door panel was loose and whistled to the one with the clipboard. The tension heightened perceptibly, but Jack continued to smile blandly even as the inspector pried open the panel and felt around inside. A moment's suspense, and then the inspector frowned irritably, finding nothing. He slammed the passenger's door shut.

The one with the clipboard curled his lip disdainfully and turned to Jack. "And what's in the boxes, señor?"

The gambler's blue eyes flickered in confusion. He followed the inspector's eyes to the space behind the driver's seat. Several dun-colored boxes were piled there, a blanket half thrown over them. Clearly Jack had never seen them before, and the clipboard official could tell he was nonplussed. Jack tried to cover the clumsiness of the moment with a chuckle, lifting his brows impishly as he drawled in response, "Hand grenades, of course."

"Open them, please," commanded the other coldly.

Jack bent and pushed up the backseat, lifting out one of the boxes. From the corner of one eye he could see the inspector on the opposite side of the car standing with his carbine ready. Jack laid the box down on the hood of the Town and Country, and with only the barest wince, he lifted the top away.

He wanted to burst out laughing. Inside was a bright array of Christmas-tree ornaments. Struggling not to show his relief, he reached in and pulled out a hand-blown glass Santa. He dangled it from the tip of his finger and smiled merrily at the customs man, who burst out laughing himself.

"I tell you what, my friend," said Jack Weil smoothly. "Why don't you take a couple of these for your kids. We could all use a little Christmas, no?"

The inspector's mood had changed completely. His own eyes were as bright as a kid's. He waved away his partner with the carbine, sending him along to harass the next car. Then he laid his clipboard down and bent over the Christmas box, carefully selecting an angel and a snowman. "You want to know something crazy," he said to Jack, comradely now. "The rebels is telling everybody not to have no Christmas this year. No trees. No presents. *Nada*." He laughed derisively at such an appalling turn of events.

"No kidding," Jack retorted, clucking with disapproval. "Is that the kind of country these rebels want to have? Where Christmas is against the law? What a world."

The inspector carefully tucked the ornaments in his jacket pocket, then handed the car's papers back to Jack. He smiled for the gambler to move on, and the two of them parted, wishing each other a happy Christmas. As Jack moved to sling himself back in the car he noticed the battered station wagon emerging from the *Suzi*'s hull, squalling children leaning out the windows.

As the Town and Country glided away into traffic a group of three inspectors was giving a hard time to the next one in line, a pickup truck driven by two hapless peasants. The inspectors poked around and fired off questions as if they'd uncovered a terrorist hideout. Meanwhile the station wagon pulled into the inspection area. The seven-year-old leaped from front seat to back, tormenting his little sister, who screamed bloody murder. The mother was changing the baby's diaper on the front seat. Dad in his Harry Truman shirt smiled apologetically at the inspector with the clipboard, who took one look at this zoo of Americans and brusquely waved them on.

As the grimy station wagon swung into the moiling blur of traffic—no helpful road signs on either side, no tourist information kiosk—the vacationing Americans looked lost already. They had no choice but to go with the honking flow, hoping a strip of motels would show up soon. In any case they didn't notice the Town and Country parked at the curb in the harbor square, slipping into traffic behind them as they chugged by.

The two cars moved inch by inch, lurching stop-and-go as they left the port and wound their way up through the faded and peeling colonial quarter. Jack could see the children running their own guerrilla war in the backseat, taking no prisoners. Street vendors leaned in at their windows, offering everything from Virgin Mary statues to live chickens. The Americans shrank timidly from the gaudy aggression and carnival air of the street life, while the gambler seemed to drink it all in, as if he were home again.

Finally they turned off on Avenida del Jesu, wider and more commercial, blaring with signs that blinked even in daylight. It must have calmed the Americans to see the big billboard for Coca-Cola, rising atop an office building. Jack saw the wife point excitedly at a big motel on the left, Casa del Sol, as reassuringly garish as anything in Florida. The station wagon pulled in under the sign, and Jack drew the Town and Country to the curb.

Harry Truman and his wife were looking frantically for his wallet as Jack Weil strode up. "Sorry to bother you," he said with smooth politeness. They looked at him blankly, but he could tell they were glad he spoke English. "I'm with the U.S. embassy," Jack went on, and now the Americans puffed with nationalistic pride. "We've had a report that your car has been used to smuggle in contraband."

Simultaneously both husband and wife went white with shock. Sweat broke out on Harry Truman's brow as he began to sputter.

"Of course we know *you're* not involved," Jack added hastily. "These are ruthless people. They've got no qualms about taking advantage of innocent tourists like you. Don't worry, we'll leave your name completely out of this."

Their panic seemed to recede a little as Jack moved around to the back of the car. The children inside were still roughhousing, and their father roared for them to shut up. The edge in his voice was so terrifying, they were suddenly meek as lambs. Jack motioned to the man to open the back gate, and then Jack brushed aside the litter of toys and raised the flooring over the tire well. There were the oilcloth bundles.

The Americans gasped in horror, drawing back as- if something might explode. The wife lurched to the driver's door, ordering her kids out of the car. Jack began to gather up the bundles, stacking them in his arms. The tourists huddled together as if for a family portrait, gaping at him.

"If you want some free advice," Jack said sternly, "I'd keep this quiet till you get back home. These are not the kind of people you want to upset, if you know what I mean." They nodded dumbly. "Have a nice holiday, huh?"

He trudged across to the Town and Country, slumping the bundles one by one into the backseat beside the boxes of ornaments. As he climbed in the car and gunned the engine, peeling out into the flow of traffic, the Americans looked after him in total awe, as if they'd just been touched by some kind of national hero. This was the most adventure they'd ever had, a story they would be dining out on till the one in diapers was out of high school.

The bearded man on the Vespa had been weaving in and out of traffic for several blocks, but now he slowed to make the turn on the narrow street where he hoped to find Arturo. On the corner a tethered mule was drinking lazily from a water trough. The bearded man's foot dragged on the pavement as he took the turn, glancing into his side mirror— catching a glimpse for the first time of the olive-green car behind. It was dangerously close, and turning right in his wake.

The bearded man swayed as he tried to gather speed, the steep buildings on either side seeming about to cave in on him. The olive-green car kept pace, stalking him. He knew it was no accident they were following, even as he knew the crooked street led into a dead-end square. No one was out on the sidewalk. No one leaned out of the windows. It was as if the whole neighborhood knew, with a sixth sense, when it was time to see nothing.

The bearded man's eyes were wide with panic as he rode in terror with the beast behind him. Just ahead was the little square with no way out.

In the Malecon district, all was glitter. The flashy deco hotels seemed to preen with glamour, towering above tropical gardens gushing with fountains and stalked by flamingos. The Lido was the pinnacle of Havana chic, its two towering wings dazzling coral with turquoise balconies. The burst of white Christmas lights wrapped like diamond paving around its lobby pillars was more than a little gilding on the lily, but in the Malecon district nothing was truly excessive. Flash was the point.

The Lido portico was a constant stream of Cadillacs and Continentals, the proudest American imports. Havana women in Palm Beach dresses and New York jewels paraded here on the arms of sugar millionaires and exiled gangsters. At the Lido there was no sign at all of any trouble in the land. The Lido crowd had money to burn. Besides, they took good care of the peasant class, their servants and plantation workers. If anything had been wrong with Cuba, the Lido crowd would have been the first to know, because they owned the place.

It was still early morning when Jack Weil pulled the Town and Country into the Lido portico. Carlos the doorman, dressed in braided velvet and gold, grinned as he opened the door and recognized the gambler. They greeted one another like old friends, though Carlos knew not to ask Jack how he was doing or where he'd been. That would have been bad luck. Here and now was all that mattered at the Lido.

Jack strode confidently through the gilded lobby shaded by indoor palms, past the big parrot cage and a moss-banked pool glittering with the tossed coins of a thousand wishes. As he entered the swank casino it could have been midnight. Men in tuxedos and drop-dead women in sequined dresses strolled from table to table. Yet Jack knew instantly that the place was only half-full, slow even for 9:00 A.M. On the bandstand a six-man combo was valiantly trying to pump up some energy, belting out a fast rendition of a hot Prez Prado mambo.

Jack was looking for someone, even as he nodded friendly greetings to several of the floor men and dealers. A slick blackjack pitman winked as he passed, "Hey Jack, long time."

Jack flashed a vague grin in return, and then he caught sight of a tired-looking man over by the baccarat tables. Jack sidled up to him and poked him with an elbow. "So how's it going, Ramos?" he asked playfully. "Where's the story?"

Julio Ramos turned to face his interrogator. The hard-bitten journalist was probably in his midforties, but he looked a decade older. Whiskey years. "Oh, the story's right here," he replied, seemingly unfazed by the sight of Jack, whom he hadn't seen in months. "I keep interviewing all your fellow Americans. And you know what's amazing, Jack? No one is afraid."

"And what should we be afraid of?" Jack retorted, his eyes still searching the room restlessly.

"You don't take any of this seriously, do you?" Ramos didn't sound angry, exactly. Maybe he was too tired to be angry. "It's just pesos to you, isn't it, my friend? You piss on our foreign money. If it's not an American dollar, it's not worth shit." He seemed to be talking less to Jack than writing an editorial in his head. "I'm telling you, Jack, there's a real revolution out there."

Jack punched the journalist softly on the shoulder. "Please—it's too early. I just got in. You mind if we fight the revolution *after* I've had some breakfast? Where's Joe Volpi—you seen him?" And just at that moment his gaze froze, sharp as the sight on a rifle. "Never mind, Ramos," he said. "We'll catch up later."

He moved off at an easy saunter, making for the double-curved staircase at the far end of the casino. On the landing stood a tall man in a business suit. There was a definite proprietary glint in Joe Volpi's eyes as he surveyed his little kingdom. If Meyer Lansky was the king of Havana, Joe Volpi was his prime minister. Yet there was nothing flashy about him, here in the gaudy aquarium of the Lido, full of exotic rainbow fish. Volpi's suit was conservative gray, as precise as a Midwest accountant's. His black-rim glasses made him look painfully studious, a professor surveying his students as they took their final exam.

As Jack moved up the curving stairs toward him, his face broke into a sour smile. Not exactly warm, Joe Volpi. Cold as meat, and he liked to tease and taunt, like a kid picking wings off flies. "Hello, Jack," he drawled. "How are you, Jack?" Volpi put out a beefy hand to shake. "We never see you no more. How come? We miss your money, Jack."

The gambler shook the casino manager's hand, but carefully, as if he feared to lose his watch. "Hey, Joe. Where is everybody?"

"It's early, Jack."

"Yeah? I heard it was getting pretty late down here. I heard you guys were in the middle of a revolution." Jack laughed easily, brushing aside all politics. "So I figured there'd be a lot of loose money around. People cashing out . . ." He cast a glance down on the gaming tables, as if to appraise the little fish.

"Yeah, they're cashin' out, all right," Volpi admitted. "You know what they do, Jack? They give the money to their wives. Then the wives buy these junk statues from the holy fathers. They shove a few grand up Saint Anthony's ass, and they're on the plane to Miami." The sneer in Volpi's voice made it clear what he thought of such nickel-and-dime maneuvers.

"This revolution bull is just a lotta hysteria," Volpi went on. "It's the whole other end of the island. Six hundred miles from here." His hand waved indifferently toward the east, his pinkie finger glittering with a triple emerald. "That's where your rebels are, Jack. All two dozen of 'em."

"Mmm." Jack continued to study the room below, the gamblers as restless as rats in a maze. "Let me tell you something I learned in the Pacific. Nothin' like the sound of gunfire to stimulate a little action."

"Is that so, Jack?" Volpi nodded sagely, considering these words of wisdom. "So where are the big players today, huh? 'Cause somebody blew up an ammo dump in Cojimar last night. Very, very loud noise. So how come they're not here playing?"

"Oh, they're out there," Jack replied quietly, half to

himself. "They just . . . don't smell blood yet." His eyes moved from the scene below to Volpi. "And what's the action like on the top floor?" he asked, nodding upward. He could almost taste those private games in the penthouse suites.

"I closed 'em," Volpi growled in disgust. "Take my word for it, Jack—nobody's thinkin' about high-stakes poker. Situation's too confused."

Jack reached out a hand and slapped the railing. "Joe, that's *why* they come to play. They're looking for something they can *do* something about." He sounded like a radio salesman, a hundred-and-ten-percent belief in the product. "Listen, they know the party's almost over. The real big players out there . . . oh yeah, they're ready."

Joe Volpi looked at the gambler with the same sour smile, and yet there was astonishment in his eyes. Volpi had been standing at this railing for months now, watching them play in dribs and drabs, the dealers practically asleep. He was a man who believed in sudden changes of weather, but it hadn't rained for him in a long time.

"Sounds like you want to play some serious poker, Jack. I'm just guessing, you understand. . . ."

"Mmm," Jack repeated in the same neutral tone, one hand idly stroking the brass railing, as if it were Aladdin's lamp. "I was thinking—I *could* run a game out of my apartment. But then I'd have to hire me a cook, couple of waiters, plus rent a little muscle." He sighed wearily at the thought of all that overhead. Then he said very evenly, "Hell, I'd pay a ten-point rake not to have the aggravation."

At last there was an offer on the table. Neither man spoke for a moment. They'd been in this game for a long time, and it was only natural in the course of things that they crossed one another's path. But it didn't mean they harbored any sentiment for each other, good or bad, especially not trust. Cautious admiration was about as far as it went.

"I'd bring 'em in, Joe," Jack declared, nothing if not self-confident. "And once they come here to the Lido, they'd have to walk by all the action down there." He swept a manicured hand, taking in the carnival of tables in the room below. "It'd heat things up real good, having a big game upstairs."

Volpi nodded slowly throughout the gambler's pitch. Finally he sniffed and twitched his broken nose, a pug from a long time back. "I always said, Jack," he drawled, "if you ever thought about anything else besides snatch and poker . . . you'd be a friggin' genius." Jack continued to stare out across the casino, not acknowledging the joke in any way. Volpi's sour smile settled again on his face, till he looked once more like a junkyard dog. "I'll think about it," he added without inflection.

"There's other casinos," Jack replied almost casually, upping the ante.

"That's not a smart idea, Jack. Don't forget, Lansky still runs this town."

The gambler looked at him, smoother than ever, as if the buried threat meant nothing to him at all. "Don't think too long, Joe," he declared softly. "The revolution might go away."

When he turned to go down the thick-carpeted stairs, he froze for an instant before he took the first step. Bobby Duran had just entered the room, gliding among the morning players, beautiful and on edge. She hadn't had time to change her clothes, except to slip on a peach silk jacket over the white blouse. And yet she was as fresh as if she'd spent a month on a yacht, anchored in a quiet bay, the water still as glass and deep as sapphire. Watching her move among the tables, Jack seemed to forget they were on his turf. He looked lost for a moment, like he didn't know which card to play next.

She stopped at an empty blackjack table, stalling for time. She handed a twenty to the dealer for chips. He began to deal the cards: a four to her, a six to the house, a ten to her, then a house card down. He waited for her to make the next move, and her face was a sudden mask of hesitation, as if the stakes were a whole lot steeper than twenty bucks. The dealer raised his brows expectantly. She looked like she was about to cry.

"Stand," said a voice at her shoulder.

"What?" she asked, wilting with relief to find him there, feeling his breath on her neck.

"Don't take any more cards," he explained—patient, as if to a child.

She smiled and shook her head dreamily at the dealer. He hit himself with a nine and broke. An impeccably good loser, he quickly swept Bobby's chips toward her, adding ten to her twenty. Her cheeks flushed with—was it embarrassment or delight?

"Now let me buy you a drink," said Jack, and she scooped up her chips and moved unquestioningly by his side. Yet as they walked away out of the morning casino, where the night before never ended, they kept a discreet few inches between them, not even grazing their sleeves. Perhaps it was just an instinct for caution, in case they were under surveillance. Perhaps they both knew the uses of distance. In any case, they strolled across the lobby and into the bar as if they were the barest acquaintances—each someone the other had once met on a ship, only the name escaped them now.

Even at 9:00 A.M. the bar was more lively than the casino, though of course it was a different sort of night that never ended here. Jack nodded to the head barman, then guided Bobby to a turquoise leather booth in the corner, again without touching her. They slid in across from each other, and only by the way she clutched her purse in front of her did she show how nervous she was.

"What'll you have?" asked Jack, one eye out for a waiter. Bobby fumbled to open the purse, as if she couldn't bear it till the money part was over with. "Come on, put that down. Relax," he said, reaching to move the purse from the table to the banquette.

But she jerked her hand, catching the strap, and the purse spilled. A bunch of things tumbled out, falling under the table onto the floor. Again she seemed to be about to weep

34

from weariness. "No problem," Jack assured her, ducking his hands beneath the table. Like a magician pulling out rabbits, he brought up one thing after another, laying them on the table before her. "Keys, lighter, cigarettes, wallet," he announced cheerfully, holding open the bag so she could slip them all back in. "Good as new. Some things are easy to fix, right?"

She smiled in spite of herself as the waiter glided up, nodding at Jack in recognition. "How about a daiquiri?" asked the gambler, and Bobby shook her hair and said to the waiter, "Ginger ale. Please."

Her eye caught a familiar figure sitting at the bar: Marion Chigwell. The sycophantic writer waved jauntily in their direction, making Bobby visibly wince. She stiffened slightly as she looked at Jack, hating to be seen in public. "I think I'd better give you your money," she said, and it sounded as if she'd bolt the moment she'd done it. She opened her purse again and felt around with her hand. She pulled out the Lido parking ticket. Then she looked confused, because something was clearly missing.

She looked up. Casually Jack removed the remaining money from an envelope. ". . . two, three four," he declared, counting out the hundreds. "Yeah, it's all here."

She stared at him, dumbfounded. He grinned and reached across as if to sweep a curl of stray hair from her face. But he snapped his fingers beside her ear and showed her a fifty-cent piece gleaming on his palm. "Impressed?" he inquired dryly. "What'd you think? That I was just some jerk trying to pick you up?"

She didn't take the fifty cents. "And why should I change my mind, Mr. Weil?"

"Call me Jack. And what's your name?"

"Millicent Smith," she replied without a pause. He shook his head no, but she ignored his skepticism. The deal was hers. "What do you *do*, Mr. Weil?" she asked. "A man with so many talents. Are you a professional magician?" She drew out the adjective with a certain playfulness.

"Investments," he replied succinctly. "Marsha? Shirley? No, you're not a Shirley?" He seemed genuinely troubled at not being able to come up with a name that suited her. Then he brightened. "Catherine—that's it."

"Roberta," she declared, and just at that moment the waiter arrived with the drinks. He set the ginger ale down before her, the daiquiri in front of Jack. Delicately Bobby lifted the paper umbrella from her glass and twirled it between her fingers.

"So what's in the bundles, Roberta?"

She rose from the booth and gathered her purse. "I believe we're fair and square, Mr. Weil," she said. "You don't have to know anything more." And she swept away toward the lobby, ignoring once more the frivolous wave from Chigwell at the bar.

Jack caught up with her as she passed the parrot cage, its flash of iridescent wings and the babble of a jungle. He strode beside her, still keeping that tiny distance between them, and said, "I'd like to see you again sometime."

Her eyes never flickered. "I told you, I'm married."

Jack Weil grinned as they came to the lobby entrance. "You know something?" he asked, laughing at himself. "You didn't."

She cast her eyes down, and for a moment the proud facade cracked and let in a little light. "I'm sorry," she said quietly. "It was unintentional."

"That is definitely too bad," the gambler declared gravely. They were standing off to the side of the flow of traffic into the Lido, close by a bank of orchids and a bubbling fountain. Again, it could almost have been a jungle clearing. "But hey, this isn't like the States, is it? People in Havana know how to fool around. I think it's the climate, don't you?"

Bobby Duran didn't answer. She spun the paper umbrella between her fingers, thinking her own thoughts.

"What I mean is," Jack went on smoothly, "I keep a little place here. Just a flat, but it's one of the older buildings. Lotta charm, reminds some people of Paris. And real discreet."

She looked at him now, neither startled nor disgusted. Relieved, perhaps. "You're very straightforward, aren't you, Mr. Weil?"

"Oh, I can be suave as all hell, believe me, Roberta. You mind if I call you Bobby? It's just I figure you know a lot of suave guys already. So I got no edge in that department." He grinned puckishly. "Buy hey, how many *crude* guys do you know?"

She laughed, more effortlessly than he'd ever heard her. She seemed free at that moment, entirely self-possessed, as if no one had ever hurt her, especially a man. And in her freedom was a beauty so bottomless it took his breath away. He was half a step behind when she reached out a hand and laid it on his arm. "It's very important, Mr. Weil, that nobody know about our arrangement with the cars. Nobody." She locked eyes with him, deadly serious. It was as if the playful flirtation a moment before had never happened.

"If it's important to you," the gambler replied in a husky voice, "then it's important to me." And when she nodded and made a move to go, he stumbled to say more so she wouldn't leave him yet. "I guess . . . you know what you're doing."

"I do," she replied, smiling serenely, her eyes already searching for the car valet.

"Nice silk jacket . . . and those aren't rhinestones in your ears either. What do you need with a revolution, Bobby? Tell me that."

Her face flushed, and she bristled like a thoroughbred penned in a stall. "Look, Mr. Weil, you did me a favor, and I'm grateful." She couldn't keep the disdain out of her voice. She didn't much want to. "But you're arrogant and selfish and much too sure of things. What do you know about Cuba?"

The cords went tense in his neck, but his manner was smooth and charming as ever. "I know who's in charge," he replied emphatically. "And I know how to stay out of trouble." He shrugged, but it came across more sheepish than indifferent. "That's all I usually need to know about any place." And he reached over and took the paper umbrella from between her fingers. "For luck—do you mind?"

The valet came over, and she handed him the claim check, but her eyes never left Jack's. "Do you believe in luck?" she asked him, almost plaintive.

"No," he replied with a sad smile, twirling the tiny umbrella.

"I have to go," she said abruptly, as if the conversation was beginning to feel like quicksand. She glided past him, not planning to ever look back, then stopped as her face flushed crimson.

For the car that the valet had brought was the green Cadillac, which wasn't so surprising, since this was the car she had left with him. The valet beamed politely, holding the door open for her.

"Thanks. That's mine," said Jack, grazing her shoulder slightly as he moved to get in. He flipped a claim check out of his jacket and handed it to the puzzled valet, along with a twenty-dollar bill. "Please get the lady's car now," Jack demanded. And the valet nodded, twenty being just the right amount to ask no questions.

Jack climbed in, the engine exploding to life. As he eased out of the portico, he passed abreast of her. He winked like a man on a lucky streak and said softly, "Some other time, huh?"

She pretended not to hear. And by then he was gone.

III

THE GREEN CADDY wove in and out, passing a dead bus and an open-air market. The vendors crowed excitedly, telling the neighborhood women with the string bags to stock up now for Christmas, because who knew how many chickens and plantains would be in the stalls by the end of the week? Underneath everything now was the threat of disruption and shortages. In the street markets of the colonial quarter, there were as many rumors buzzing as flies.

Jack Weil grinned as he rounded the corner, nosing through a crowd of street urchins. He seemed intoxicated by the upheaval and pulsing energy of the quarter, watching the sun pour down on the streaked pastels of the old stucco. He passed an open hydrant, its gush of water spouting deliriously at the sky, children scampering half-naked in and out of the back spray. Outside a shuttered café, a man sat crouched on the stoop with a cock under his arm, calling for bets and challengers.

Jack pulled the Caddy up to the curb outside a tall ocher building, a Spanish colonial mansion of the old style. The stucco was cracked in a hundred places, some of the cracks sporting tufts of grass. The ground floor was given over to shops—a pharmacy and a laundry. Yet the facade was still noble, with rows of peaked Moorish windows and rickety iron balconies that no one dared step out on anymore, and the great wooden doors that were wide enough to admit a carriage opened grandly onto an inner court with its shaggy overgrown garden.

Two brown urchins still wet from the hydrant came running as Jack stepped out of the car. He let them fight for his suitcases and drag them behind as he swung back the massive door. He and his bearers had hardly reached the staircase leading out of the courtyard before a figure appeared to greet him, jingling keys and wheezing. La Polaca, they called her, the Polish one, though in truth she was mostly Hungarian with a little Greek. She puffed on a hand-rolled cigarette and studied her tenant skeptically.

"So why you don't write?" she demanded with wounded pride. "I would have clean the flat."

"No, you wouldn't," retorted Jack with a pleasant smile. "Hot water running?"

La Polaca shrugged, as if that was a very complicated question. They headed up to the landing together, La Polaca fighting for breath and defiantly dragging on her cigarette all at once. She studied her great ring of keys, carefully selecting one, and opened the heavy oak door to Jack's apartment. The urchins scampered in first, carrying Jack's valises, and dropped them in the middle of the floor.

It was just as he'd left it, many months ago. La Polaca bent to pick up a few yellowed pieces of mail just inside the door while the gambler emptied his pockets of change and sent the children away whooping as if they were rich. On the center table was a cup of coagulated coffee. A fine layer of dust seemed to cover everything, thick in the air and palpable where the sun streaked in through the chinks in the shutters.

"I didn't think you would ever come back," declared La Polaca, stubbing out her cigarette.

"Why?" he replied jauntily. "They pass a law against poker?"

"No . . . but everything else." Then she held a finger to her lips, indicating the subject was forbidden. She handed him the mail she'd gathered off the floor, and he tossed it in a wastebasket under the table.

"Professor still upstairs?" he asked, moving to open the tall shutters.

"Still here." She chortled merrily. "Still screwing widows at the Nacional. *Twins* this time, from Chicago. Says it's half as boring." La Polaca shrugged. "I think *twice* as boring."

The sun streamed in as Jack threw open the casement windows. He took off his jacket and patted the pocket, reaching in and pulling out the paper umbrella from the Lido. He seemed surprised he still had it. He placed it in a chipped bowl on the table as La Polaca crossed to the window, looking down suspiciously into the street.

"How I would do in Miami, Jack? What do you think my chance is there?"

"Lousy," he replied flippantly. "What's a fine Hungarian lady going to do in Miami? What's wrong with Havana?"

When she answered, it was almost as if she were relating a dream. "You know the sound a tank makes?" she asked, practically whispering. "This terrible squeak when it come down the street. I keep hearing tanks." She fell silent, moving away from the brightness of the window.

Jack continued to bustle about the room, straightening cushions and tossing away the shriveled potted plants. "Hey, Polaca, this isn't Budapest."

She gave him an indulgent smile, which held a certain gentle pity. "You're okay, Jack," she said, genuinely pleased to have him back. "They keep the windows closed in the casino. The only noise is the cards shuffling, the clink of the chips. What do you care what's in the street, huh?" Nothing about her words was meant to judge him. If anything, she wanted to protect him. She moved to the door and beamed at him coquettishly. "I go find the broom," she said, and disappeared down the stairs, her hacking cough ringing up the stairwell.

Jack closed the door and strolled to the window, tapping

a Pall Mall from the pack and lighting up. He flipped the match out the window and watched it float down to the street. His eye fell to a deck of cards on the windowsill. Automatically he picked it up, shuffling as he returned to the center of the room. He slapped the deck on the table, as if waiting for a phantom partner to make the cut.

His eyes squinted nearly shut as the wreath of smoke from the cigarette clouded the air about his head. He rolled up his sleeves. Then he did a very curious thing. He turned his left forearm up and rubbed his fingers along the skin, stroking the powerful veins. For luck, perhaps, except he didn't believe in luck.

He spoke to the empty room. "Jack Weil is back," he said with a certain defiance.

Nobody contradicted him.

In the Malecon district the wind blew steadily out of the west, and the tide broke over the seawall, sending up a fan of spray that dazzled in the midday light. Across the wide shorefront avenue, a pair of lethargic National Policemen sat dully on a pile of sandbags, their carbines propped beside them. They looked blankly out at the whitecapped sea, as if they were meant to watch for pirates. Nearby, from a window in one of the ramshackle beach hotels, a radio bawled the hit parade, all the way from Miami.

"Drinking rum and Coca-Cola," warbled the Andrews Sisters. "Go down Point Couva-Mana . . ."

It blared so loud, you could hear it a hundred yards in all directions. Beyond the police and their sandbag bunker, beyond the next shuttered hotel, the music floated down an alley sifted with sand like a dusting of snow, blown from the beach across the way. A tin warehouse stood at the end of the alley, the front of it scarred with jagged red paint that read *FUERA YANQUIS!* The music seemed to vibrate the walls of the warehouse, shimmering like a tambourine.

"Both mother and daugh–ter," swelled the Andrews Sisters in gaudy harmony. "Working for the yanqui dollar!"

Gray light filtered through the grimy windows of the

warehouse. Inside were mostly piles of machine parts, greasy and rusty by turns, which looked as if they couldn't remember what machines they belonged to. But in the center of the cluttered space, shining like a showroom, stood the white Town and Country, its trunk flipped open. Ricardo, the gigolo revolutionary, chuckled as he heaved out the oilcloth bundles. One by one he handed them over to an older man with one strong arm and a tucked sleeve.

On a worktable nearby, pieces of a portable radio transceiver waited to be assembled. Monica, a gaunt, intense young woman with dark hair, studied the assembly plans. Pacing back and forth in front of the dirty window was Tomas, the bespectacled scholar. Only he seemed to hear the yammering of the pop song, or at least he was the only one being driven crazy by it.

Tomas turned and barked at the others, "It's five o'clock! Where is he?"

No one answered, for no one knew. Ricardo and the one-armed man Bufano transferred the bundles to one end of the worktable. Carefully Ricardo began to unwrap the oilcloth. Monica picked up the crystal and fitted it into its zinc casing. She was as careful and deliberate as if she were making a bomb.

"Something's wrong," Tomas said, seething. "Where is he?" Always very excitable, Tomas. He paced back and forth in a rage, furious as a panther. And the others continued to pay no attention. They didn't dare worry about the things they didn't know yet, or else the revolution would have been over before it ever got started.

By nightfall it was raining, one of those mad tropical cloudbursts that come like the end of the world and then move restlessly on, dancing from island to island. A white streak of lightning illuminated the green Cadillac, pelted with rain at the curb, the gutter beneath rushing with water like a mountain stream. Someone had had the foresight to put the top up, though the vinyl leaked in a couple of places.

Inside his apartment, casements thrown open to the rain,

Jack Weil sat and listened to it rain as if it were a symphony. Beneath a curling poster of a bullfighter, he dealt himself a poker hand for the fifteenth time, playing against two ghosts. He laid all the cards face up, and he was third man out with a pair of nines. Somewhere in the back of his mind he remembered an old wives' tale about never playing in a lightning storm.

As he gathered the cards together, there was a distant sound of machine-gun fire—softer than the thunder, but more insidious. He sat up straight and waited. No follow-up burst of fire. Down below in the street, a car accelerated with a screech on the wet pavement. Once again Jack Weil rubbed the inside of his left forearm.

He put down the deck of cards and took the paper umbrella out of the bowl. He opened and closed it, then put it back. Finally he grabbed the phone and dialed, the nervous tension breaking as he cranked the rotary hard, spinning it like a roulette wheel. Whoever answered barely had time to say hello.

"I got a message for Joe Volpi," the gambler said with a sneer. "Tell him Jack Weil got tired of waiting. I'm out playing cards."

And when he dropped the phone in the cradle, he suddenly became aware that the fury of the storm had passed. He threw on his jacket and slipped the deck into his pocket. By the time he came out on the street, the rain had dwindled down to the barest drizzle. If the old wives were right, now was the time to play some poker.

He drove due east through the old Spanish quarter, the farthest place he could get from the big hotels. Nobody from the Lido would ever be caught dead here—but then, there was more than one kind of dead on this seedy, garish strip of hooker bars and penny casinos. Even after the gust of tropical rain, the street was noisy and dirty and quarrelsome, like a drunk that couldn't get sober anymore.

Jack parked the car in a muddy alley and went on foot down the glistening sidewalk, pushing his way through the braying legions of lottery salesmen. Every shabby casino on

44

the strip looked the same, down-and-out, the doorway into a little room in hell. The slots looked rigged. Even the green felt on the tables seemed to be covered with fungus, rotting in front of your eyes. Still, the hollow players in the shadows waited for a lucky streak, but most of these had long since played their last hand.

Maybe he chose it at random, maybe he'd been there before. Or maybe the neon was just a little gaudier and the pair of hookers lounging in the doorway a little more voluptuous. Jack stepped in off the sidewalk and cased the place. A bank of slots and a couple of craps tables. Mostly it was a bar. A lizard-looking dude stepped up to the gambler, rubbing his hands as if to get the blood going. "Señor," he said with a tiny bow, but Jack was already out the door.

Restlessly he crossed the street, staring into the big glass windows of another tawdry, run-down casino. A guitar trio wandered the club floor, playing "Malagueña." Again the energy was all dead-end, like trying to play cards in a mortuary. The gambler didn't even bother to go in, but hurried away down the street, darting in and out among the swaying drunks on the sidewalk.

It was a good half hour later, by which time he'd checked out every two-bit joint in the quarter, before he got any sort of positive buzz. The casino stood on the corner of a square, facing an old mission church. The flow of the crowd going in and out was fairly constant, mostly sailors and workingmen, but at least they weren't half in the bag. A scrawny Santa stood outside the door, swinging a tinkling bell over a papier-mâché chimney.

Jack could see through the plate-glass window that the operation was a little more substantial, roulette tables and ceiling fans. He dropped a handful of change in Santa's chimney and strolled inside. Behind the bar two strippers on a platform went through the motions, jiggling their pasties. Jack spotted the cadaverous proprietor at the end of the bar, a Syrian who kept touching his slicked-back hair to see if it was on straight.

Jack Weil sauntered over and introduced himself. While

they conducted their curt negotiations, the strippers behind them went for broke, the full bump and grind, trying to get the gambler's attention. But he was already following the Syrian to a private table beyond the roulette pit. In fact, he had hardly cracked open a new deck of cards before the serious poker players began to materialize, sniffing out the action.

A stocky Cuban in a Panama hat and a British seaman came forward as if drawn by a magnet, hurriedly buying chips from the Syrian. Jack nodded and smiled as they took their seats at the table. A Chinese businessman pulled out a roll, and as he paid the Syrian for a stack of chips they looked like a pair of ancient traders on the old spice route. Jack grinned at the international flavor of the game that was pulling together—a regular United Nations of poker.

A black bus driver in a blue uniform was right behind the Chinese, but he seemed hesitant to join in. "Come on, pal, have a seat," Jack encouraged him. "Ante is *dos* pesos, *comprende*? We're playing straight draw." By then the man couldn't resist, and they were five around the table. "Let's play poker," said Jack Weil, a low thrill in his voice, and the deal began.

It was hours later, the smoke as thick as mustard gas. The jukebox was three notches louder, trying to keep the all-night crowd awake. Two different strippers, big in the chest, were grinding away on the bar platform, their movements dreamy as swimmers. No one was paying them any mind, for all the attention was focused on the poker table.

The Cuban in the Panama hat was raking in a hefty pot, a thousand dollars easy. The Chinese and the bus driver had long since dropped out with empty pockets, but others had quickly replaced them. In fact they were standing in line to get into the game, for the dealer with the blond hair and the easy smile was losing big.

"You bluffed me, I know it." Jack Weil grinned at the Cuban, giving him a helpless shrug. "What's the word for 'bluff' in Spanish?" he asked the crowd around him.

The Syrian watched him intently, not quite sure what his game was. Yet the proprietor could hardly complain, for he'd sold more chips in this one night than he had all month.

They kept pouring in till the first streaks of daylight glowed through the dusty front window. By then, there was just a lone black stripper dancing by herself on the platform above the bar. She practically forgot to take her clothes off, doing her best for the dazed lineup of unshaven faces nodding over their drinks.

And the poker game went on and on, the kibitzers standing three deep. At the table facing Jack were a couple of band musicians still in their tacky blue tuxedos, a hung over tourist who had Miami written all over his face, and a red-faced American sailor. Sitting beside the gambler was one of the black strippers from the middle of the night, her arms folded demurely over her breasts.

His grin as fresh as ever, Jack Weil laid down a full house, queens over sevens. Finally he'd won a fat one. He raked in the bills in front of him like a kid with a pile of candy. Carefully he counted out a few hundred and held it out to the Syrian—the house cut. "All for you, amigo," he said. "Also some very black coffee when you get a chance."

The sailor picked up the cards to shuffle, and Jack draped an arm idly about the chair where the stripper sat. He squinted around at the ring of kibitzers and suddenly brightened as he recognized a face. "Hey, we must be getting pretty classy," he declared softly. "Baby Hernandez is here."

Hernandez stood out sharply among the wilted, all-night crowd. The young sugar tycoon was freshly shaved and powdered, dressed for the Lido. His lime cologne cut through the fetid air like a breath of spring. He smiled winningly at Jack, because Baby Hernandez liked everybody and everybody liked him. "So," he purred, smooth as hundred-proof rum, "what they say is true, huh, Jackie?"

"What's that, Baby?"

"That you'll play anywhere." Baby's smile wasn't quite a sneer—not quite.

"Anywhere they'll have me," Jack drawled. Then his eyes sharpened with a glint of challenge. "You in, Baby?"

A beat of uncertainty, and then the sugar tycoon said, "Deal. I got to make a call." He turned on his heel and moved toward the pay phone at the bar. Jack's lips parted in a small grim smile of satisfaction as he watched Baby Hernandez dial.

It was very, very soon afterward that a big white yacht of a limo came shouldering down the narrow street and pulled to the curb outside the cheap casino. The limo was even more out of place than Baby Hernandez, who, after all, liked to go slumming when he was in a certain mood. The crisply uniformed chauffeur jumped out and opened the rear door. Joe Volpi stepped on the sidewalk with the sourest look imaginable, as if he were walking in dog shit. Never did a man like Volpi deign to cross the border into this crummy world of losers. He looked slightly nervous to be here, as if the crumminess might rub off.

Shadowed by his bodyguard, Volpi stepped into the sleazy den. The place was jumping at 7:00 A.M., a whole lot busier than the Lido. The crowd was so thick beyond the roulette pit that you couldn't even see the huddle of men at the poker table. Volpi's bodyguard shoved a way through, and he heard the gambler's patter before he saw him.

"Deuce, trey—possible straight," declared Jack Weil in an antic mood, unshaven and red-eyed but high on adrenaline. He slapped the cards down as he dealt round the table. "Nine to five, office hours. Pair of ladies. Four of clubs. Oh–oh, the suicide king," he said, laying the ace of spades on the red-faced sailor. Then he hit himself. "Seven and three belong to me," he groaned, then nodded across to the Cuban in the Panama hat, who held the two red queens. "Ladies' turn to bet."

He looked up over the heads of the players and caught sight of Volpi, standing gloomily just behind the sailor. "Well, well, well," the gambler said softly, then spread his hands as if to show off the elegance of his setting. "Good action, congenial surroundings. That's all I ask for, pal."

Then he lowered his eyes to the card players, looking from one to the other. "Last hand, boys," he informed them, then grabbed a stack of chips. "And I'll raise two hundred."

Volpi turned abruptly and moved back through the crowd, grimacing at the close contact. The Syrian stood at the door, bowing as if the king himself had entered his lowly establishment. Volpi ignored his fawning presence and hurried out to his car. When he ducked inside the red plush interior of the limo, he heaved a weary sigh and reached to the bar for his bottle of antacid.

A few minutes later Jack Weil stepped out of the casino, taking a deep breath of the morning air. He shook his head in mock wonderment at the sight of the long white limo, then let the chauffeur open the door for him. He sat down opposite Volpi in one of the overstuffed jump seats and locked his hands behind his neck, stretching and groaning at last with exhaustion. Softly the car glided away.

"Guess what, I won the hand," the gambler declared, grinning over at the manager of the Lido. "You must be good luck for me, Joe."

Volpi's voice was as cold as his eyes. "I didn't appreciate the message you left, Jack."

The gambler shrugged. "I got impatient."

"You're not in a position to get impatient. Impatience is a mistake right now." The words were tight with warning, and yet there was something weary in Volpi's whole posture, as if he was reading from a script he had tired of long ago. He rubbed his temples and sighed. "Okay, you can run a game at the Lido. Ten percent, just like you said."

Jack rolled his head on the cushion and looked out the smoked window at the street. They were stopped at a light, where a cluster of day workers ate their breakfast out of paper bags. They still looked hungry, even with their mouths full.

"Poor sons of bitches," Volpi said quietly, following

Jack's gaze. "They're gonna trade that schmuck Batista in for what? Another tyrant, that's what." He made a scoffing sound and brushed a speck of lint from his trousers.

"I want more, Joe." There was dead silence from the seat opposite. Casually Jack tapped out a cigarette and lit it. "I played every Elks Club and Moose Hall from Chi to Miami. And I remember every hand of every two-bit game. You understand?"

"What do you want, Jack?"

"I want a shot," the gambler retorted, blowing smoke. "One shot—at a game I could never get near. With guys that don't even think about how much they're playing for. Now do you understand?"

Silence again from Volpi's corner. And yet it was clear in the Lido manager's face that he was hearing something very rare—a raw nerve of honesty that wouldn't reveal itself again. Vulnerable and dangerous at the same time. And most definitely the words of a man who wouldn't be toyed with.

"I want you to talk to Lansky," Jack continued precisely. "I want the house to back me."

Joe Volpi sniffed, like he'd developed a sudden allergy. "Yesterday all you wanted was to run a game at the club. And I'm givin' it to you. Now you want to be bankrolled." He opened his palms in a helpless gesture, as if to say he was dead broke.

Jack stubbed out his cigarette in the ashtray. "You know what happened to me last week?" His voice was strangely antic again, a man about to tell a joke. "I realized I'm not gonna die young. What's the use of kidding myself? I'm never gonna get a shot at one of *those* games—not unless I grab it now." He leaned toward Volpi, elbows on his knees. "This is the time for me, Joe. This is the city. History's not gonna strike twice."

They both rocked slightly as the limo glided to a halt in front of Jack's apartment. The urchins of the quarter were already scampering around the car. Joe Volpi shook his head, not a big fan of history. "You're tired, Jack," he said.

"Yeah, I'm tired . . . of some things."

"Slow down," Volpi declared. "One game. The way we talked. Let's see how you do." He coughed softly. Maybe he was getting a cold. "It'll take me at least a day to put it together. We'll see how it goes. One world at a time, Jack, okay?"

The chauffeur opened the passenger door, letting in the blinding morning light. The red plush looked like it belonged in a whorehouse. Jack Weil nodded and stepped from the car. "Get some rest," called Volpi, almost as if he was really concerned for the gambler's welfare.

And the limo sailed away, the urchins running after it squalling like a flock of gulls. The gambler yawned and stretched his arms wide. The morning sparkled after the rain. For once in his life he looked like a man with history on his side.

It was dusk in the garden district, the stately villas set back behind old brick walls, the hillsides swathed with lush green lawns. Royal palms lined the lazy S-curve of the street, and of course there were no sidewalks, for no one who really belonged here would have been out walking like a common peasant.

The steel-blue Chevrolet came around the turn and headed into a cobbled driveway. The driver was Bufano, the one-armed revolutionary, but when he got out, he was dressed in proper white pants and a blazer, the hollow sleeve tucked in his pocket. He looked as distinguished as a military man. From the passenger's side emerged Monica, the radio wizard, sporting an airy sundress.

As they strolled across the courtyard to the house, they could have been any of the neighbors—upper-class, secure, dull as old money. Except across the street, on the wide veranda of the villa opposite, a man and a woman were watching them. The man nodded over his newspaper, and the woman stood up from the porch swing and strode purposefully into the house. Like the scream of a silent alarm, too high-pitched for the human ear. The sound of Havana.

IV

LA FLORIDA BAR and Café, on a stylish corner in central Havana, flanked by jewelers and Paris boutiques, was where the smart set hung out. The chic facade of the "Floridita," which was what the in-crowd called it, was all brass fittings and polished teak. It could have been an elegant bistro on the Left Bank, and it did its damnedest to look that way. Even on a weeknight like this—the air full of dark gossip about pipe bombs and rebel invasion—it wasn't surprising to see the limos lining the curb outside the Floridita. Through thick and thin, the high life had to go on.

Inside the bistro was jam-packed, the everyone-who-was-anyone crowd jostling and gossiping, spreading rumors. They all spent so much time table-hopping, they barely ever sat down, like children playing musical chairs. The music was a trio in the main dining saloon, playing a swank arrangement of "Volare." The women were deeply tanned and seriously thin, wearing little nothing cocktail dresses and casual diamonds. The men were always a bit older, running somehow to catch up, fueled by too many martinis.

Marion Chigwell, lightweight Yankee writer, shared a table tonight with Julio Ramos, tough-guy reporter. A very peculiar match, these two, but at least they shared the ink-stained fingers and swollen livers of their common profession. Chigwell's bow tie fluttered as he vented his sweeping opinions.

"But who the hell is he?" Chigwell said dismissively. "Castro who? He's just a voice on the radio."

Ramos sipped his whiskey and shrugged. "Look, nobody know's what's gonna happen. Even the rebels. They don't all want Castro—some want Prio." He made a weighing motion with his hands. "All they know is they want change." Then he gave a sneering nod at Chigwell's drink on the table. "It's supposed to be the daiquiri here, my friend. The *mojito* you drink at the Bodeguita. Where you getting your information? From peasants?"

Both men turned their heads at once as Jack Weil made his way to the bar. The gambler waved to the writers, then paused at a table or two. He looked completely rested tonight, sporting a white linen jacket. Looked like a winner. Nothing about him suggested the sleazy joint where he'd spent the previous night. He had this remarkable capacity to slough off the past, like a snake shedding its skin. He was a new man tonight, ready for anything, especially of the female kind.

He scarcely had time to reach the bar and order himself an *anejo* before they closed in on him. Two sexy girls on vacation, burning for a party. Patty was a poodle-cut blond in a Marilyn dress cut very low in the bodice. Her pal Diane wore a dark ponytail and was naked under a white cashmere sweater. They were clearly in heat and proud of it. Both out of high school, but only just. In the States they would have been carded at the door.

"Hey!" said Diane, tapping Jack on the shoulder. "You speak English?" A real ice breaker, Diane.

"All the time." The gambler smiled.

"I told you he was American," she declared, pulling Patty into the circle. Then to Jack, grave as a schoolgirl, "Listen, we can't figure out—"

"What you want is a daiquiri," Jack retorted, snapping his fingers to call the barman.

Diane pouted. "What if I don't like it?"

Jack slipped his hand around her waist. "You will," he assured her. "My name's Jack, by the way."

Diane smiled, stretching her taut body like a cat as she introduced Patty and herself. And before they knew it, Ramos was sidling up on a small poaching mission. A whiskey grin creased his face, and his nose twitched like a bird dog's. "Your first trip to Havana, ladies?" the journalist queried.

"Hey Ramos, where's the story?" Jack taunted.

The journalist nodded his head in a courtly bow, taking in Diane and Patty. "These two beautiful flowers are the story," he purred. "Welcome to Hemingway's favorite bar."

Patty gasped. "We know," she breathed excitedly. "We were hoping we'd see him."

The journalist tilted his head toward Jack with a puzzled frown. "He didn't tell you?"

"Tell us what?" Diane whispered, walking right into it.

"Son of a gun." Ramos clucked, softly punching the gambler's shoulder. "Good old Ernie, shy as a friggin' debutante."

"Ernie?" Patty's voice was trembling now, unbelieving and yet . . .

Ramos nodded sagely. "Ernest Jack Hemingway."

Diane scoffed, for she was the worldly one. "Yeah? And where's his beard?"

"Shh," replied the journalist, a finger to his lips. "He's traveling incognito."

They all laughed merrily as Jack presented the girls with their daiquiris. Chigwell appeared behind Ramos and cleared his throat, smiling hopefully. The only reason Ramos let him into the circle was that it enabled Ramos to get himself closer to Patty. "I'm Chigwell, I write for *Gourmet*," said the irrepressible writer, always sounding as if he was out to sell a few subscriptions. He nodded at Jack. "Weren't you on the Key West ferry a couple nights ago?"

"Hmm," said Jack thoughtfully, as if trying to remember. "Was I wearing a beard?"

"No—no beard."

54

The gambler shook his head. "Couldn't have been me then." At which the two cupcakes shrieked with laughter, Diane wriggling seductively in the curve of Jack's arm.

"How long you here for, ladies?" asked Ramos, looking as if he was about to take a bite out of Patty's shoulder.

"Just through New Year's Eve," Diane drawled. "Hey, what about Castro and them? Is all this dangerous?"

"Nice seeing you again, Jack," Chigwell piped in, glancing at his watch like the White Rabbit. "Listen, I got three restaurants to try before midnight. I better move my tail. See you, Ramos. Ladies." And he was off, veering through the crowd with his bow tie bobbing.

Diane took a big gulp of her drink, the whole political question having already floated out of her head. "Ooo, that's good," she moaned, as if she were giving a preview of how she played in the dark.

Ramos leaned close to Jack. "You think he's a fruit? Miss Marion?"

The gambler squinted his eyes, mulling it over. "I don't know," he replied after a moment. "But he's sure as hell lying about something." Then he gave a grimace of distaste, clearly not wanting to spoil a sexy evening with too much sober speculation. He squeezed Diane's hip, so that she arched her back expectantly. "All right, ladies, let's plan your evening before the party gets away from us."

"No," protested Ramos, "*I'm* the one who's gonna do the planning. I'm the native, after all." He swelled out his chest, endearing in his sudden self-importance, a swagger in his stance like one of Hemingway's heroes. "We start at a place where the tourists don't drink. Follow me!"

He raised his arm as if he was leading a cavalry charge, then turned to lead the way through the buzzing congestion around the bar. Patty and Diane looked questioningly to Jack, who nodded for them to follow in the journalist's wake. "Christian Science Reading Room," he informed them, arms around both their shoulders as they headed out.

The four of them went laughing down the sidewalk, past the fleet of limos, and piled into the green Cadillac. The night was irresistibly balmy, kissed by jasmine, as they wound their way through streets strung with multicolored Christmas lights. Diane cozied up to Jack in front, and Ramos rode in the back with Patty, waving his arms like a politician in a parade.

"You Yankees are all the same," the journalist bawled into the night. "We die for years fighting Spain for independence, then you come in at the end for twenty minutes and call it the Spanish-American War!" He waved an imperious finger at Patty, who blinked at him uncertainly. "You've always treated us like an American colony!"

"I just *met* you," Patty retorted with slightly ruffled dignity. She pulled her skirt an inch closer toward her knees.

"Don't pay any attention to him," Jack called from the front seat. "His grandma did it with Teddy Roosevelt. The Ramoses are terrified that they might be part Episcopalian."

He turned down a bustling avenue where cha-cha music blared from countless bars and strip joints. They had definitely found the party. Christmas trees were everywhere, in pots along the sidewalks and blinking in the windows of the bars. Pimps and hookers pranced up and down, dressed to the teeth. A red-nosed plastic reindeer perched precariously on a stoplight.

The Bodeguita del Medio was in startling contrast to the Floridita, but just as popular and maybe even more chic, in a downtown sort of way. It was only a small café on a narrow street off the avenue, yet the line went halfway around the block. Ramos gestured for Jack to park in the alley beside it, then led them all around to the front of the line. The bouncer nodded and let them by as if they had diplomatic immunity. The girls were suitably impressed.

Inside it was even more crowded than the Floridita, but here there was none of that Frenchy elegance. The atmosphere was Spanish Cuban, unadulterated by uptown chic. Lanterns flickered against the walls, and the music was provided by three guitarists who called themselves Carlos Pueblo and Co. The clientele was younger, much less manicured. Dressed down instead of up: *guayaberas* instead of jackets. People were having a raucous good time, partly because it was Christmas, partly because the world was about to collapse.

Jack had his arms around both girls as Ramos went over to say hello to the owner. Jack bent his head and whispered into the ponytail, "Want to try a *mojito*?"

"Sure!" She laughed. "I want to try everything!"

The gambler smiled and bent the other way, murmuring to the poodle blond. "How about you, Diane?"

"I'm Patty."

"Just testing you," said Jack, and they all laughed. "You want to try everything, too, Patty?" He grazed his hand up and down her arm, and she uttered a soft groan that apparently meant yes.

Suddenly two large men in bad suits came pushing through the crowd from the back of the café. The revelers seemed to part like a wave, and a brief ominous silence shivered over the room as the sharks headed out. When they were gone, it was as if a siren had sounded an all-clear. The merriment rose again, and if it was artificial, nobody wanted to say.

Ramos came over to Jack and the girls. "You see those guys? Batista's police. SIM, we call 'em."

"What did they want?" asked Patty, still rubbing up to Jack.

Ramos smiled. "They want to keep something from happening."

Diane poked Jack playfully with her elbow. "Hey, I thought you said Havana's safe."

The gambler smiled. "Not me, honey. I don't think anywhere's safe."

Ramos gasped and clutched the back of a chair, as if he were having a coronary. "My God," he whispered, a mix of awe and urgency. "It's Duran."

Jack was aware of a stir by the door, a break in the din, but whoever had just come in was all but concealed by the crowd. He craned his neck to see, but he didn't really care that much, and besides, his hands were full.

"Jack!" The journalist's voice was near frantic with excitement. "It's Duran—Arturo Duran." When Jack looked back at him blankly, Ramos was furious with impatience. "This is a very special man," he declared, in a tone that was practically religious.

"Oh yeah . . ." the gambler retorted vaguely, a man who never passed a church without holding his breath.

"He's been in the mountains," Ramos continued, leaning so close to Jack that the gambler winced from the smell of years of whiskey on his breath. "They say with Fidel. Maybe Duran's the one who can pull all these factions together." At that moment of passion it was clearer than ever where the journalist's sympathies lay. To hell with the objectivity of his chosen profession. He was as fierce as any guerrilla.

Again Jack turned his head to the bustle at the door, and this time he saw the man who commanded such fervent loyalty. A handsome Cuban in his midforties, clearly an aristocrat, with large, expressive eyes and a neatly trimmed mustache. But for all the elegance of his demeanor, the impeccable cut of his European clothes, there was something indefinably ascetic about him. A man who had learned how much to give up and who knew in his bones what to hold out for.

Diane and Patty were already tugging the gambler impatiently toward the bar, and he'd half turned away from Arturo Duran when the crowd at the door parted again. A woman moved to Duran's side, and Jack Weil's heart stopped. It was Bobby. Hastily the gambler withdrew his arms from around the two bimbos. He gripped the journalist's elbow. "Hey," he said, his mouth gone suddenly dry, "who's—who's the woman?"

"His wife," replied Ramos, his eyes still fixed on his hero. "Roberta."

Arturo Duran and his wife were trying to make their way to the bar, but they kept being stopped by well-wishers, people who pumped Duran's hand. He accepted these attentions with some embarrassment, yet he endured them.

The owner of the Bodeguita stepped forward to bow and scrape. That was the moment when Bobby tossed her luxuriant mane and let her gaze drift around the café.

When she saw Jack, she seemed to falter, as if a stab of pain from an old wound had knifed her. For an instant she and the gambler were both frozen, eyes locked. Then her husband turned from the owner to take her arm again, and her body went soft and supple again. She leaned close and murmured into his ear, and one could see the easy intimacy they shared. Duran smiled.

Then he moved resolutely along the bar toward Ramos and Jack and the girls, his wife following half a step behind. Ramos's face was bathed in a sort of stunned rapture, watching Duran approach, but it turned into naked shock when Duran put a friendly hand out to the gambler. "Well, hello there," the aristocrat declared, smiling warmly. "It's been a long time." The handshake was firm. "You have a moment?"

"For *you*?" retorted Jack. "You kidding?"

As he let Arturo lead him away to the end of the bar it was hard to say what pleased the gambler most. The expression on poor Ramos's face was priceless. And then there was the sudden proximity to Bobby, which had already left Jack more intoxicated than half a dozen *mojitos*. He looked like he'd just been invited to join a game where the ante was ten thousand bucks.

Bobby moved graciously forward to cover the gambler's absence. "I'm Roberta Duran," she offered charmingly, as if she was the hostess and this was her party.

"I didn't know your husband knew Jack Weil," said Ramos, his mouth still slightly agape.

"Oh yes," she said, smiling at the American girls.

"I'm Diane, and this is Patty," said the one with the ponytail. Just now they seemed younger than ever, especially next to Bobby. They looked like they weren't sure whether they should curtsy.

And at the end of the bar Arturo Duran sized up the gambler with an appraising eye that was half-amused. He seemed to know intuitively the depth of Jack's uninvolvement in political matters. "You don't know who I am, do you?" he asked, managing to say it without the least conceit or arrogance.

"Just that Ramos gets all choked up when he talks about you," Jack replied. He was doing his own appraising.

Arturo Duran shrugged. "You know Latins," he said with wry dismissiveness. Then, more earnestly, "I wanted to thank you for what you did. My wife tells me you were amazing."

Jack couldn't keep himself from glancing back at Bobby, conversing animatedly with Patty and Diane. Her careless elegance and unaffected manner were as palpable as her lily perfume. He almost didn't hear Duran's next words. "I hope you can have some supper with us."

"Uh, thanks," said the gambler, flustered and not sure why. "I can't. My friends are . . . um . . ."

"Please," Arturo coaxed him. "Just something very fast, the way you Americans eat." And he snapped his fingers and laughed, a man with deep affection for the sprawling country to the north. "And then you can rejoin your friends somewhere. Surely they won't mind. It's not that I dislike Ramos, you understand. He's a fine man, but he is a reporter after all." Because Jack was mute, unable to raise any further objection, the business of supper at least appeared settled. "Please," Arturo repeated, clinching it now, "it would make us both very happy."

Jack nodded yes, drawn in spite of himself into the force field of the other's magnetic intensity. They rejoined the others briefly, Jack promising to hook up later with Ramos and the girls. The journalist made sure there were no objections from Diane and Patty, expertly steering them out— anything he could do for the cause of Arturo Duran. Meanwhile Bobby and Jack greeted each other in the most rigorously casual manner—travelers who'd met on a ship, but as if they couldn't quite place which passage it was.

The owner led the three of them into the dining area beyond the bar. Somehow an empty table had materialized out of thin air, for otherwise the room was packed. As soon as they sat down a waiter was there with a batch of *mojitos*. "I think you'll like the food," Arturo Duran assured his guest, then hastened to qualify, "though it's really just peasant fare. Nothing fancy."

"I've eaten here," Jack replied, staring at his drink so he wouldn't stare at her.

"Mr. Weil keeps an apartment in Havana," Bobby explained, loosening the scarf at her neck.

"Ah," said Duran. "So you spend a lot of time in Cuba." It wasn't quite a question. Clearly he was still appraising the American, trying to figure out where the playboy stopped.

"I come down to play cards," Jack said without inflection.

Arturo nodded. "So you're a gambler."

"Well, I try to keep the gambling to a minimum."

Arturo shot him a puzzled look. "And how do you manage that?"

"By being very good at it."

Bobby laughed deliciously, and even Arturo smiled. Jack couldn't keep himself from looking at her any longer. The Paris scarf was stenciled with an equestrian motif, vivid against the pale coral of her dress. Her cheeks were pink, though she wore no makeup. It was probably just a touch of the sun, from her time in the green convertible.

Plates of food began to appear, though no one had placed an order. Black beans and rice, yucca and pork, a heap of green tomatoes. Peasant food, as Arturo had promised, and of course there would be no bill to pay.

"Yes, a gambler," Bobby allowed, reaching a hand to squeeze her husband's arm with bold affection. "A man willing to take risks—isn't that right, Mr. Weil?" Jack sat perfectly still, his silence all the agreement he would give her. "A man who knows how to keep those risks to a minimum. Just the kind of man we need."

A chill came over the room, and Jack looked to his left. The two SIM men were back, standing in the doorway.

Their eyes were dead behind their shades as they scanned the tables. Jack murmured under his breath, "I'd sure love to have that sunglasses concession."

Bobby's laugh betrayed no fear. The gambler looked at Arturo, more fascinated than ever. "These guys don't worry you?"

"Not so much," he replied, leaning over to spoon some pork onto Jack's plate. "Not because I'm so brave," he hastened to add. "But you see, Mr. Weil, there are two categories of people in Cuba under Batista. The torturable and the nontorturable. My family is an old one, Castilian, very well known. So . . ."

He gave a modest shrug, almost a reflex with him, as if to say he took credit for very little. Right now he seemed most concerned that his guest eat heartily, and thus the gambler dug in, trying not to feel he was being fattened up. The pork was superb, all the more sophisticated and subtle for its peasant roots. Jack said so, managing to compliment at once the chef of the Bodeguita and the rich, intricate island nation he considered his second home.

Arturo Duran smiled. He obviously found it a good deal easier to accept flattering words about his country than about himself. He watched the two of them eat with pleasure, though he scarcely touched his own plate. The ascetic in him was always testing, like a saint struggling with faith.

"I hope you know how important it was, what you did for us," he said to Jack.

The gambler glanced at Bobby, who looked back at him with that same bold and disarming frankness with which she'd approached him on the *Suzi*. Jack Weil was a great bluffer, but he found he couldn't meet the vivid intensity of those eyes. The stakes were too high. He looked back at her husband, and Arturo was writing a phone number on the inner flap of a pack of Bodeguita matches.

"Yeah, well I'll take your word for it," the gambler responded with as much indifference as he could muster.

"You're a card player, Mr. Weil, and by your own admission a good one." Arturo smiled, and Jack felt suddenly like an amateur by comparison, a two-bit bingo player. "You move among the sort of people who could be of great value to us. If I asked you to do something more. . . ?"

Jack's face flushed. "I don't play cards for that," he retorted coolly. "That's politics." The last word rolled off his tongue with a spin of unutterable contempt.

Arturo pushed the pack of matches close to the gambler's plate. "In case you change your mind."

"I won't."

The aristocrat smiled more broadly still, shaking his head indulgently. "That's very American of you, Mr. Weil. Politics is what life is all about, from wars to famines to revolutions. And yet you say you're not interested."

"Not *my* life," Jack retorted, but even to him the words came out sounding petulant, like those of a kid who wanted his own way or nothing.

"Everyone's life," said Arturo, gazing rather mournfully at the food on the table. "Isn't politics just a kind of hope?"

Jack laughed tightly. "Don't ask me, pal. I don't know what it is."

"I think you're making Mr. Weil uncomfortable," said Bobby, pulling the ends of her scarf till it hugged her neck.

Arturo studied Jack Weil's face. He had already made his appraisal, whatever it was. Now he seemed more bemused than anything, as if he understood he was sitting with someone radically different from himself, and thus shouldn't waste the opportunity to learn how his opposite ticked. Till now, the only opposite men he'd ever known were his mortal enemies.

"Perhaps you think it's . . . unseemly," declared Arturo, choosing his words like one picks one's way through a mine field, "for me to ask my wife to do these dangerous things."

"She's *your* wife," the gambler replied, but not rudely or with hardness. He was simply trying to say it was none of his business. If anything, he sounded as if he wished he didn't care—but wishing didn't make it so.

"You see, we have only one objective," continued Arturo Duran. "To overthrow Batista. To do so, it becomes necessary to get one's hands dirty." Unconsciously he studied his own hands before him on the table, perhaps to see if they were dirty enough. The saint again—testing, always testing. "If we had *more* than one objective—let's say to be attractive and charming . . ." He smiled at something private, an old memory. "Well, then Batista might rule Cuba forever. Please don't misunderstand, Mr. Weil. I'm not here to be your judge. In many ways I envy men like you. How you manage to keep a certain innocence, in the face of everything."

But his wife was not nearly so poised or philosophical. Her cheeks flushed as she slipped an arm about her husband's shoulders. She spoke without anger, but the words were no less like bullets. "Perhaps it isn't innocence at all," she said. "Perhaps Mr. Weil really *doesn't* give a damn."

"Hey, I know politicians." The gambler shrugged, perverse as ever, finding it easier to respond to the toughness in her, the unconcealed contempt. "I play cards with 'em. In fact I *love* to, because they're easy to beat." He laughed, short and dry. "Hell, it's the *only* place an ordinary Joe can beat a politician." There was a look of challenge in his eyes, as if he dared anyone here to say he wasn't that ordinary Joe. "Listen, I better catch up with my party."

Bobby nodded graciously, the lantern light rippling across her hair. She was the lovely hostess again. "It was good of you to take the time, Mr. Weil," she declared with genuine sincerity. "I hope your friends will forgive us."

Jack looked over at her, smiling serenely, and his own face was strained. Her toughness and contempt were so much simpler. And he seemed to have lost—misplaced— that effortless casualness with which he'd taken leave of her in the portico of the Lido. This was good-bye instead. The word that defined a gambler's life, always on his way out of somewhere, yet right now it stuck in his throat.

But Arturo wasn't finished. "Why are they easy to beat?" he asked, more fascinated than he wanted to be.

Jack turned to face him again, relieved to have a reason not to look at her. "Because sometimes in poker," he said, "it's smart to lose with a winning hand so you can win more later with a losing hand." He spoke this axiom with a tone of utter authority, as if it had been handed to him on a stone tablet. "But a politician can never quite trust it to work that way. Because they always want the power *now*."

The aristocrat looked back at him with a start of appreciation, all the more remarkable since Arturo Duran was not a man easily impressed. He'd spent too much time with men who'd made their peace with tyrants, never questioning, dulled by oppression.

Bobby's voice was soft, but the challenge was loud, "I think you care a lot more about the world than you pretend, Mr. Weil."

"Oh really?" drawled the gambler, almost a taunt, as if goading her on.

"Someone has to be responsible for changing things," she said. "Or nothing ever changes."

"Maybe." He nodded. He looked down at his hand on the table, startled to find himself fiddling with the book of matches. He palmed it and tightened his fist. "But I don't really feel qualified to decide who should make the changes."

"Then why did you help?" asked Arturo.

"That was a business deal."

Arturo smiled. "Then why did you give back the money?"

It was a damn good thing it wasn't a poker hand, for Jack Weil's face was jarred, a man who'd just dropped an ace. He shot a glance at Bobby, who lowered her gaze and trailed the end of the scarf across her lips.

Arturo continued. "She told me the envelope was back in her purse when she got home. I understand you're something of a magician as well as a gambler."

Jack was silent. The guitar trio came strolling by, bowing toward Bobby as they passed, strumming an Andalusian love song. It was Arturo who held all the cards right now, though he didn't look remotely like a gambler. His smile was good-natured and almost impish, without a twinge of jealousy.

"Perhaps you *do* believe in something after all," he remarked dryly. "Perhaps you believe in beautiful women, Mr. Weil."

It was Jack who stood up first, but they were all ready to go now. The gambler stuffed his hands in his pockets and murmured a formal thanks to his host for supper. Perhaps he would have said something to Bobby next, but the owner of the Bodeguita was already bustling over. Bobby and Jack exchanged a glance, but anything final went unsaid. The voluble owner made fussing noises, angling for compliments, gushing with praise of the lady. Jack made a gesture that was half a shrug and half a wave, but at least he didn't have to say good-bye.

He stepped away and began to weave through the crowded tables toward the front. He didn't look back, and nobody followed, but somehow he didn't have the air of a man who was getting away. Still as suave as ever, Jack Weil turned heads as he made his way out, the dream game of a lifetime shimmering on the horizon. But not entirely free anymore, not like he was. He stepped out into the glittering city—Christmas trees and jasmine—and his brow was creased with brooding, like a man who'd been found out.

The book of matches was in his pocket.

V

IT WAS AFTER midnight now, and anything was possible. The crowds of revelers at the Floridita and the Bodeguita were at full volume, no room at the inn, but now that the witching hour had come they would start peeling off in twos and threes to explore the deeper mysteries of the night. The casinos would start revving up, along with the strip shows and the private pleasure domes. Night in Havana was its own kingdom of special favors and secret assignations, the stuff that daylight would never even dream of.

The restless dancers in the night parade included the scarecrow figure of a man in white, wheeling his pushcart of flavored ices through the narrow streets of the colonial quarter. As the cart creaked over the cobblestones, its bells tinkling seductively, couples arm in arm stepped forward to buy a sweet, feeling like kids again. The scarecrow scooped shaved ice into paper cones, then drizzled each with bright syrup, yellow and green and red.

As he handed the cones around to his laughing customers, rooting to make change in the pouch of money at his waist, a beggar emerged from a nearby doorway. The ice eaters turned their backs and ignored the pleading, outstretched hand, and the scarecrow hissed for the mendicant to go away.

Then suddenly the whole scene was lit up as a black car

lurched around the corner and came thundering down the cobbled street. They all looked up, vendor and beggar and customers, as the black car shrieked to a halt just a few yards away. It seemed as if someone inside must have a terrible yearning for a cherry ice. Then the rear door swung open, and a body was dumped in the gutter, landing stiffly in front of the horrified spectators.

With a squeal of tires the black car was gone. The ice eaters hurriedly dispersed, no one even bothering to check if the body was alive or dead. The scarecrow raced his pushcart away, disappearing round the corner. Only the beggar was curious enough to go over and peer at the dead man's face, its blank eyes staring at the midnight sky. It was the bearded man who'd ridden the Vespa.

Everyone on the street ducked into their houses or walked the other way. The beggar went over to the curb and picked up a newspaper. He opened it and spread it like a shroud over the dead man's face, then turned and shuffled back to his doorway. Tonight in Havana, this was all the funeral the bearded man would get. It was more than most. If you wanted to have a proper ceremony these days, you had to die in your own bed.

And did one more body make any difference to the fear and tension that gripped the city? Not really. The luxury of the night was its own denial. The shadows hid the violence, and the revelers went for the light, drawn like so many moths to the safety of the neon and the streets that never slept.

Arm in arm, tipsy couples strolled the busiest thoroughfares, too excited to sleep yet. Bobby and Arturo appeared as lighthearted as any of the others, her head bent lazily on his shoulder as they walked, with no particular destination. You would have had to look closely at their eyes to see how watchful they were, a certain inner radar tuned to red alert. They passed a gang of American sailors who whistled appreciatively at Bobby's stunning figure. They skirted around a boisterous line jostling to get into a nightclub.

At the corner of the square they passed a row of taxicabs.

Casually Arturo glanced over his shoulder, checking the traffic along the street. No black car was creeping along in their wake, and nobody followed on foot. Arturo seemed to make a flash decision, steering his wife quickly to the taxi at the head of the line. He opened the door and practically shoved her in, then turned and strode the other way as fast as he could.

The cab took off through the square, turning onto a boulevard that was bumper to bumper with cruising traffic. Young Cuban men sporting American chrome crawled forward in a din of music, ogling and whistling at groups of girls. "Sweet Little Sixteen" wailed like an anthem, and peanut vendors and newspaper hawkers waded among the cars, selling their wares.

The taxicab crossed the Prado intersection, the Via Veneto of Havana. A tall Christmas tree rose up from the central garden circle, a crèche with life-size figures grouped at the base. Though the traffic was madness, several young people were actually dancing in the street, pounding a drumbeat on the hoods of the cars as they went. And as the taxicab turned away from the Prado, it passed a green Cadillac convertible inching onto the main drag. But just at that moment their heads were turned in different directions, and thus Bobby and Jack missed their final chance of the evening. Truly like ships in the night.

Jack Weil was preoccupied, his eyes sweeping the sidewalks, looking for Ramos and the cupcakes. He looked more earnest than ever, as single-minded as a sailor on his first shore leave in six months. Just down the street he spotted the Tropicana, the neon swoops of its sign towering over the other clubs on the Prado. Jack smiled and put on his left blinker, trusting his instincts.

As he waited to turn in, a well-dressed and smooth-skinned woman stepped off the curb and sidled up to the Caddy. She was so poised and elegant as she leaned down to address the gambler, she might have been about to remind him of a meeting on some other ship, first cabin deluxe. When she smiled, her teeth were gapped and crooked, the only sign that she wasn't the rich girl she dressed like. Sweetly she said, "Blowjob Americano, señor?"

Jack Weil grinned. Even for a man who thought he'd seen everything, he'd never come up against such a particular distinction. Apparently there was an American brand of everything. "Some other time, sweetheart," he retorted pleasantly. "But I've already got *two* dates tonight."

The hooker shrugged philosophically and waved him away, wishing him double good luck as he swung the car into the entry court of the Tropicana. He let the attendant open his door, then trotted up the steps to the valet-roped entrance. He seemed to have entirely recovered his playboy self-confidence. As he came inside the club, the walls rippling with light from a mirrored ball revolving on the ceiling, he looked as if he was home again, ready for anything.

The women in long dresses, the red-faced men in tuxedos who looked as if they were choking on cash—they'd all been making the same rounds all evening, from the Floridita to the Lido and now the Tropicana. The route of the night was as strict as the Stations of the Cross, and nobody missed the 1:00 A.M. show at the Tropicana. Jack moved through the peacock crowd at the bar, craning his head to look through the glass wall that faced out onto the garden.

A hand came down on his shoulder, and he turned. He faced a middle-aged man with curly gray hair, dressed to kill, his eyes as bright as the diamond studs on his shirt-front. "Santos," Jack acknowledged warmly, gripping the other man's hand. "How's it going?"

"Twilight of the gods, Jackie," retorted Santos, one arm sweeping to indicate the high-priced swells around them. "Eat, drink, and be merry, huh? 'Cause tomorrow . . ." He let the thought trail off in a shrug, then winked and gave Jack's elbow a gentle push, as if to coax him to enjoy the spoils while they lasted.

Jack moved closer toward the glass wall, his eyes studying the lush indoor garden. Suddenly he caught sight of Ramos, sitting with Patty and Diane at a ringside table. He watched them for a moment like a spy and made no immediate move to let them know he was here. After all the trouble of tracking them down, he seemed to wonder why he'd bothered. Almost unconsciously, he cradled his left arm against his abdomen and began to stroke the forearm with his fingers, rather as if he were looking for a pulse.

The Academia Dance Hall was the opposite of swell, a combination waterfront dive and sock hop. From the outside, facing onto the docks, it looked like a condemned warehouse, except for the wave of students standing in line to get in. They must have had very strong constitutions, because the stench of fish from the packing houses was overwhelming, enough to make a cat faint. Luckily these were very bohemian types, as Beat as their compatriots in New York or Paris, and so they liked their atmosphere gritty and louche.

Inside it was packed, the university students rocking to a preppy combo that was pouring out a tinny rendition of "That'll Be the Day." The dancers looked like their dearest ambition was to be on "American Bandstand." More serious types congregated at the bar, a lot of black berets and facial hair, mirror images of Che. The shop girls trying to catch their eye weren't up on guerrilla theory, but they liked the look and the attitude.

Arturo Duran appeared at the door, completely failing to be inconspicuous. He looked a bit like a professor come to chaperon the dance. His eyes restlessly scanned the bar till he spotted Bufano, his one arm holding a large shopping bag. The barest nod passed between them, and then they both headed around the dancers toward the kitchen.

As they disappeared through the swing doors one of the couples stopped dancing: Monica and Ricardo. They split off in different directions, Monica bound for the ladies' room and Ricardo to saunter out for a smoke. They just didn't want to be seen moving right after the others into the kitchen. Nothing must call the wrong attention to this meeting ground, the only safe place where all of them could gather.

When Arturo Duran and Bufano entered the cramped and greasy kitchen, there were two men in soiled chef's whites and three disheveled waiters all stooped around a small radio. Through a storm of static and crackle, a voice was calling urgently from the little box. "Rebel Radio here," shouted the voice in the night. "Can you read us?"

The cooks and waiters jumped away in fear when Arturo cleared his throat, one of them knocking the radio to the floor. All relaxed immediately when they saw who it was, but shuffled uncertainly, almost as if they wanted to kneel before him and kiss his ring. The old ways died very hard.

Arturo and Bufano moved past them, down a small hallway. The aristocrat unlatched the back door to the alley, admitting Monica and Ricardo. Just on their heels came Tomas, blinking behind his spectacles, a shopping bag in his arms equal in heft to the one Bufano was carrying. Monica took the keys from her purse and opened the lock on the storeroom. She flicked on the light inside, illuminating a dim bare bulb in the ceiling. One by one the rebels entered, Arturo closing the door behind.

They moved with no time to waste. Bufano and Tomas set down their shopping bags on the baker's table in the center of the room. Carefully they lifted out the pieces of the radio transmitter and coiled antenna. Arturo checked his watch as Monica moved to connect the elements. It would only take her three or four minutes. She was their radio genius, proof positive that women would claim their proper place in the revolutionary power structure.

It was 12:59 by Arturo's Cartier watch, an ironic remnant of the oppressor culture, which owned the people by owning the clocks. They would make the connection and transmit at exactly 1:05. Five minutes after that they would all be gone, and the underchef in the grimy white apron would be at this table kneading dough. Everything was planned to the minute, for the night was never long enough for the work of making a whole new world.

*   *   *

The darkness thrummed with the sound of bongos. Then one piercing beam of light swept the exotic foliage, as if searching the perch of a jaguar. The bongos rose as the light snaked down to the Tropicana stage, a form undulating into its white pool. She stood revealed, a breathtaking *mulata*, easily six feet tall, an Amazon queen. A strip of dark fabric was tied about her breasts, and below she wore a long batik skirt slit up the middle. The light widened as she swayed to the accelerating beat of the drums.

And now behind her came another, just as regal and tall, and then another. They began to sashay back and forth along the lip of the stage, swooning with their own beauty, and now the lights came up bright as the Carib sun at noon, when it turned the water to mercury.

At the best of the ringside tables, a portly Cuban rum tycoon clapped slowly, practically falling out of his chair with pleasure, and still the *mulatas* kept coming, one after another. A Cuban admiral blew kisses toward the stage. Beside him two American navy brass sat up stiffly, their eyes bugging out. The *mulatas* strutted for all of them, the warriors and kings of commerce who jammed the nightclub. Half their movements were those of models slouching along a runway, and half were the sway of priestesses bearing sacrifices to an angry god.

The *mulata* line of the Tropicana was Cuba's eighth wonder of the world. They were twenty in all, the most exquisite women imaginable, shaded from palest cream to deepest coffee, filling the stage now as the audience went wild. And just as they reached the crescendo of their full dazzling presence, Jack Weil slipped into the empty chair beside Patty at ringside. He smiled and squeezed her hand, nodding up at the line of dancers as if he had produced them himself.

Ramos across the table had had too much to drink, his head half slumped on Diane's shoulder. Sleepily he peered across at the gambler, and he rallied enough to sputter triumphantly, "Jack! You made it!"

The show was just beginning. The *mulata* line on the ringside stage continued its seductive prancing, the girls kicking their skirts behind them, revealing their long flawless legs and the teasing hint of no underwear. Now the lights expanded, revealing a second-tier stage behind and a third above that as well. An Afro-Cuban band was on the second stage, steel and wailing horns, and the bongos and conga drums on the third, playing in wild syncopation.

The jungle garden was alive with spectacle, a glass-enclosed Eden open to the tropical sky. There were stars twinkling in the branches of the palms and eucalyptus, and a pair of singers duetting a passionate love ballad from tree houses on opposite sides. Dancers gyrated on every level, beautiful and damned at once, the last exultation of a pagan wilderness, crying for pleasure instead of war.

At the bases of the trees colored fountains began to play, and the *mulata* line began to move down a runway through the audience, mysterious as a frieze on an ancient temple. The audience applauded madly, the circles upon circles of white-linen tables floating off into the darkness, votive candles flickering. Here was the pinnacle of Havana glamour—American money, Cuban money, Venezuelan, Brazilian, every currency that owned the world, as if heaps of gold were on every table.

A delirium of pleasure, all for the delectation of the ruling class. Jack leaned across Patty, rubbing up against her breasts, and spoke over the swirl of steel and percussion, "Having a good time, ladies?"

Both of them grinned in return, Diane's eyes widening with desire. "It's okay," she teased the gambler, "but I'd still like to see the *real* Havana. You know?"

Jack laughed appreciatively, the master of the revels. The two girls were practically panting with erotic fire, swept up now in the wild thunder of the pagan rite. And Ramos, poor Ramos, was fast asleep on Diane's shoulder—missing the story as usual.

*   *   *

When the service door opened in the alley behind the Academia, Ricardo and Tomas came out first, darting off into the darkness like a pair of cats. A half minute later Monica emerged with Arturo Duran, and they made their way down the alley, pretending to be a strolling pair of lovers. Last came Bufano, closing the door behind and heading off in yet a third direction. Through the thin walls of the dance hall, strains of "Cherry Pink and Apple Blossom White" covered the dispersal of the rebels.

As they headed away from the docks Ricardo and Tomas looked just as scruffy and bohemian as any other students. They passed a waterfront coffee shop, the wavering blue neon in its window washing across their faces as they went by. They didn't bother to notice the old man wiping the counter inside. Or the seedy-looking workman sitting at the window table with his plain wife in a faded flower dress. As soon as the two young men had passed, the couple stopped eating their plates of fried plantains. The workman pressed his cheek to the window to watch which direction Tomas and Ricardo were headed. His wife leaped up, not half so slovenly as she looked, and made a beeline for the pay telephone.

Most people tried to be nothing at all, of course. For thousands of years they did the best they could to see and hear and speak no evil. But here in Havana on the brink of Christmas, the speed of events was making its own demands. If you weren't a rebel or a government soldier, then you'd better be passing information to one or the other. The only ones who were truly neutral were the dead.

An hour later, in a pinball parlor off Calle Santa Maria, Bufano the one-armed man had racked up eighty thousand points. The pinball bells were ringing like mad as the steel ball bucked and rolled through the bumpers. Though players stood and worked every machine in the line along the wall, it was Bufano who had gathered a small crowd of onlookers, cheering him on.

Then suddenly his audience evaporated, hurrying away to mind their own business. Bufano was too absorbed in the play of the ball to notice. He also didn't notice the two hulking men in suits and dark glasses bearing down on him. They grabbed him and shoved their guns in his sides, and the ball that had racked up so many dizzying points stopped dancing and sank into the hole. As the two men hustled Bufano out of the parlor not a single other customer turned to look. Nobody saw a thing.

Down in the colonial quarter, it was just nearing 2:00 A.M. in Monica's apartment. The young woman sat in a bathrobe at a small table, her hair pulled back in a bun. Quietly she studied a textbook—*Particle Physics*—for she still had a final exam day after tomorrow, revolution or no. In the corner of the bed/sitting room her grandmother lay fast asleep, white hair braided on the pillow, a gold cross on a chain around her neck.

There was a slight rustle in the hallway, no more than a rat would make, and then the door burst open. It took three thugs to corner and capture the wiry young electronics wizard, who made no attempt to resist. She raised her arms above her head and pleaded that they leave the old woman alone. A SIM agent clasped her hands and roughly bound them with handcuffs. The grandmother tried to stand up, beseeching them in Jesus's name. But Jesus had no currency with the goons, and one of them hit the old woman hard, throwing her against the headboard.

Now Monica began to fight, hissing and clawing, but uselessly. Two of them dragged her out, and the one who'd silenced the old woman bent over her unconscious body and ripped the cross from her throat—gold was gold. A moment later there was dead silence in the modest bed-sitter, the textbook thrown to the floor with its useless formulae, a trickle of blood on the grandmother's chin. The Christmas presents she'd wrapped for her beloved Monica were hidden under the bed, but they wouldn't be having Christmas this year.

In the shantytown by the docks, the scholarly Tomas was running, running, his gaudy sport shirt soaked with sweat. He had broken free from the two SIM men who ambushed him in the foyer of his dormitory, and he'd managed to flee to the quarter of the desperate poor. Here there were no streetlights, not even streets to speak of, just an endless jumble of shanties—tin, straw, cardboard. But he'd somehow lost his glasses in the melee, so the night was a blur of shapeless shadows as he ran. Dogs barked on all sides, marking his trail wherever he fled.

He knew they were right behind him, and there was no place left to hide, but he ran because he wanted to die running. Every second of freedom was precious as gold, even as it sifted away like sand in an hourglass.

As each rebel was silenced and captured, nobody knew that the others had been taken. This was the final delusion of the revolutionaries' passion, that someone among them had managed to escape. No matter if they all had to die, somewhere the secrets were free. And if any of them was going to make it out alive, it would surely be Ricardo, who drove the old Buick through the tropical night with the radio blaring. Sporting a leather jacket and jeans, a Lucky Strike dangling from his lips, his jet-black hair blown back in the night wind, he was the spitting image of James Dean—a poster of whom graced the wall above his bed. Except in Ricardo's case he was most definitely a rebel *with* a cause.

He approached the tunnel to Guanabacoa, his mind already racing ahead to the sultry girl who waited for him in bed. An upper-class girl who loved him for being a patriot, but more than anything liked their secret assignations, which felt to her like Romeo and Juliet—for her father was a cabinet minister in the Batista government.

Ricardo flipped the cigarette out the window and glanced at his face in the rearview mirror, already feeling the tightening in his pants, knowing exactly how sex and politics mixed.

Then, as he entered the tunnel, the car in front of him suddenly slammed on its brakes. Ricardo lurched forward as he shrieked to a halt, barely missing the bumper. He began to curse with rage at the moron who'd almost gotten them both killed, and was about to hurl open his door when another car hurtled up behind the Buick, smashing its fender and sending it up against the wall of the tunnel. A shower of sparks sprayed over the scene like fireworks.

And still Ricardo cursed with fury, railing at the peasant drivers—as if he'd forgotten the highest goal of his life was to free those peasants. He struggled to get out of the Buick, ready for a macho display of force, and only then did he see who it was approaching from either side. Men in suits and dark glasses, pistols in hand. Suddenly Ricardo knew he wouldn't be making it back to Guanabacoa and the sultry girl, that sheer brute power had won out again.

In a word, the gigolo revolutionary was history.

It was later than any of that in Jack Weil's apartment, dark except for the glow of the streetlight filtering in through the gauzy curtains. Down in the street, a man and his wife were having a screaming fight as they walked drunkenly home, and it sounded almost comforting in a city braced for the sort of explosion that couldn't go home and sleep it off. The gambler stood at the window with his shirt off, letting the night breeze cool him down.

There was a fumbling noise on the sofa behind him. "Hey," called Patty, swatting a lamp shade. "Where's the lights around here?"

"Don't turn on the lights," he said, not sharp but very firm. It was as if he was a sentry watching the night for enemy fire.

Patty slumped back against the cushions, taking another deep drag from a marijuana cigarette as fat as a panatela. "Hey," she called out again, "this isn't doing a thing for me."

Diane appeared out of the darkness, waltzing with herself. She was stark naked. She knelt beside her friend on the sofa and snatched the reefer away. "Gimme that," she exclaimed in a playful pout. "I like *everything*."

As she danced away from the sofa, the coal of the cigarette looping like a firefly, Patty leaped up to chase her. The poodle blond was much more modest, still wearing bra and panties. They raced each other around the center table, laughing giddily. When Jack turned away from the window, drawn at last to the siren song of the nymphs, his face was curiously still, not drunk enough at all. He was thinking too much for 3:00 A.M., and much too much for a gambler.

The girls darted into the bedroom, Patty pleading now for another puff of the drug that did nothing for her. They giggled and passed it back and forth, like a couple of kids behind the barn. When Jack came up and slipped an arm around Patty's waist, she shrieked in mock terror, struggling to get away. With an expert flick of his hand the gambler unhooked the bra, burying his head between her breasts. She stopped struggling and half swooned, ready to pitch over onto the bed.

His lips caressed first one nipple, then the other, till she moaned deliriously. Then he whispered softly against her neck, "Which one are you?"

Patty laughed, not offended at all. "I'm not sure. Does it matter?" The gambler grinned and shook his head, which struck Patty as so funny that she turned to Diane, slouching on the end of the bed with the reefer. "Hey, which one are *you*?"

Diane coughed a little. "Damned if I know," she retorted, and by then they were all bitten with the laughing bug, tumbling in a heap on the bed. So late in the night the only way to play was dealer's choice, and every card was going to be wild. For that kind of game it didn't really matter who any of them were, as long as they felt no pain.

The birds had already begun their predawn racket, louder in the garden quarter than any machine-gun fire. Streaks of coral and purple mottled the dark sky. Here at the top of the quiet, hilly street, the view was extraordinarily peaceful, from the tall cluster of hotel towers in the east to the harbor in the west. Farther out, jeweled islands dotted the milky pewter of the morning sea.

As the three gray American sedans turned up the hill, silent as a funeral procession, the bird song seemed to shiver—the way it did in the jungle when a jaguar padded through hunting for his breakfast. The three cars stopped at the crest of the hill, before a large Caribbean bungalow set in a small park and surrounded by a whitewashed fence.

In the old days of the colonies, the house had been part of the city's fortifications, a general's quarters. The walkways were paved with crushed shells, and a pretty gazebo perched at the edge of the lawn, the whole of the ocean spread below it. A house that had only known the most genteel sort of life, always a faithful retinue of hot-and-cold-running servants.

Out of the cars came several men, tumbling from every door, every one in a dark suit and sunglasses. So identical in their drabness and their blankness, they might have been almost funny, especially since the sun wasn't even up yet. But the machine guns they carried weren't funny at all, nor their grim sweep through the wrought-iron gates as they fanned out around the bungalow to cover every exit. By the time they had surrounded the house on the hill, the birds had stopped singing entirely.

Wordlessly two of them smashed in the beautiful green glass doors at the front, an echoing crash from the rear of the house as their fellow agents broke through. A kitchen maid began to scream, and the butler in the pantry crawled behind a cabinet. But the SIM men weren't interested in the servants. They swept through to the dark wood spiral stair in the entry hall till the whole house seemed to be full of goons.

Two of them, armed with machine guns, barreled up the stairs, just as Arturo Duran appeared at the upper banister, still foggy with sleep and pulling on a robe.

His eyes widened, but he made no attempt to run as they grabbed his arms. His backbone locked to attention, so he easily stood taller than they. If he needed to brace for anything, it was Bobby stumbling out of the bedroom. *Her* eyes blazed, and she threw herself in a fury against the nearest of the brutes, gripping his arm just above the butt of the machine gun. She didn't care that she was unarmed herself—

ridiculously vulnerable in a satin slip and her hair wild to her shoulders. She hissed in a language beyond words, more like a force of nature than a woman.

The agent grabbed her hair and yanked her head back, pulling her off him. She fought like a cat, clawing, and he swung the barrel of the gun toward her. Arturo Duran bellowed like an animal in pain, "Bobby—no!"

The power of his voice, thunderous with pride, froze them all like statues. She stopped fighting, letting her arms go limp, and stood panting. The agent still had a fistful of her hair, but he let his weapon go slack, pointing it toward the floor. By now there were half a dozen of them on the landing, enough to quell a whole platoon of defenseless men. The ones who held Arturo marched him forcefully toward the stairs.

"Her, too," barked the one who seemed to be in charge, who carried no gun himself and much preferred to order a man to shoot.

Arturo Duran went rigid and snapped his head around. "No," he commanded again, but this time it sounded more like pleading.

No use. They dragged him away down the stairs, his heart pounding with fear now, a man who never flinched, but the fear wasn't for him. The one who was holding Bobby shoved her toward the stairs, and she wheeled on the thick-jowled man who was their leader.

"Not till I get dressed," she seethed in defiance, as if he wasn't even worth spitting on. And she turned and stalked back in the bedroom, daring them to shoot her in the back.

Two of them waited dumbly at the bedroom door, watching her throw on a dress and grab a pair of shoes. For a second there, the machine guns in their hands were like toys, foolish and clumsy and drooping. Buttoning up, she swept from the room to follow her husband, the agents hustling after her like a retinue. As she came down into the arms of her jailers—head high, every nerve seething with contempt—it was she who seemed to command an army.

VI

MIDAFTERNOON AT THE Floridita was good
for nothing but washing the floors and polishing the bar
glasses. The dining room wasn't open for lunch because the
crowd that turned it into a Left Bank bistro at night was
usually too hung over to look at food. There were always a
few in the bar, of course, wistful types who dawdled over
espresso, looking to soak up a little Papa Hemingway, as if
this were the clean, well-lighted place.

Today an American couple, bored to tears with each
other, sat in the corner booth. He was reading the green
sheet from Hialeah, and she was too dressed up, her flow-
ered hat like marzipan. Two men in business suits, vaguely
European, hunkered down at the bar and talked about spending New Year's in New York, but they were careful not to
imply they were only buying one-way tickets. It wasn't
good form to talk about running away.

On the last stool sat Ramos, staring at a newspaper. The
glass of tea and the plate of rolls by his elbow were untouched. He didn't actually seem to be reading. His eyes
were fixed on the same blur of words, as if he was drinking
up the news telepathically. No one would have suspected he
was a journalist himself. Gripping the edges of the paper in
his hands, he looked more like a priest who'd lost his faith.

Jack Weil stepped in through the revolving door, pushing
it very slowly as if the ride might make him dizzy. He

looked fit enough, freshly shaved and sporty in an open-necked shirt, and the spring was still in his stride. But he definitely would have turned down the chance to go deep-sea fishing, or anywhere else that tilted too much.

"*Anejo* and coffee," he said to the barman. He seemed to examine his own face in the mirror above the bar, though in a guarded sort of way—as if he wasn't quite prepared to play cards with the face that looked back at him. Then he noticed Ramos slumped at the end of the bar. "Hey, pal," he said, his normal enthusiasm ringing a trifle hollow, "we lost you last night."

Ramos continued to stare at his paper, deaf to the gambler's greeting. The barman served Jack, who sank the *anejo* into the coffee and took a sip like it was medicine. "So, Ramos," he said, trying again, "you hear the one about the Bulgarian, the hermaphrodite, and the Harlem Globetrotter?" Silence still from the end of the bar. "See, they're rowing across the Pacific in a dinghy. . . ." Suddenly the gambler seemed to lose the thread of the story. He sipped his spiked coffee again. "Hey, you want to hear or not?"

By way of reply, Ramos slid the paper down the cold slab of the marble bar toward his friend. Gingerly Jack moved to take a look, but reluctantly, as if he'd have happily waited till he'd finished his breakfast. The shocking headline was like an explosion on the page: REBEL GANG ARRESTED! Below it, a blown-up photo of Arturo Duran, eyes closed and very dead. The picture was grainy, but Jack could still see the torn clothes and the smears of dirt on the aristocrat's face. It didn't look like it had been an easy death.

"Somebody found the body this morning," Ramos said dully. "The police say that SIM picked him up for questioning, and he tried to escape, so they shot him." He uttered a dry, mirthless laugh, as if he'd heard it all before. Then he seemed to force himself to focus, and his voice grew stronger. "It must have been right after you left him, Jack. Did he say anything? Was he worried?"

The gambler stared at the paper, as hypnotized as Ramos

had been. "He said he was nontorturable," Jack replied tonelessly.

"Yeah? So they just killed him. Wasn't that decent of them?" His bitterness was withering. "Fuckin' SIM."

Jack reached out a hand for his coffee cup and missed it, but it didn't seem to matter. He made no attempt to reply to Ramos, and that was all right, too. Then a figure emerged from the back office behind the bar—the day manager. He wasn't as fawning as the owner, but the day-light crowd didn't require its collective ass to be kissed. At the Floridita they knew when to leave their best cus-tomers alone.

"Señor Weil," said the manager, "Joe Volpi was in here looking for you. He says to tell you he's been able to ar-range that party." He checked a scribbled note in his hand. "The Veradero Suite at the Lido."

"Yeah, okay," the gambler replied vaguely, and yet he barely seemed to take the information in. More than a little ironic, since he'd been waiting half his life to hear it. He glanced over at Ramos, and his blue eyes were hard and glittering with intensity. "What about his wife, Ramos? What happened to her?"

The journalist shrugged wearily. "It just says 'disap-peared.' "

The manager looked a bit anxious now as he cast his eyes at the clock above the bar. He clearly didn't want to get on the wrong side of Joe Volpi. "Two-thirty, Mr. Volpi said," he declared with a certain urgency.

Jack Weil nodded and turned on his heel, abruptly mov-ing to leave. Yet it still didn't appear as if he'd quite con-nected with what the manager said. The call had come at last, summoning him to the penthouse suite, and he looked like he didn't remember where that was. He batted through the revolving door and stalked away down the street, a man who might end up anywhere before the day was done.

It was a solitary cell, with a window a foot square facing an airshaft, so the bare glimmer of light made the place seem like an underwater cave. Bobby Duran paced the narrow floor, three steps either way. Compulsively she kept pushing her hair back away from her face, but it fell forward again, dirty and limp and wild. There were deep shadows under her eyes, as if she hadn't slept in months. The dress she'd put on so defiantly was damp and disheveled, torn at the buttonholes.

She stopped and stared at the wall beside the window, hugging herself and shivering with a chill. The wall was covered with names and dates, disconnected messages— GOD SAVE—all scrawled in the stone with a shoe nail or the handle of a spoon. The messages of the damned. Bobby seized her head in her hands, covering her ears as if she heard screaming.

Yet the only sound was the guards unlocking the door. One brought in food on a tray as the other stood blocking the way out. Bobby whirled around and hissed at them, "Where is my husband?"

No answer. The guard laid the tray on the stool beside the cot and turned to go. The other one pulled the door shut behind them, the thunk of the key in the lock like a dagger in Bobby's heart. She heard them walk away and clamped a hand to her mouth so she wouldn't scream.

Jack Weil sat in the barber's chair, staring at himself in the mirror as the barber snipped at the back of his head. A manicurist bent over the arm of the chair, working at the cuticles on Jack's left hand. He wasn't in obvious need of either one—the haircut or the manicure—but the instinct for fastidiousness was stronger than the need. He wouldn't dream of showing up for a penthouse game without looking impeccable. Being groomed was like putting his armor on.

His stare in the mirror was blank. Suddenly he pulled his hand away and removed the sheet that covered his clothes. "It's enough," he said abruptly as the barber stood away and bowed meekly. "Can I use the phone?"

"Of course, señor." The barber gestured toward the corner. The gambler peeled off bills for both of them, then headed for the phone. From his pocket he took out the pack of matches from the Bodeguita. He dialed the number Arturo had written—heard it ringing—then hung up.

The barber came over with a whisk broom. Jack let himself be brushed, and now there was pain in the blanks of his eyes. He didn't know what he wanted anymore, or he knew and didn't dare give it a name.

The interrogation room was very simple, a couple of stools and a table, and a drain in the center of the floor for washing away the unpleasantness. A woman was kneeling against her will, her head thrust in a bucket of water, held down by a burly corporal. The woman's shoulders bucked and struggled violently, but the corporal's hand was like a vise.

"You know nothing of the radio transmitter," said a man's calm voice from across the room. This was Colonel Menocal, head of SIM. He wore a light, soft, civilian suit, and he stood just far enough away not to be splashed. "Not the schedules? The frequencies?"

He made a gesture with his hand, almost bored, and the corporal released the woman's head. Bobby exploded up for air, gasping and choking, her eyes wild. Menocal smiled, elegant as a matinee idol. He probed again. "Not the group's contact in the mountains?"

Bobby coughed violently, then swept her hair from her eyes and gave him a defiant look.

"You were married to Arturo Duran," said Menocal, "and yet you have no idea of the activities of the Duran group. Or the identity of even one of its members."

Now Bobby's look changed to terror, though she stayed mute.

"Yes, he's dead," declared the colonel with a tiny smile. "So it doesn't really matter anymore, does it?" He crouched and looked directly into her stunned and horrified eyes. "When is the next broadcast? We can wait, you know. We have the radio. It's too late to save anyone."

Bobby cast her eyes down, staring at the bucket of water, longing to drown in it now. But she said nothing.

Jack Weil and Joe Volpi stepped from the elevator on the top floor of the Lido. They walked along the black and white marble floor toward a door at the far end of the corridor. On either side of the door stood a couple of goons, one reading a tabloid newspaper, the other an action comic book. They hadn't exactly been recruited at the library.

"The heavy hitter is Roy Forbes," Volpi murmured to the gambler. "Canadian. Tin mines. *Loaded.*"

"And who're the wrestlers?" Jack retorted, nodding toward the goons.

"Bodyguards. One of the players is a little—how should we say?—unpopular these days. Colonel Menocal." And when Jack shot him a puzzled look, he added, "Head of SIM."

Jack blanched, but just for a split second. As he and Volpi passed the guards and entered the suite the gambler was a study in coolness. He didn't bat an eye at the lavishness of the oval blond wood room, the silk-upholstered chairs, the antique mirrors and paintings. By the semicircular bar three waiters stood so still they were almost invisible. On the far side of the room, on a sofa by the fireplace, two gorgeous hookers sat studying their nails. On the coffee table before them was a lavish buffet with caviar and oysters.

There were several men in the room, but Jack managed to lock eyes with none of them. Instead he examined the playing table in the center, overlaid with a beautiful green circle of felt. Beside the table was a maple stand on wheels, holding stacks of chips, new decks of cards, and marker pads. Volpi moved immediately to the stand so he could supervise the buy-ins. One of his best men from the casino downstairs was exchanging chips for cash.

"So Jack, who do you know?" Volpi asked, smiling around expansively at his roomful of high rollers. "Willy you know."

An aging man with a smashed nose, somewhat thick in the torso, nodded from across the table. "*Wie gehts,* amigo?" he offered pleasantly, all but clicking his heels. Jack knew him as a semipro, both gambler and fixer. About as trustworthy as a diamondback rattler.

Jack nodded in response, trying not to make it look like an effort. "Hey, Willy. Somebody told me you were sailing off Venezuela."

Willy shrugged and winked as if they were old buddies. He understood that Jack was implying he'd gone for a swim in cement shoes, and chose to believe he was being complimented for not getting wet. He sat down heavily at the table as Joe Volpi nodded to the man beyond him. "You know Baby," Joe declared to Jack.

Baby Hernandez, the king of rum and molasses, flashed an icy grin. Then Joe was introducing them both to Roy Forbes, a man with a long mean face as craggy as the Newfoundland coast. Forbes, being the richest, scarcely acknowledged the others. All he wanted to do was play cards, and he took from his pocket an obscene wad of cash, moving up to buy in. Jack recognized the pock-faced man behind him as Sonny, the owner of another casino.

Jack's eyes searched the room for Menocal, but no one was wearing a uniform or looked cruel enough. "Buy-in's a grand, Jack," Joe Volpi informed him, and he dutifully drew a roll of cash from his own pocket. He handed Joe six thousand-dollar bills.

And Baby Hernandez drawled, "So you're just gonna stick your toe in the water, huh, Jack?"

Another man, brawny as a linebacker, tore himself from the buffet and approached, chowing down on a sandwich. "Yeah, what's the story, Volpi?" he demanded, jerking a thumb at Jack. "You letting this bum in the game?"

"Fuck, I let you in, Mike," retorted Volpi with his sour smile. "One bum's just as good as the next."

Perhaps the irony broke the tension. In any case, a second later all their attention was drawn to the door of the suite as Colonel Menocal entered. Not in a uniform at all, Jack noticed with surprise, but a Palm Beach linen suit, and not especially cruel looking either. As he walked over, smiling at the group of players, he looked like one of those harmless sports who divided his time between the racetrack and the casino. This seemed even more chilling, somehow—the unlined face, the vapid smile, the banal chitchat as he was introduced round the group.

"Colonel Menocal," Volpi said, "I don't think you know Jack Weil."

Menocal smiled and thrust out a hand. "*Con mucho gusto,* Jack," he said smoothly. They shook. And when Jack looked in his eyes, he saw how deeply satisfied the colonel was with the world, how happy he was in his work. In charge of all terror and torture, and yet he beamed like an archbishop.

Menocal took out an envelope of money—a great deal of money—and handed it over to Joe for chips. Meanwhile Jack picked up a new deck and cracked it open, trying to shake the distraction of the colonel's presence. "Table stakes," he announced briskly. "Twenty-dollars ante. Dealer's choice."

The high rollers took their places round the table, each with his little kingdom of chips. Forbes leaned forward and stuck his craggy face at Jack. "We playin' against Joe Volpi's money or yours?" The sneering put-down wasn't remotely subtle.

"All mine, I'm afraid," Jack replied with a stiff smile. Then he announced to the table, "In honor of Mr. Forbes . . . Canadian stud. You know how to play, Mike?"

"Sure!" Mike McClany said, with enthusiasm, sucking the crumbs of the sandwich through his teeth. "Four-card straight or flush beats a pair."

Jack nodded to Menocal. "That okay with you?"

"Of course."

One by one they began to ante into the pot. Jack started the deal. Mike drummed his pudgy fingers on the table and grinned at Jack. "I seen your friend Dante de Cenzo in Miami," he said. "Did he tell you I practically own this joint now? The feds made 'em sell. You can't own a joint in Vegas and Cuba both anymore. So Volpi and Meyer, they came to me." He poked his thumb at his barrel chest.

"Little louder, Mike," Joe Volpi drawled. "The bugs aren't workin' too well tonight. They may not pick up every word unless you talk real clear."

Mike McClany scoffed. "Hey, this is public knowledge."

"It is now, Mike," Volpi purred, his loathing for his boorish, not-so-silent partner undisguised.

"When you play poker, Mike," Jack said impatiently, "you gotta ante first. It's one of the main rules."

As Mike fiddled with his chips Jack glanced up to find the colonel watching him closely. Just at that moment there was a burst of distant machine-gun fire from across the city, somewhere toward the mountains.

Willy laughed. "It's getting to sound like Shanghai around here. I was there in '49. Sensational, absolutely sensational. But I stayed too long. The communists came in—I lost a fortune." He shrugged philosophically, as if he could dance in his cement shoes. "Trick is to get in, get out."

Jack nodded to Sonny. "Ten bets."

"This is not Shanghai, my friend," declared Colonel Menocal suavely. "Nothing is going to change here."

Abruptly Jack turned to him. "Any chance Mrs. Duran is alive?"

Joe Volpi took a sharp intake of breath, appalled by the gambler's forwardness. First rule at the Lido: You don't mix cards and politics. Menocal frowned at Jack, trying to figure him out. "Who?" he asked carefully. Jack didn't repeat the name but held the colonel's gaze, unwavering.

"Play poker, Jack," Joe Volpi barked.

"Whose bet is it?" Forbes wanted to know.

Menocal smiled. "It's Jack's bet," he said.

* * *

The interrogation room was lit by a single pale bulb, as if Batista was trying to economize in every way he could. Bobby was slumped on the low stool with her head down, and it wasn't certain if she was even conscious. Her blouse and hair were drenched. Across the room in the shadows, near the water-torture bucket, a large rectangular box had just been wheeled in on a dolly.

The young corporal on guard moved forward and gently touched Bobby's shoulder. She raised her head, but her eyes were dazed. The corporal tapped a cigarette from his pack and offered it to her. She made no gesture either way, as if she was beyond responding. He touched her lips with the cigarette, and finally she shook her head no.

He leaned forward toward her. His voice was soft and intimate. "How old are you, señora?"

"Thirty-three," came the toneless reply.

"I'm eighteen," he said. "Almost."

"Young for a fascist," Bobby retorted, some blood in her voice now.

The corporal smiled. "Would be a feather in my cap if you gave *me* the information my colonel wants. I would be a sergeant, maybe." His chest puffed at the mere idea as he straightened up. "Come here, señora."

She watched him move across the room to where the bucket stood. She shrank back on the stool.

"No, no more swimming for now," he assured her. "I want you to see something." And now his voice hardened into an order. "Stand up, please. Come here."

Bobby stood up from the stool, her carriage still erect, a vestige of the pride and passion that coursed through her veins. She moved to the dark corner, tilting her head curiously at the sight of the long rectangular box. Then suddenly the corporal switched on a flashlight in his hand, training the bright beam on the body of Monica, laid out in an open coffin.

"Don't you know this pretty girl?" asked the corporal, his voice almost playful, as if this was a private joke between them.

Bobby's eyes filled with tears, till the sight of the dead woman blurred. She moved her head from side to side, more in disbelief than denial. She swallowed hard. When at last she found her voice, there was something deeply formal about her words, as if she was speaking to a church full of friends and loved ones. As if she could find some meaning in all of this by fiercely proclaiming the virtues of the bright and beautiful woman before her.

"Her name is Monica Eloy. She was seventeen years old—not quite your age. She was a science student at the university before it was closed. She had a scholarship."

The corporal practically trembled as he listened. Somehow he had managed to break the wife of Arturo Duran, and now she was going to give him a king's ransom of information.

"She made her own clothes," Bobby continued softly. "She could sew very well, so she made her own clothes." It seemed the tears were about to spill. She swallowed even harder. "She made that dress herself." And she gestured sadly at the torn print shift on the frail body.

Then she turned to the young soldier, who barely breathed he was so excited. Bobby Duran tossed her ragged hair, a flash of the old defiance. She spoke with murderous calm, "And I'll drown before I tell you one thing more. And *you'll* die a corporal, you son of a bitch."

She turned and went back to the stool, like a queen in exile, and just as regal.

It was deep in the middle of the night by now in the penthouse suite. The poker players had been at it for hours, and the air was yellow with smoke. Half-eaten plates of food were strewn about, because the waiters had long since been dismissed, too distracting for Roy Forbes. Also the hookers. Poker was everything now. Forbes sipped tensely from a glass of milk, like an old man who'd outlived all his bad habits. His stack of chips was considerably smaller.

Joe Volpi watched the table like a hawk. Baby Hernandez and Mike McClany had folded. Jack had three hearts and a club showing. Menocal had two diamonds, ace high. The pock-faced Sonny had a king high and two little diamonds. Although he was still officially in, and he might be due for a Christmas miracle, it was really down to Menocal and Jack, head-to-head.

The colonel studied Jack across the table for a long moment. "What am I supposed to think, my friend?" he asked. "When you raised, I thought you had sevens back-to-back. Now you want me to think you have hearts." He paused thoughtfully, a man who was used to getting into other people's heads, by whatever means he could. "But then you wouldn't have checked, would you? Eight hundred."

As soon as Menocal pushed his chips into the center, Sonny folded. The heat was too hot. But Jack smiled with a certain serene satisfaction and announced, "Call your eight and . . . tapped."

With that he pushed all the chips he had—almost eleven thousand—toward the pot, which began to look like the end of the rainbow. Menocal studied Jack again, as if adding up the cost of his clothes. Clearly the colonel didn't think the gambler's tastes were expensive enough. He nodded to Volpi that he would meet the raise. Then he said quietly to Jack, "I think you're trying to steal it, my friend."

With a neat flourish the head of the secret police turned up his hole card: ace of spades. "Pair of aces, Mr. Weil," he declared.

Jack nodded, then turned up his own hole card: ace of hearts. Very politely, the soul of courtesy, he said, "Unfortunately, Colonel, four hearts beats a pair." And almost apologetically he began raking in the huge pile of chips.

There was dead silence around the table. Menocal's face was utterly blank, no emotion at all. And as Jack stacked his chips, Joe Volpi stepped forward and bowed obsequiously in Roy Forbes's direction. "Up to you, Mr. Forbes," he said. "You want to call it a night?"

"Yeah," replied the industrialist, sharp as a dog barking. They all stood up at once, breaking the spell of the game at last, most of them looking like they were nursing a bad case of heartburn. The colonel extended a hand to Jack. "Clearly it doesn't pay to underestimate you, Mr. Weil."

Jack grinned. "Doesn't bother me."

A small, delicate pause, in which the colonel examined his hands, but not to check if they were dirty. Indeed, he seemed to be admiring them. When he spoke, he addressed the tips of his fingers. "I think Mrs. Duran is being questioned by the authorities," he said.

"You're the authorities, aren't you?" the gambler retorted.

The colonel's mouth stretched in a small, mirthless smile. "Yes," he replied, with a false modesty worthy of an archbishop destined to be a cardinal. Then, to the group at large, *"Hasta leugo, amigos."*

As he moved toward the door, his pair of goons in tow, Mike McClany tried to waylay him. "Buy you some breakfast, Colonel?" he asked, knowing what a coup it would be to have such a powerful man sitting in one of the public spaces, as if the Lido were an annex of the presidential palace.

"Sleep would be better, *gracias,*" the colonel replied, barely breaking stride as he and the bodyguards swept out. It felt as if the room itself unclenched slightly, now that he was gone.

Mike turned back to the others. "Baby? Some breakfast?" He seemed obscurely terrified at the notion of eating his waffles and sausages all alone.

"I can't," said Baby Hernandez, moving to peer out the door, making sure the colonel had made it into the elevator. He turned once more to the group and gave a weary shrug. "I have to fly to Oriente," he explained, meaning that he had a meeting with the rebels, very off-the-record.

Willy laughed. "You trying to buy insurance on the revolution?"

"The rebels tried that shit with me." Forbes sneered. Again that air of fine disdain from being the richest man in the room. "I told them to shove it."

"They can burn my fields like that," Baby retorted, snapping his fingers. "They can't burn your mines." And he walked out followed by Willy and Mike, who pleaded with them to have a plate of eggs before they headed out.

Which left Forbes, Joe Volpi, and Jack, standing in a group by the green-covered table. "Everything satisfactory, Mr. Forbes?" asked Volpi, concerned as any maître d'.

"Except for losing," replied the industrialist dryly. "Sandwiches were good, though."

Volpi purred and rubbed his hands together. "We could make the stakes more . . . interesting next time."

Forbes nodded. "Yeah," he said, "maybe we'll get together again." Despite the declaration, his tone was heavily noncommittal. "So long, Weil."

As soon as he'd left the suite, swinging the door shut behind him, Joe Volpi whirled on Jack. "What the fuck are you doing, man?"

Jack ignored the outburst. "Where would he have her?" he demanded sharply.

Joe Volpi swallowed his fury and changed tactics. He put an arm around the gambler's shoulders and spoke in an almost avuncular way, distinctly creepy but not unendearing. "Leave it alone, Jack," he reasoned. "What kind of action did you come down here for? I think this Forbes is gonna come through. You might get to play that game you been waiting all your life for. This thing tonight, this was like a test. Now I told you I'd talk to Meyer. Don't screw it up, okay?"

Jack shrugged off Volpi's arm. His eyes blazed with concentration. "Where, Joe?" he asked, goading the other man. "Come on, you know where all the bodies are buried around here." Then a half second's pause, in which the gambler's face went naked with raw need. "Get me in to see her, Joe."

"No." Volpi backed away a step, as if unable to bear the intimacy of the moment.

"Hey Joe, gimme a break." Coaxing and smooth, Jack the seducer. "Didn't I save your ass in the war?"

Volpi flashed his sour smile. "I was in Vegas, Jack. The whole time."

"Well, I *would* have, pal," the gambler replied cheerfully, clapping Volpi on the shoulder. "I would have dragged your wounded butt ten miles to the nearest field hospital. That's how loyal I am, ya know?" He began to steer the reluctant Volpi toward the telephone on the bar. "Besides, I'm gonna make you guys a gold mine when we have the big game—or should I say a tin mine?" He picked up the receiver and held it out to Joe. "And all I need is this one little favor. . . ."

VII

THE PRISON LOOMED above the Malecon sea-wall in the chill dawn light, its black stone walls like glacial ice. It had been a prison for hundreds of years, one of the oldest fortifications in the city, with dungeons as twisted and deep and hopeless as a medieval inquisition. The high tide sprayed against the bases of its towers, proving once again that no force of nature would ever bring it down. By the years of pain and madness it enclosed, the old prison had achieved an almost separate reality.

In front of the looming iron gates, a green Cadillac convertible was parked among the unmarked black sedans of the secret police, an incongruous toy. Admitted within the gates of hell, Jack Weil was led across the cobbled prison courtyard and into the heavily guarded warden's compound. He walked carefully, almost on tiptoe, as if he didn't want to wake the dead. As they passed under an archway and into the warden's stronghold, Jack heard distantly through the stone a scrap of a popular song—Rosemary Clooney, it sounded like. Under the song was a muffled scream that went on and on, in a sick sort of harmony.

The guard ushered the gambler into a small, seedy office. Behind the scarred desk sat an even seedier sergeant, unshaven and clearly a rummy. His grungy uniform appeared to be crawling with lice. Jack held out to the unsavory man the official pass that Volpi had managed to secure. The sergeant took it between two fingers, gingerly, as if it was even more soiled than he was.

"Mmm," he grunted with evident distaste. "For one look at the prisoner. I warn you, sēnor, is rather dark down there. Not such a good place for looking." He heaved himself to his feet and snatched up a ring of keys.

"I don't want to look at her," the gambler replied evenly. The sergeant stopped and gave him a curious look, interested at last. "I want her out," said Jack.

The sergeant laughed coarsely. "Only somebody more important wants her *here*, Chico—"

"He's asleep," the gambler said, cutting him off. Then he drew two airline tickets from his inside jacket pocket. "And by the time he wakes up, you and your wife will be in a hotel in Miami, having a sloe-gin fizz by the pool." He slapped the tickets down on the desk. "After all, Lieutenant, a month from now who *knows* who's going to be boss down here?"

The sergeant hesitated, beads of sweat on his forehead. Then Jack pulled a roll of cash from his pants and began to count out hundred-dollar bills. Crisp from the mint, the greenbacks fell softly on the desk. "Two thousand," Jack declared. "American. For expenses."

The sergeant pulled in his gut and seemed to stand an inch taller, as if he accepted the promotion to lieutenant Jack had unwittingly given him. He scooped up the money with a cupped hand, gathered the tickets, and stuffed it all between the tarnished buttons of his uniform. Then he smiled and gave the keys a jingle, like some kind of ghastly Santa.

"You wait outside, sēnor," he said.

In her solitary cell Bobby huddled on the wooden bunk, arms around her knees as she rocked back and forth. After a long moment she turned her dazed eyes to the wall, then reached out a finger to scratch at a clear space with her nail. It wasn't clear what word she was trying to write, maybe just an *X* to mark the spot of her pain. Then she swiveled her head at the sound of the key in the lock.

The sergeant said nothing but merely jerked his head, indicating she should follow. She did so, nothing to fight with anymore. Her shoulders were slumped and her spirit broken as she walked beside him through a labyrinth of passages, up flights of spiral stairs. It didn't even seem to cross her dulled and ravaged mind that he hadn't bothered to put handcuffs on her.

She wouldn't have been the least surprised if he'd led her out into the prison yard to face a firing squad. Perhaps she might have even been relieved to have it over with. She certainly didn't understand what they were doing in an office or why the sergeant drew a finger across his lips to ask for silence. Her heart was too dead to hope right now.

Then suddenly he was handing her an envelope from the desk. She opened the flap and reached inside, bewildered, as if this was all happening in a dream. Her hand came out holding her wristwatch and her wedding ring. She fumbled to put them on, even though they raked her soul with memories that hurt. The dead heart was beating again, but was raw like an open wound.

She looked up at the sergeant, still waiting to see what the trick was. He was holding her elegant bone-colored bag with the gold clasp, an absurd luxury in this place of desolation. He handed it to her, and she took it. Once more he drew his finger across his lips and motioned her to follow. She finally believed she was going to be freed as she walked beside him down a long flight of stone stairs, her footsteps ringing hollowly. Free like a castaway, floating alone on the open sea.

It was just dawn as Jack saw her emerge through the iron gates. Her eyes fluttered against the red gold of the low sun, and she clutched her bag tightly against her breasts as if it held everything she owned. She stood in the parking lot, uncertain which way to go, and when he stepped away from the Cadillac to greet her, she looked at him like he was a stranger.

"You want me to take you home?" he asked gently. No answer: she still seemed dazed. "I don't think you should stay there, but maybe you want to pick up a few things."

She swallowed with difficulty. It seemed a great effort to speak, but she understood she owed him something. "I'd like to walk a little," she said at last, almost as if she thought she needed permission, or as if she feared she might not remember how. "I'd like to get a cup of coffee, and I'd like to walk."

He nodded and opened the car door. She moaned a little as she got in, the muscles stiff in her neck and shoulders. He tried not to think about what she'd been through, taking it like she did—one step at a time. He drove them a quarter mile along the Malecon seawall, stopping at a café-bar that was just opening its shutters. Neither of them spoke as they sat at an outside table, watching the surf turn blue as the sun rose higher.

A waiter brought them bowls of milky coffee and then began to swab the tile floor with a string mop, sloshing it in a bucket of water. For a long moment she stared at the bucket, stunned by its ordinariness, the lack of any threat. She shuddered involuntarily at the memory of the other bucket, then turned her gaze to watch the water spilling across the floor. The fanning pattern made by the mop, the gleam of the wet tile—it all seemed so unbearably sweet for being so plain.

"You have a cigarette?" she asked in a husky voice.

Jack slipped out his pack of Pall Malls and tapped out a cigarette. She took it awkwardly between her fingers, as if they were slightly numb from frostbite. She let him light it for her, recognizing the matches from the Bodeguita. "You think you could eat something?" he asked tentatively, not wanting to say the wrong thing.

"Oh no," she replied gravely. She took a deep drag and blew it out and watched the smoke, tossing her hair slightly.

He'd made no mention of her disheveled appearance, the torn buttons at the neck of her dress, but the morning sun was already softening all of that. Her hair was luxurious again as it dried in the breeze off the water.

"He's dead," she said quietly, her eyes far out to sea now, as if looking for a sail. "Are they all dead?"

He shook his head because he didn't know. He said nothing about her loss because it would have sounded empty. When they'd finished the bowls of coffee, he paid the waiter and trotted across the street to catch up with her as she walked along the seawall. Trailing her hand along the rough stone balustrade, she moved as deliberately as a sleepwalker—or a dreamer puzzled to find herself released from a nightmare into beauty. The choppy sea below the wall was gold and navy blue, gloriously alive.

He stayed beside her, measuring his pace to hers, until she stopped and leaned against the wall, the first moment she'd truly rested since she left the jail. Jack stood next to her, hands in his pockets, and they looked wistfully out toward the horizon. Till finally she said, "What are you? A gangster?"

He laughed. "Do I look like a gangster?"

"Why did he let me go?" Her voice was almost a whisper, as if she still didn't quite believe she was free. Jack didn't answer, but then she didn't seem to expect him to either. She walked a few paces farther, then tilted her head and looked at the light on the water. "You can see the fish," she said irrelevantly, and yet she sounded heartbroken, as if she longed to point out the fish to her husband.

Jack waited for her to turn around. When she did, her gaze was direct and inquiring, bold again the way it was before they came and smashed into her house. Jack held her eyes with his, and the moment suddenly threatened to become too naked. She might break down. He might pity her. There was no way to predict where it would go from there.

She was the first to look away. "Where are you from?" she asked, just to fill the awkward silence.

"I don't know. Philadelphia." It was either a lie, or it mattered so little he could hardly remember.

"I used to have good friends there."

"I bet I don't known them."

Now she wasn't afraid to look, becaue they were both smiling. She caught at her blowing hair, which the sun had laced with gold. Behind her the ocean belonged to no one, freer than all of them, endlessly rebelling as it slapped the long seawall. A shower of spray exploded over the balustrade, and he pulled her away before it doused her.

"Hey, I think we should get out of here," Jack declared, one hand still on the small of her back, as if they were dancing.

"I'd like to walk." And she sidled out of the circle of his arm, but gently and with something like regret, so it didn't leave him empty.

"It's a long way," he said, but not pushing.

"I'll be all right." She reached out a hand to his, the hand he dealt with, squeezing it briefly. "Good-bye."

And he let her walk away along the wall, still with the pace of a dreamer, her beauty restored by the morning light. He turned to cross the boulevard, hands in his pockets, feeling the roll of cash he'd won. He got into the car and watched her some more in the side mirror, moving ever farther away. He couldn't stop thinking about the good-bye, whether it sounded final because she was bound for a place where he could never follow her.

Except he was a gambler.

He cranked the key, and the engine exploded. He raked the wheel hard to the left, taking off from the curb into a tight U-turn. He glided the Caddy along the seawall, catching up with her, then slowing almost to a crawl so he could stay exactly abreast of her. Finally she turned with her enigmatic smile, watching the car move with her. She seemed almost hypnotized.

"Get in," he said, but the smile stayed fixed, as if she hadn't heard him. He reached over and flung open the door. "Come on. Get in."

Clara," she said softly, "Arturo's family has a *finca*. Just before Santa Clara . . ." She was like an amnesiac swimming up out of a deep underwater cave. "The rebels are using it. They don't know that . . ."

Her voice trailed off. She seemed unable to pronounce her husband dead again. Jack turned back to the stove and cracked the eggs, sizzling them in the butter. "So, Bobby, where are you from?" he asked, cheerful and energetic, like a short-order cook in a diner. "Where'd you grow up?"

Her eyes pulled away from the dark horizon, watching him flip the eggs and stick the bread under the broiler. "Sweden," she replied.

He snapped his fingers. "I was gonna say one of those Scandinavian countries. Something kind of . . . dusky about that voice. You got family there?" She nodded. "You in touch with them?"

"No," she said with a small toss of her hair, as if she was trying the gesture out again. "Just Christmas."

"It's Christmas now," Jack replied, expertly sliding the eggs from the pan to the toast.

"Not this Christmas."

"Well, you ought to be in touch," he declared, capping the eggs with a second slice of toast. Then he moved to the cupboard to take out a couple of mugs. "So, anyway, you came over here from Sweden. Just to warm up?"

"No, I didn't come here first." She was trying to concentrate now, as if it was very important to get the sequence right. "I was in California. Hollywood."

He gave a low whistle as he poured the coffee. "Hey, you get around, don't you? What were you doing out there?"

She uttered a soft, one-note laugh, more like a sigh really. "I saw Garbo when I was a kid."

"Garbo?" He frowned as he set the plate and mug before her. "Oh yeah, that's right. Swedish!"

Bobby nodded, the corners of her mouth beginning to curl with irony. "Yes. And she seemed to know Robert Taylor. . . ."

"Yup. *Camille*. I'm sure they were real good buddies." He was grinning at her.

"Anyway, he was so pretty . . . I just had to meet him. So I went to California to be an actress. Like everybody else."

"So you could be pals with Robert Taylor." He tilted his head, beaming with delight, triumphant that he'd managed to tap into her irony.

"Except I never met him," she admitted. She hadn't touched the sandwich yet, but she took a sip of the coffee. "Instead I married a writer. But then he was blacklisted, so we had to leave the States." She shrugged—win some, lose some.

"He was a commie, huh?" She shrugged again, as if the word was very inexact. "Well, I've known good commies and bad commies. I'm sure he was a good one."

"He wrote Westerns."

"Ah," said the gambler. "I like Westerns. I don't know what they have to *do* with anything, but I like them."

She reached to the plate and tore off a corner of toast. Jack tried not to gloat, for it all still seemed very tenuous, her remembering and her fragile grip on reality. "He hated Mexico," she said, chewing thoughtfully. "He started drinking. And then it was finished." Suddenly she gasped, half rising from the chair. "I should have got some clean clothes. . . ."

"Don't worry," he said soothingly, "we'll get you whatever you need." She settled again with a sigh, picked up the knife beside the plate, and carefully cut the sandwich in half. "So how'd it go for *you* in Mexico? You get to do some acting?"

She smiled at the memory, picking up the sandwich and taking a bite. She glanced at Jack, and he winked. "Mmm," she murmured playfully, pointing to her mouth. And when she'd had another gulp of coffee, she seemed almost exhilarated to tell him the story. "Oh yes," she said sardonically, "I was a very big actress in Mexico." She laughed like a trill of music, and he found himself holding his breath.

"I was always 'La Gringa,' " she continued, tilting her chin and lowering her eyes in a pose of comic glamour. "My favorite was when I played the daughter of a mad scientist, and he replaces my brain with the brain of a gorilla."

They were both laughing now. She took another hungry bite, then tossed her hair for real. "Of course my sweetheart doesn't know any of this," she said. "And he comes to the lab one night, and he says, *'Querida! Qué pasa? Te comportes de un modo bastane raro!'* And I go like this."

She sat straight up in the chair and began to growl as she pawed the air. Jack leaned against the fridge, doubled over with laughter, as she rolled her eyes and gabbled like a monkey. Then she couldn't stop laughing either, and suddenly the tears were running down her cheeks, and she was crying at the same time. Then just crying.

Jack stood awkwardly, not quite knowing how to help. She wasn't sobbing, she was far too exhausted for that. But the tears streamed down her face, and she gasped in pain, as if the torturers had come back. Jack moved to her, putting out a hand to stroke her hair. She turned her face away and pulled herself together. When she began to breathe regularly again, Jack withdrew his hand—balling it into a fist as if he'd touched fire.

"I met a lot of nice people in Mexico," she said. "That's where I met Arturo. So now I'm in Cuba." She shook her head in a sort of amazement, as if her life had changed so many times she hardly recognized it anymore. "In the last seven years I've spent maybe two weeks in the States. What's it like these days?" The question was heavy with yearning, a longing for something left behind.

"Well," said Jack, retrieving his coffee mug from the stove, "the Dodgers moved to L.A. The Giants moved to San Francisco. That about covers it. Oh, and you can watch yourself on television in front of the RCA Building."

She was eating the sandwich again, hungrily now, like a refugee who didn't know when she'd see her next meal. He was almost embarrassed to witness the nakedness of her appetite. She was too real.

"You want to go back, Bobby?" he asked in a different voice. " 'Cause I can get you a seat anywhere you want to go, anytime. 'Cause I don't think you're safe here much longer."

"Safe," she repeated questioningly, as if the word had no meaning where she lived. She took a white dish towel from the table and wiped her mouth and her hands, simple as a farm girl just then. "Jack Weil," she said, savoring the bluntness of his name. "Tell me, Jack Weil, why are you doing all this?"

"For old times," he replied, smiling. "Remember, we used to be smuggling buddies. Besides, I never knew a movie star before—especially one with the brain of a gorilla." Yet he couldn't sustain the lightness. He wanted to reach for a reason he'd never spoken before—never even imagined. "I don't know," he said uncertainly. "I like you. You're . . . you don't say everything."

She didn't answer, but she heard him. And he actually saw the moment when the weariness hit her at last, like a tidal wave. Her eyelids drooped, and her arms went rubbery.

"Hey, I think you better sleep for a while," he said gently.

She sighed. "First I'd like to take a shower."

"Sure. It's right over there. I'll get you a robe."

He strode through the flat to the bedroom, pulling a silky boxer's robe from his closet. When he returned to the kitchen, she hadn't moved. She took the robe and laid it on her lap, stroking the green fabric with her hand.

"We almost did it," she declared mournfully. "We were so close."

Right now he wanted to touch her more than ever. For the first time it hurt not to. "Hey—I'm sorry," he said awkwardly. "He was a real nice guy."

"Yes. He was." He thought she was going to cry again, but whatever it was went deeper just then than tears. "You have no idea," she added softly. Then she stood up and turned her piercing eyes on him, anxious in case that last remark had somehow left Jack out. She smiled. "After we left you at the Bodeguita, we walked for a while. He said he'd like to play poker with you sometime."

She stepped by him and out of the kitchen, leaving behind her the faintest hint of her lily perfume. He heard her pad across the darkened living room and into the bathroom, closing the door behind her. He stared down at her empty plate, then at her bag. For a second it seemed as if he would explode with feeling, but he probably didn't know what the feeling was. Instead, almost unconsciously, he held up his arm and rubbed the inside of the forearm, stroking it for luck. When he heard the water running in the bathroom, his features were blank—what they called in his trade a poker face.

He walked into the living room and switched on the lamps. Then he sat at the center table and reached for a deck of cards. He began to play blackjack with himself, but he hardly saw the cards. He heard the water stop, and a minute later she stepped from the bathroom, wrapped in the green silk robe. She was toweling her hair dry, softly humming. He kept on playing blackjack—kept on losing.

"Can I borrow some clothes?" she asked. "I don't think I could stand putting that dress on again." And when he moved to get up, she waved a hand to stop him. "No, no," she said playfully, "let me pick."

She swept the towel like a turban around her head and moved into his bedroom. He switched to poker hands, playing against two of his faithful phantoms. He heard her rustling in his closet, strangely excited to think of her touching all his clothes. There was a rattle of machine-gun fire in the distance, which clenched his gut. He didn't want to think about the outside world right now. He'd had enough of it.

Then she appeared at the bedroom door. She wore a pair of pleated white linen trousers and a brick-red shirt, the whole outfit loose and oversized and therefore sexy. She turned her body in a half twirl, modeling for him. "Well," she said, laughing, "could I pass for Jack Weil?"

"You could be twins," he drawled.

"I'd rather take a nap in here," she said, and moved across to the shuttered window. She pulled the shutters open, and the sun poured in. Unlike him, she didn't seem to need to keep the world outside. She settled herself on the sofa so the sunlight could fall on her hair and finish drying it. She snuggled against the cushions and smiled at him. "You don't have to stay."

"Thanks, but I live here." They grinned at each other. "Anything else I can get for you, Mr. Weil?" he asked. "A blanket, maybe?"

She shook her head dreamily, eyelids heavy again. "Maybe you'll put on a record," she said.

He moved past the sofa to the hi-fi cabinet, plucking up the first album that came to hand: *Kay Starr at the Copa.* Clearly his luck was holding. He slid the disc out of the sleeve and set it on the turntable. A moment later the room was bathed in a big-band sound, and the singer was crooning "Always Remember."

He looked down at her curled on the sofa, her face turned from the brightness of the sun. She was already fast asleep, so if she heard the music at all, it was only to score her dreams. His own conflicting emotions seemed to evaporate at the sight of her looking so safe. And suddenly it hit him how exhausted he was himself.

He moved to the bedroom, lulled by the music. He didn't even bother to take his shoes off as he lay down, because he thought he would get up as soon as the record was over. He only needed forty winks himself, and besides, he couldn't think of anything he'd rather do today than watch her dream.

For he was the sentry here.

VIII

HE WOKE TO the ringing of the phone, with no sense of the time at all. Above him the ceiling fan turned slowly, pushed by a lazy breeze. He was on his feet by the end of the second ring and moving urgently into the living room, but not because of the phone. Because of her.

She was gone. He knew it even as he came around the sofa, feeling her absence like a sudden stroke of bad luck. The clothes she'd borrowed were folded neatly, and there was a note on top. His heart pounded. The phone was on the fifth ring. He snatched up the square of paper—he'd never seen her handwriting before. He couldn't even begin to list the things about her he'd never seen.

You're a decent man, Jack Weil. So long. Bobby.

He grabbed the phone on the eighth ring, just to make it stop. He didn't say hello. Joe Volpi's voice was filled with excitement, "Jack? Congratulations, baby. Meyer's interested."

"What?" the gambler asked vaguely, stalling for time so he could read the words over and over.

"Forbes got a couple of heavyweight Canucks coming down from Montreal."

"Yeah, okay . . ."

"Something wrong, Jack?"

"No," the gambler said hoarsely. "Nothing's wrong." The words of the note had already started to blur, till they seemed like only the record of murmurous sounds, a laugh and a sigh together. *So long.*

"Be at Meyer's Christmas party tonight," instructed the oily casino chief. "He wants a look at your face. If he's gonna back you for this kind of dough, you better give him a real good look. You come around eight—the Royal Suite. And there'll be a nice little Christmas ornament for you—"

Jack nodded curtly and put down the phone, cutting him off midsentence. The gambler didn't like being told what to do. He seemed completely uninterested in the prospect of meeting the King of Big. All he wanted to do right now was stare at Bobby's note. But he hadn't even sat down before the door to the apartment shook with knocking. He knew in his bones it wasn't La Polaca. He crossed to the vestibule, slipping the note in his pocket.

When he opened the door, it was like a parody of a ceremonial entrance. The two bodyguards from the Lido game, brutes in soiled white suits, stepped aside like an honor guard, revealing Colonel Menocal. The impeccable colonel, his eyes glazed with arrogance, strode past Jack into the flat. He glanced around like somebody used to taking over, as if his job gave him eminent domain.

"Where is she?" he asked sharply.

"Who?" Jack retorted, slouching against the kitchen doorway, hands in his pockets.

The colonel's eyes bored into him. "What are you up to, Jack?" he asked, sneering. "You becoming political all of a sudden?"

"Oh sure. Didn't you know? I'm down here running for Congress."

Menocal turned from him contemptuously, raking the room once more with his flashing eyes. He caught sight of himself in the oval mirror on the wall beside the bathroom door. Abruptly he strode over and yanked the mirror from the wall, dashing it to the floor at his feet. It shattered as if a bomb had exploded.

The silence afterward was creepy, the colonel standing in a pool of shards. His voice was a whisper of rage. "You paid two thousand dollars for her company, my friend. That's high for a Havana whore."

Jack strolled across the room to the cupboard above the hi-fi. He didn't seem at all rattled by the colonel's presence. He took down a bottle of whiskey and a pair of glasses. Then he crossed to the center table, pouring himself a shot. "Colonel," he said, lifting the glass in a gentlemanly toast, "I have to tell you, I made a big mistake on that." He swallowed the shot in a single gulp, smacking his lips. "She's got too much baggage, that one. Too much going on, if you catch my drift." He shrugged. "I think she's gone back to the States."

He offered the bottle to Menocal, just a friendly drink between a couple of card players. The colonel drew back icily, as if he refused to be drawn in. "Of course you're a liar, Jack," he said. "But then, it's your profession, isn't it? I'm just here to remind you what a good life you have in Havana. You play cards—you eat well—you fuck whenever you want. So I ask myself, why would you want to get involved with these fanatics? Because they want to *change* all that."

He stepped out of the pool of the broken mirror, not the least bit superstitious that he might have just brought himself seven years of bad luck. Colonel Menocal was the sort of man who'd been making his own luck all his life. "Leave them alone, Jack," he added pointedly, just this side of a threat. "And if you hear from Mrs. Duran, I want to be the first to know. You understand?"

Jack said nothing. He poured himself a second shot, and the colonel moved to leave, his bodyguards falling into step behind him. The second one, the dimwit who read the comic books, remarked to the gambler in a superior tone, "Don't drink so early, señor. Your liver is not even awake yet."

Jack lifted the glass, toasting the goon, and drank it down. When they pulled the door shut, he heard them clumping down the stairs, imagining the horror of La Polaca as she watched them from behind her curtains. Jack Weil didn't seem to care in the least that he'd just been visited—just been *warned*—by the most dangerous man in Cuba. He poured himself a third shot and drew Bobby's note from his pocket. Then he sat down to read it in earnest—poring over it like a hand-drawn map, as if somehow it would lead him back to her.

Christmas was doing the best it could, but it was a constant struggle to keep things merry. High on the wedding-cake roof of the presidential palace, machine-gun emplacements were set up all along the balustrade, which winked and glowed with ropes of colored lights. A loud-speaker at either end blared "Silent Night" in an endless loop, yet the speakers looked ready at any moment to pierce the air with sirens.

In the courtyard in front of the palace rose a huge white-frosted Christmas tree, shining like a beacon over the city. In front of the tree, where the presents should have been, were sandbag fortifications. These served as makeshift bunkers for what looked like a whole division of Batistiano troops. Beyond the sandbags was a cordon of military trucks and a unit of antiaircraft, all of it siphoned off from the Marshall Plan at five cents on the dollar. All around the perimeter of the palace grounds, the wrought-iron fence was reinforced with swirls of barbed wire. Behind the main gates, decked with Christmas greens, was a pen in which two drugged reindeer scratched for fleas, looking totally lost.

It was either Christmas or Armageddon, whichever came first.

The city was a frenzy of parties tonight, in every drunken quarter. The holiday was the last excuse to forget all the tension and uncertainty. The tourist hotels and casinos were ablaze with light. The best champagne was trundled out of the cellars—what were they saving it for? The limousines, the diamonds, mink on a balmy night—by common consent, now was the time to go for broke.

The best party, the only party, the one they would all kill to get into, was happening at the Royal Suite at the Lido. A vast, high-ceilinged deco set, sleek as the first-class lounge on the *Ile de France*. "Jingle Bells" was the song of the hour, upbeat and rhumba tempo, provided by an orchestra in white tails. The perfect accompaniment to the papier-mâché palm tree revolving in the center of the room like a giant ballerina, dusted with artificial snow and glitter. Along one wall was a lavish buffet table, fit for a coronation or a wedding in Little Italy.

The guests of Meyer Lansky were ornamental and noisy, filling the air with a greedy, forced gaiety. The buffet was attacked rather than sampled. The drinks went down too fast because there was always more where that came from. Meanwhile, the more serious party nibbles—ganja from Kingston, cocaine direct from La Paz—were being consumed in the bathrooms and in quiet corners of the balcony.

It was a mixed group—the swell and the sleazy. The stylish women preferred strapless dresses, because they showed off to best effect the bronze and cocoa of a Carib tan. Well-cared-for older gentleman, sporting madras dinner jackets, preened at the attentions of the society sweeties who escorted them. You could tell the upper-level members of the Mob by the dead stares in their nerveless faces. They weren't really meant to wear suits except to their own funerals. The Mob wives were mostly Italian mamas, who never traveled south for the winter without a gallon jar of red sauce.

Circulating here and there were entertainers from the high-priced clubs on the Strip, glad-handing and nearly delirious with their own glamour. And of course you had the ubiquitous hustlers and dealers, who would have looked obscurely dirty even in Santa suits.

The conversation was as empty as everyone could get away with. They dropped names like stones on one another's feet. They got huffy and swore they would call the embassy if somebody didn't get this country in order pretty quick. They decided with breathless intensity that Eddie was really in love with Liz. The usual bull, except there was a frantic edge, a thin whine of hysteria just under the surface, as if the *Ile de France* at any moment might just kiss an iceberg.

Jack Weil moved through the thick of the crowd, swimming through a sea of strapless shoulders. He didn't appear to know anyone, which seemed to suit him fine. He kept an eye out for Joe Volpi; but mostly—he knew it was irrational—he combed the sea of partygoers for Bobby. There was no way that she would be here, but he couldn't be anywhere now without searching.

Suddenly he found himself face-to-face with a longhaired blond in a skintight aqua dress. She looked like a mermaid. "You must be Jack," she breathed, leaning so close that her breasts pressed against his white dinner jacket.

"Yeah," he replied guardedly.

"Hi, I'm Audrey," she said with a giddy smile.

"Okay," retorted the gambler. In the back of his mind he heard Volpi purring: *a nice little Christmas ornament for you.*

She clutched one of his biceps. If she got any closer, she was going to mount him. "Can you tell me which one is Meyer Lansky?" she asked excitedly. "I'm dying to meet him."

"People usually die *after* they meet him," said Jack, but he could tell from the wrinkled look on her brow that irony wasn't her strong suit. "I don't see him," he added, keeping it simple. He put his two hands on her waist and moved her back a couple of inches, just to relieve the pressure.

"Would you introduce me?" Audrey asked coyly, swiveling her hips in his hands. She was so full of love moves, she couldn't get out of her own way.

"Sure," Jack promised, smiling at her touching faith in the helpfulness of men. "Just don't stick your tongue in his ear—okay, Audrey? I hear he doesn't like it."

Audrey nodded gravely. He wondered how old she was—nineteen, twenty-one—and where she would be at thirty, over what hill. Again that brooding intensity shivered the blue of his eyes, too serious for a party. Then the grinning presence of Mike McClany came bustling over in a blue tuxedo, a heaping plate from the buffet in one hand. As usual he looked as if he was wagging his tail behind him, so excited was he to own a piece of this paradise.

"You see Joe?" Jack asked curtly, dispensing with the amenities.

"He's here," said Mike, wedging himself between Jack and Audrey. Then to the bimbo, his eyebrows jumping like Groucho, "Well, hello there."

Jack's eyes darted to a woman a few feet away, who tossed her mane of copper hair as she laughed. No—not Bobby. "Oh yeah, Mike," said the gambler, slightly dazed, "this is . . . uh . . ."

"Audrey LaShelle," the bimbo offered cheerfully.

"Audrey here is just fascinated by the resort business," Jack continued. "She's just dying to meet Meyer. I'll bet you could help her with that—couldn't you, Mike?" He beamed at the two of them like a matchmaker.

"It's a genuine pleasure, Mike," said Audrey, more breathless than ever, pressing against his shoulder.

He almost tipped his plate, he was so enraptured. "It's genuine for me, too, Miss LaShelle," he intoned in his best Rotarian manner, gazing at her as if she was a Christmas bauble.

Jack had already moved away, relieved of the baggage of Volpi's little present. He craned his neck and scanned the crowd, trying to spot the casino manager. For all his guff and bluster, Joe Volpi was probably the closest Jack had to a buddy in Havana. Which, considering the bristling attitude they exhibited with each other, didn't seem to leave much room for bonding and affection. Put it this way: They were never going to play golf. And if there was only one ticket out of a place like this . . . hey buddy, go find your own.

Jack slouched against the bar and ordered himself an *anejo*. Somebody nudged his shoulder, and he turned to discover Baby Hernandez beside him—something he should have been able to do blind, given the cloud of lime cologne that surrounded the sugar tycoon. "Jack," Baby declared effusively, full of holiday cheer, "*you*'ll understand. We were just discussing three at a time."

Then Jack became aware of the loping and shaggy figure on Baby's other side: Marion Chigwell. The vapid journalist looked as Andover/Yale as ever in his blue blazer and rep tie. He scooped the hair out of his eyes and nodded giddily at Jack.

"See, I gave myself a little Christmas present," said Baby Hernandez. He ticked them off on his fingers. "A Chinese, a *negrita*, and the other one was, I think, Danish. Very pretty ladies. But you know something? I felt left out." He guffawed at his own predicament. He was very drunk.

But Jack had already sidled around him to get closer to Chigwell. He clapped an old-school hand on the journalist's shoulder. "The other night with Ramos," he said, "didn't you say we came over on the same ferry?"

"Oh yes, that's right, we did," Chigwell retorted eagerly, clearly thrilled that the gambler had finally noticed him.

"There was a very elegant lady in a white silk blouse. . . ."

"Roberta Duran." Chigwell nodded, shaking flakes of dandruff onto his shoulders. "Yes—you danced with her. She's a friend of mine." He preened with self-importance, then seemed to feel he was being indelicate. He clucked and shook his head. "Terrible . . . about her husband."

He was so ridiculous, Jack wanted to grab his lapels and bang his head against the wall. But he kept his own smile fixed and friendly and asked, as casually as he could, "You haven't seen her, have you?"

Chigwell shrugged. " 'Disappeared,' they said." A very broad concept in Havana, which usually meant erased.

"She was released," Jack prompted.

"Oh, I'm so glad," replied the supercilious WASP. Then

he shrugged again. "Well, it's easy to lose track of people in Havana. Especially these days."

He didn't know anything. Jack swallowed his rage of impatience and turned to Baby Hernandez again, sucking the olives out of his martini. "Where's Joe?" he demanded.

Baby rolled his eyes in the direction of the band. "He's down the hall," said the sugar tycoon, feeling no pain himself. "Getting the bad news."

Abruptly Jack walked away from the bar, not another moment to waste with decadent fools. He threaded his way once more among the strapless shoulders, past the white-tailed orchestra, and slipped from the main salon down a hallway lined with Picasso etchings. He wondered how soon those etchings would be pulled from their frames and tucked in a fleeing suitcase. He opened a door and saw a bed covered with the fur coats of the strapless women. On top of these, a portly man was dry-humping a showgirl, who smiled and waved at the gambler as he closed the door again.

He moved to the next room down the hall, its door ajar. Joe Volpi stood in the middle of the room, feet spread and torso hunkering slightly forward, like a dazed prizefighter. As Jack stepped in he saw that Volpi was leaning toward a radio, riveted on the voice that crackled through the static. Two Cuban waiters with trays in their hands were listening, just as dumbstruck.

"This is Radio Rebelde!" crowed the radio voice. "Transmitting from the free territory of Cuba!" Then a blur of rapid, excited Spanish that Jack didn't catch.

Joe Volpi turned and saw the gambler. For a moment there was a look in his eyes that Jack had never seen before. A look of total defeat and surrender, as if the last game had been played and there were no more chips in the bank.

"What's he saying?" Jack demanded, as the radio voice rattled on.

The mask of smug indifference had already fallen once more on Volpi's face. He stared with contempt at the radio, then turned and barked at the waiters, "Hey, morons! There's nobody serving out there! What *is* this!"

The two waiters blinked at their boss, as if they were seeing him through different eyes. They hefted their trays and moved to the door, but with a certain deliberateness, like they had all the time in the world.

"The rebels just cut the island in half," Volpi snarled. "There's fighting in the streets of Santa Clara."

A flicker of something half-forgotten flashed in the gambler's eyes like a coin in a wishing well. "Santa Clara?" he repeated, savoring the words as if they were a message from Bobby.

"Yeah, and our half's smaller than their half," the casino manager continued with rueful irony. "They're a hundred and fifty miles away."

And then the door slammed behind them, and they both turned sharply, as if a gun had just gone off. There was Meyer Lansky, the King of Big himself. A good-looking man in a homely sort of way, trim and crackling with energy, as if he lived on the balls of his feet. Seething right now.

"Hiya, Meyer," said Volpi. "This is Jack—"

But Lansky stepped past Jack like the gambler was invisible. He sneered at Volpi. "So what happened to the fucking offensive we paid for, huh, Joe? All this bullshit you been handing me about reinforcements. So where the fuck are they?"

Joe Volpi smiled his sweetest sour smile and put his fingers together like the steeple of a church. "Well, there's supposed to be an armored train on the way. With enough troops—"

"What is this?" bawled the king, hands groping the air as if he couldn't find his scepter. "China? Siberia? The Boxer fucking Rebellion?" He was practically screaming in Volpi's face.

Joe looked miserable. "Meyer, they're trying to—"

"Shut up and listen, Joe," Lansky retorted, poking a finger for emphasis. "Here's what you're gonna do tomorrow. You're gonna talk to the Batista people and tell 'em how upset I am. You got that?'' Volpi nodded sheepishly. Jack could hardly stand to witness his humiliation. ''Then you're gonna tell 'em they better start fighting *real fast*. Or they're gonna be one sorry bunch of faggots!''

Lanksy began to pace, too excited to stand in one place. Jack didn't move a muscle, staying as invisible as he possibly could. ''You remind them,'' hissed the king, ''the only reason there's civilized *plumbing* on this godforsaken island is because Americans came here in '98 and beat the shit out of Spain! Batista's own friggin' palace had an outdoor crapper! *We* installed one inside!''

He was like a politician playing to the gallery, this feisty little historian of plumbing. He could have been Teddy Roosevelt himself, so self-righteous and pro-America. There wasn't any question whose side God was on. And if Meyer Lansky didn't carry a big stick himself, it was only because he had legions of stick carriers ready to jump at his bidding.

''The only reason the son of a bitch got an army in the first place is we *gave* it to him!'' Lansky turned on his underling, whose sour smile was beginning to look a bit sickly. ''So you tell him he better start using it! Or else we take our business elsewhere! You got that, Joe? We *invented* Havana, for Chrissake. And we can move it someplace else anytime we want. You tell 'em that, okay?''

Lansky's face was beet red, his voice hoarse with fury, as he turned on his heel and slammed out of the room. Not once had he so much as glanced at Jack Weil. The gambler stared at the floor, embarrassed for Volpi. The room was silent except for the crackle of static over the radio, as if waiting for the next rebel announcement. The party noise from the main room reverberated faintly through the walls, like the memory of a former age.

Volpi cleared this throat, discreet as a mortician. ''You want to go for a walk, Jack?''

The gambler nodded. ''Sure. This party sucks, if you ask

me." He caught Joe Volpi's eye, and the two men smiled as they headed out, cool as a pair of mercenaries.

They strolled along the Upper Prado, where the crowds in the street were making merry at an ever-more-frantic pace, as if they were playing a dwindling game of musical chairs. Nonstop music pervaded the night, pouring from dance halls and restaurants. But the voice of Rebel Radio persisted as well, spilling from a thousand radios in counterpoint to the carols and the rhumbas. There was something almost dreamlike in this world on the brink of vanishing—a sense of finality, the last dance and the last drunken laughter. You couldn't stop moving, somehow, or else you wouldn't be there anymore.

"So," Jack finally asked, after they'd walked for several blocks in silence, "are we rained out, Joe?"

"What?" Volpi retorted, startled as if he'd just awakened. "No, no," he hastened to reassure. "Game's still on. He'll back you, all right. You got my word, Jack. Hey, he's always havin' a tantrum, Meyer, but that don't interfere with business."

They ambled past a sidewalk café, where every table was full to bursting. The revelers hoisted drinks and after-dinner coffee as an all-girl orchestra serenaded them with intricate tropical blues. There was something wonderfully defiant about the scene, especially when a convoy of military trucks came roaring by on the boulevard. The soldiers huddled knee to knee in the truck beds, clasping their carbines, and the languid crowd at the café cheered and raised their drinks as if it was all a parade.

Jack and Volpi turned at the next corner into a narrow street, where a housewife was selling tiny cups of coffee from her windowsill. Jack thought of La Polaca and those who survived the great jagged edges of history, wrapped in their housecoats and curlers. "So Meyer's bettin' Batista *and* the rebels," Jack declared thoughtfully. "Got his money both ways, huh?"

Joe Volpi didn't answer but that was enough of an answer

for Jack. The casino manager smiled and looked up at the lines of clothing strung over the street, rippling like banners in the evening breeze. "I love this town, Jack," he said with feeling. "They call it the Paris of the Caribbean—the Pearl of the Antilles." He took a deep breath as if to drink it all in, then spread his arms like an impresario. "It's a real city!"

They came to a square with an old stone water trough in the center, its bubbling spigots green with moss. A Chinese pimp stepped out of the shadows, leading a girl so white she must have been an albino. The two men ignored the silent offer but nodded politely. In the next block painted girls were in almost every window, brushing their hair and smoking cigarettes. Two leaned over the windowsills and made kissing sounds. They were close enough to touch, but the two men pressed on, lost in their own thoughts.

"There's other cities, believe me," Jack observed, choosing his words like a man playing chess.

Volpi sighed, shaking his head. "I came here in '38."

"New York is good," Jack continued judiciously, almost ticking them off on his fingers. "Frisco. New Orleans is good." It wasn't clear whether he was trying to convince Joe or himself. Then, abruptly, "When're you going to know about the game?"

Volpi didn't answer right away. They left the street of the whores and came into a wider avenue. Across the way the limos were stacked up outside a Spanish club. The building was high colonial, with tall French windows and a rich baroque tangle of wrought iron. In the windows, holding cocktails, were the white-haired descendants of grandees. The last hurrah of the ancient regime.

"Forbes gets in tomorrow night," Volpi said at last as they paused beneath a street lamp to study the aristocrats. Then the casino manager's voice changed. "They won't let me back into the States, Jack. I'm—not a citizen anymore." He laughed, dry and self-conscious, as if he'd just discovered his fly was down.

Jack frowned. "But what'll you do if they take the city?"

Joe Volpi scoffed: piece of cake. "Meyer's been talking about Santo Domingo," he said, picking up the pace again. "You ever been there, Jack?" Now he laughed for real. "It's nowhere, baby. Hell, it's *east* of nowhere. Maybe I'll go to Costa Rica. I got a friend retired there—a widow." He smiled at Jack like a co-conspirator. "Always have an ace in the hole, my friend. This is one lady I never forget her birthday, 'cause I always figure it's going to fall apart in Havana someday. She used to run a cathouse here—very high class."

Suddenly the avenue widened out into Cathedral Square. The whitewashed face of the church was bathed in floodlights for the holiday, the plaza in front dominated by a fountain with three stone angels. The water splashing in the fountain played in the echoing square like the gush of a mountain stream. They gazed at the scene mutely for a minute, these two who were trying to stay just ahead of the whirlwind about to come. It was surely an illusion, but Cathedral Square seemed immune just then to the rough-and-tumble of revolution.

"So when are you leaving, Joe?" Jack asked quietly.

"Last," came the curt reply.

And then, as if by silent agreement, they moved to go their separate ways. They didn't say good night, and of course they knew better than to wish one another good luck. To a gambler, that kind of wish was *bad* luck. So they just separated, Jack with his hands in his pockets, strolling around the perimeter of the square. He pretended not to notice Volpi crossing the square toward the church.

A couple of women came out the side door, in shapeless black dresses and lace scarves. Grandmothers too worried to sleep, perhaps, and praying that the young men would survive the contortions of politics. Joe Volpi stood aside to let them pass, bowing respectfully. As he disappeared into the church himself you could see in his earnest face a glimpse of the long-ago altar boy, gravely lighting the candles for a Mass in Little Italy.

* * *

124

Schreiber's Deli was a sanctuary, beloved of refugees. In the heart of the colonial quarter, it might have been dropped here, bagels and all, direct from the Lower East Side. The no-nonsense signs above the counter were in Spanish, Yiddish, and English, and the noise and bustle of the late-night patrons were reassuringly those of a melting pot. The bee-hived woman at the cash register was called Stella, and she looked it.

Jack Weil picked up a light coffee and a danish from the counter, then headed toward the back, where the booths were. He looked perfectly happy to eat his 4:00 A.M. breakfast alone, but his face lit up as he passed the first booth on the right. "Well, hello there, Professor," he said cheerfully.

A small, compact gentleman with white hair and a bushy white mustache looked up from his chicken soup. He wore an elegant three-piece suit and had the squinting eyes of a jeweler. Now he grinned in delighted recognition. "Hiya, sonny," he greeted the gambler jovially. "La Polaca said you were back. By God you look good!"

The professor gestured for Jack to sit down, which the gambler did with pleasure. "So," Jack teased, "you been spending time at the Nacional, huh?"

The professor nodded, slurping a spoonful of soup. "Twin sisters from St. Louis and loaded with mazoola," he replied, then sighed and shook his head. "But I tell you, Jack, it's a deal of work separating those ladies from their spare change. What I call a mining venture. The gold is very deep. And with all this uproar . . ." The professor waved a dismissive hand at the street outside. "They could fly the coop at any minute. *C'est la vie,* my friend."

"Did you hear the rebels are fighting in Santa Clara?"

The professor nodded and sighed again, drawing a big white handkerchief from his pocket and dabbing at his mustache. "We're being overtaken by history, my boy," he intoned. "The wheel turns. But I hope you'll stay to the bitter end." He winked. "This sort of thing is very good for *your* line of work."

"No," said the gambler, "I'm going. One more game." He seemed surprised at his own decisiveness. Then he grinned impulsively. "You want to go with me, Professor? Take the ferry—drive straight through to Vegas?"

The professor made a face. "Nonsense," he scoffed. "Atom bombs and sandy pussy. What's your hurry, kid?"

Jack laughed. "I'm ahead, that's why. For once in my life. Because I knew this would be the last roll." He took a hungry bite of the danish and washed it down with coffee. "I've always stayed in Havana too long. Every time I came down here I thought . . . this is where anything's possible. I'm gonna find the best fuck and the biggest game of my life." He paused for a moment, gazing into the middle distance, as if the cocky young man he used to be might walk in off the street. "And I've almost . . . I've come so close. . . ."

The professor was peering across the deli at a pair of middle-aged women in mink stoles and diamonds. It wasn't clear that he'd even been listening to Jack as he mentally appraised each stone and sniffed the air to see if the women were easy marks. Then he turned to Jack and squinted his eyes till they were barely slits. "Havana's a state of mind, sonny," he said.

"I don't know," the gambler retorted, folding his hands before him on the table as if he were holding a poker hand. "See, I met this woman. I know her seventy-two hours and I . . . I don't know." He stared at his hands as if he didn't know how to bet anymore.

The professor smiled, pleased to be consulted in matters of the heart. "Take the advice of an old man," he said, "and stick with her. There's nothing like a woman. They love men—even schmucks." When he laughed, he looked ten years younger. He stretched his arms behind him along the back of the booth, savoring his role as philosopher. "The biggest schmuck you ever knew, Jack—a real lox— and somewhere, somehow, he's got a woman gaga over him. I tell you, women are perfect. The rest . . ." He shrugged with huge disdain. "The rest is bullshit."

Jack Weil shook his head slowly. "I can't," he said, but finally not trying to hide the pain in his voice. "She took off. I mean, I think I know where she is. She's down there where they're fighting. But I'm damned if I know why." Then he broke the bond of his clasped hands as if he were folding, beaten by the dealer. He groaned with weariness. "Aw, it's time to get out, Professor."

The professor eyed him closely, not quite believing. "So when are you leaving, sonny?" he asked, and it sounded like a dare.

Jack stood up. "Tomorrow," he replied hollowly. "And what are you gonna do?"

The professor's eyes widened, remarkably gentle when he wasn't doing his jeweler's squint. He reached out a hand and rested it lightly on Jack's. "If a man's life is a single day," he said, "then it's 10:45 for me, my friend. P.M. I don't have to do anything, really." He spoke with an extraordinary sense of relief. Then he squeezed Jack's hand. "But *you* do. It's not even dusk for you yet."

They stared at each other for a long moment, suspended in amber as the jostle of the deli went on around them. Then the gambler patted the old man's shoulder wordlessly. When he turned to go, the professor called after him, one more time for good measure. "Cover your ass, kid," he said, the coarseness and the hustle vivid once more in his tone. No one in Schreiber's Deli would ever have known he'd spoken so gently a moment before.

Jack stepped outside, startled to see the first streaks of gray in the eastern sky. How many dawns had he witnessed after a long night of cards? Yet this one seemed to have his name written on it, pearl shading to pink almost in front of his eyes. He stretched his arms over his head, a man who seemed more rested somehow for having no sleep at all. Then he turned and walked forcefully west, back toward the street where he lived. By the time he'd covered two blocks he was practically running.

IX

THE GREEN CADILLAC, its top down and the wind whipping, raced past the shantytowns of Regla. On his right Jack could still see cranes and docks beyond the smoky slums, but he'd already left the big commercial piers and the city itself behind him. The shantytowns were the refuse of Havana, strewn around the edges like fallout. The road was full of potholes, and he had to keep swerving to hold his speed. Kids on either side of the road waved and cheered as he throttled past.

In twenty minutes he was driving through open country, the urban chaos behind him like a bad dream. Here was the Cuba made for tourists: sugarcane and jungle. The villages were barely settled, a haphazard street or two gashed out of the landscape, full of pigs and chickens. Every single one looked tenuous and provisional. The exotic names flew past on signs as Jack raced through—Mantanzas, Javellanos, Colón, Cascajal. It looked as if the jungle could reclaim them all at a moment's notice.

He switched on the car radio and fiddled with the dial. Johnny Mathis crooned "Chances Are." Coming the other way along the road was a constant stream of rusty cars and jalopy trucks, filled with families clutching their small possessions. This caravan of exile, thought the gambler, was the same the whole world over, displaced by every war and revolution. The ones who didn't have cars and trucks walked at the edge of the road beside wagons led by burros. They were all fleeing the fighting in Santa Clara, but that was all they knew, what they were running *from*. They didn't have a clue as to where they were going.

A half hour later Jack was crawling through a roadside cane village, and the smell of the sugar processing hung in the air like sulfur. No one seemed to be at work that day. All the workers milled in the streets, passing bottles of dark brown rum, declaring a grim holiday that had nothing to do with Christmas. When he'd finally inched his way to the outskirts of the village, Jack found himself confronted by a sergeant with a carbine, standing guard at a crude road-block. Just a couple of sawhorses.

The sergeant was most adamant that Jack should not be driving to Santa Clara. "You don't understand," Jack explained. "I got a friend there. *Amigo—Americano!* I have to get her out. *Comprende?*"

The sergeant puffed with self-importance. Courteously he replied that he sympathized, but the road was not secure. The American had to realize that he could be stopped at any point by rebel patrols. Worse, he could drive over a mine. The sergeant pointed into the distance, where smoke hung over the highway ahead. This was the last point, he declared, where law and order still ruled.

Jack understood about every third word. Impatiently he pulled out his roll of cash and began to peel off a couple of hundreds. The sergeant backed away with offended dignity. Just Jack Weil's luck that he happened to pick the one soldier in Batista's army who wasn't crooked. But the sergeant had had enough of him. He waved a hand and indicated that Jack should drive around the sawhorses. And as the gambler pulled away along the dusty road the sergeant bawled after him, *"Loco! Completamente loco!"*

The road was so broken, so gutted with potholes, that he sometimes could only go ten or fifteen miles an hour. Several times he winced as the belly of the Caddy scraped on a rock, and he sent up a silent prayer of thanks to General Motors that the axles were so sturdy. The stream of refugees never stopped, their faces tight with anxiety as they headed toward Havana. They almost never looked at the Caddy, so fixed were they on their own goal. But when they locked eyes with Jack, he could tell they felt exactly the same as the sergeant: *loco*.

Eventually the road was only dirt, no asphalt at all. The battered cars of the refugees were fewer and fewer. Jack came over a rise, and there was nothing but lush vegetation visible for miles. Havana was all the Caribbean he'd ever known. Out here was the unpaved paradise of the old Caribbean, as pristine and wild as the land Columbus had claimed at Hispaniola. And the farther he went, the more dreamlike it seemed to him—unless it was the sleepless night catching up with him.

After a while he couldn't have said how far he'd gone, nor how far back was the last sign pointing to Santa Clara. He carried no map. There was only his intensity, the burning to connect with her again. It was all the radar he had. The sun was already setting, shimmering and muggy, and he felt his heart racing with impatience. He was very close now, he was sure of it.

He stopped at the crest of the next rise, beneath a tree that smelled of bitter almond. He didn't even know anymore what was jungle and what was cane. The country lay before him like a sea of green. And as he leaned over the steering wheel and peered out, his eyes stinging with tiredness, he heard the pop of gunfire in the distance.

Then the right side of the windshield exploded, shattering glass all over the front seat.

His foot slid off the brake and hit the gas, lurching the car to the red dirt shoulder of the road. He scrambled out and flung himself down on the ground. There was utter silence, the gunfire having seized up all the bird song in the neighborhood. Tentatively Jack came up to a half stoop, looking out through the tall grass at the world of savage green.

Nothing at all, in any direction, not even a curl of smoke. The gambler rose to his feet and brushed the red clay from his clothes. He moved to get back in the car—then stopped.

Coming toward him up the road, weird as a mirage, was a convoy of vehicles, churning up dust as they came. Jack stood there, conflicted, not sure whether to bolt or hide. In the end he stood fast because he knew in his bones they were Batistiano troops, and he didn't want to be shot in the back running. Shooting in the back was a Batistiano specialty.

There were three jeeps and a truck, covered with mud and dust. As soon as Jack saw the scowling face of the officer in the lead jeep, he knew they were in retreat. The officer motioned roughly for Jack to get out of the way, and he stepped back, leaning against the Caddy as they passed. The glassy-eyed soldiers in the truck bed looked as if they'd surrendered long ago.

They trailed away along the muggy road, slinking toward Havana. Jack got back in the car, sweeping the glass shards from the driver's side. As he headed down the hill in the direction from which the soldiers had come he saw a cleared space by the side of the road. Coming closer, he detected the shell of a blasted building. It appeared to be some kind of government office, a way station or post office, but now it was gutted and smashed almost beyond recognition.

A little farther on was a small settlement of peasant huts, riddled by artillery fire. One of them was burning, sending up a billow of black smoke into the jungle trees. The smoke stung Jack's eyes and obscured the view ahead, but he caught a glimpse of something familiar in the field beyond the burning house. He drove forward through the acrid smoke, clamping a hand to his mouth to keep from choking.

Then he saw the object clearly: the white Town and Country, tilted up on a jack. He roared forward and jumped from the Caddy, moving across the field toward the abandoned car. Now he could see it was pretty well stripped, even the seats torn out. He turned and stared at the burning hut, trying to put it all together. Instinctively he moved toward the burning building. Then his stomach clenched as he saw two bodies lying like broken dolls in the yard behind it.

His heart pounding, he ran up to examine them. A man

and a woman, dressed like field workers, who seemed to be reaching toward each other, even in death. The gambler hated himself for feeling relieved, but all he cared about now was that she not be among the dead. There was nothing he could do for the victims of the revolution. He turned and walked away, trying not to feel anything.

As he drove on slowly the smoke and the shadows of trees had turned the sunset into dusk. Half a mile farther and he came to another tiny village of huts, this one spared the brunt of enemy fire. Two kids in the dirt intersection were playing as if there was no war out there at all. Then, as he drove closer, Jack saw they were playing with the hubcaps from the Town and Country.

He stopped, and the kids looked over at him, admiring the big American car as much as the urchins in the colonial quarter had. Jack grinned at them and began to speak in his halting, know-nothing Spanish. *"Dónde está,* uh . . . woman? *Woman,* you know? *Dónde?"* He pointed behind him down the road, then at the hubcaps. "Car? Auto? Señora Duran? *Finca?"* He slammed his fist on the steering wheel, furious with himself. "Ah shit," he grumbled in frustration.

But when he looked up, one of the kids had stepped up beside the Caddy and was pointing up the road into the trees. He leaped up on the hood of Jack's car as if it were a rocket ship, clutched the hood ornament with one hand, and waved with the other as if to say, "Let's go!"

Slowly they moved out of the village, perhaps a couple of hundred yards through the trees. Suddenly the boy on the hood gesticulated left, and Jack saw a rutted, overgrown country lane splitting off from the main road. He swung the Caddy onto it, and they began a wildly bumpy ride. Rain and neglect had long since ruined the narrow roadway, and the jungle underbrush was so thick and overhanging that the gambler felt like he was drowning in green. He couldn't imagine he'd ever be able to back his way out, but he kept going forward anyway, batting away the branches that swirled around his head.

"Arriba! Arriba!" cried the boy on the hood, excitedly urging them forward.

"Means lost, right?" the gambler bawled in reply, laughing in spite of himself. He couldn't be any farther away from the rest of his life. It was as if he had stepped off the edge of the world.

And then the swishing branches lifted like veils from his eyes as the Cadillac lurched out into an open field. The gambler blinked to focus in the dusk as the boy pointed triumphantly. *"La Finca* Duran!" he crowed.

It was like a dream within a dream, to be here at last. Across the shaggy field of gently blowing grass stood a white frame house with a deep veranda. It stood on a knoll so it overlooked a great expanse of the forest. Despite the air of neglect in the uncut fields and a tumbledown stable with a sagging roof, the house still held its breath, a frozen moment in time. A jewel of the eighteenth century, when Havana was just a shabby little port.

The boy dismounted from the Caddy's hood and saluted the gambler. "Bye-bye, yanqui."

"Hey, where you going?" Jack called after him, but he'd already disappeared down the overgrown road, trotting back to his village.

Jack stepped out of the car and started walking up the long curved drive that led to the house. The way had been paved a long time past with crushed shells, so the path was faintly luminous in the dusk. In the middle distance Jack could hear the sounds of sporadic gunfire, muffled till now by the noise of his own engine. Also the occasional concussive boom of a mortar round. Memory stirred in his heart, the echo of an older war.

He had reached the top of the rise, maybe fifty feet from the house, when the front door opened slowly. Bobby stepped out onto the veranda. Even from that distance he could tell she hadn't eaten or slept since she left his apartment—when? A day ago or a month? It was as if time was no longer the measure of anything, certainly not of them.

"How did you get through?" she asked.

"By not speaking Spanish," he replied with a smile. Slowly she walked down the steps and across the grassy knoll toward him. She stopped about three feet away, and they stared into each other's eyes. "You here by yourself?"

She nodded and shrugged, as if that would tell the whole story. He was conscious of wanting to reach out a hand and touch her, almost to prove she was real. But instead he said, "Tell me something. What are you doing?"

By way of reply she turned around and led the way back to the house. She had made not the slightest gesture that he should follow, but he knew he'd passed the point of her sending him away. She wore a simple sleeveless shift, purple batik, a native woman's Sunday dress. As he walked behind her up the steps she shook the great mane of her copper hair, soft and perfumed again, the prison washed out of it.

The floorboards creaked as they crossed the veranda, the teak no longer oiled like it was in the old days. A rope hammock hung from the rafters, swaying lazily in the breeze. She opened the front door and let him go in first, but it was so dusky that he just stood there while she went to fetch a lamp. All he could see were the dark wood beams above and the old family pictures on the wall beside him, black silhouettes of young women and brittle sepia photos in heavy frames.

Across the room she lit the oil lamp, a specter in the dim light. She turned it up, and the room was bathed in gold, the woven rugs and the tables littered with mute mementos. She beckoned him to join her in the light as she set the lamp on the mantel. She turned to him, clasping her hands behind her, as if afraid she might touch something.

"This was Arturo's family home," she said, but he knew all that already. He waited, content just to drink her in. She shook her head restlessly back and forth, as if he was forcing her to talk. "The rebels have a transmitter hidden out back." Then silence. She stared at the floor. He knew it had nothing to do with how much she trusted him. Knowing would put him in danger.

She reached out a hand as if groping for something, and he pulled the Pall Malls from his pocket. She murmured with relief, any excuse to stall—taking a cigarette, lifting the glass from the lamp to light it, blowing smoke at the rafters.

"They'll try to contact Havana tonight," she said haltingly, veering at the truth like a moth around the lamp. "Actually in a little while . . . try to contact our group. You see, they don't know that everyone . . . that Arturo . . ." She passed a weary hand across her eyes, as if there was nothing to be gained from going over it again. "But Colonel Menocal will be listening," she went on bitterly. "Because he found the radio."

"Couldn't somebody else come out here?"

"If they don't know Menocal's men are listening," she went on stubbornly, "they'll say something. Names of the other resistance groups. Somebody has to stop them." She tossed her hair again, begging the question of whether somebody else could have done it. She was the one who'd come. Period.

"Menocal's looking for you, Bobby." He spoke quietly, trying not to patronize her, thinking, after all, there were things she would send him away for saying. "The other day at my place—he missed you by a few minutes."

"I'm safe here," she replied impatiently.

"Nobody's safe here!" Jack exclaimed, willing himself not to grip her shoulders. "Don't you understand? There's no *front line* in this war. And *you're* not safe anywhere in Cuba." He started to pace in front of the fireplace, trying to use up some of his nervous energy. "He's gotta be watching all the airports. Look, I know a guy who's got boats. He can—"

"Boats?" she asked, bewildered. "What are you saying?"

His voice dropped to an urgent whisper. "I'm saying you need to get out of Cuba. Now."

She barked a one-note mirthless laugh. "Don't be absurd. I can't leave."

He tried to say it without sneering. "You really think one out-of-work actress is gonna make any difference in all of this?"

"Yes," she retorted defiantly.

"Come on, what's it got to *do* with you anyway? You put this place on like a costume. You got all your lines in *español*." She was absolutely still as he paced in front of her. For some reason she permitted him the questioning of her motives, even the contempt he couldn't hide. "You're not poor, you're not hungry," he declared in frustration. "And you're sure as hell not Cuban!"

"I don't have to be Cuban to know when things are unfair."

"Things *are* unfair," he practically bellowed. "Where have *you* been?"

She shrugged. "I don't want to live that way," she said. She seemed to grow cooler, the more upset he became. And yet the passion was no less fierce in her for being a cold fire—like a blue diamond flame.

"You married into this thing, right? Well, you don't marry into revolution."

She laughed again, and this time the contempt was on the other side. "Why? Who said so, Jack Weil?" She hissed and made a motion as if to sweep dust away. "This doesn't have anything to do with Arturo anymore!"

"Are you sure?" The laser intensity of his gaze was bright, even in the lamplit dusk. "Jesus Christ, Bobby, if you need a war for things to make sense, you'll be running the rest of your life."

The blue flame flared. "Don't you tell me how to make sense of my life! I don't even know you!"

The shrillness of it stopped him cold. He ceased to pace and stared at the flickering lamp. Surely he hadn't come here to argue like this. All he could say was, "I know."

She was as pained as he was. Her voice softened. "You don't understand. You're a card player."

"Yeah. And I feel more honest playing cards than trying to make believe these mountains are mine."

She shook her head sadly, not taking any of it personally now. The argument had only made her more certain. "That's not why you play cards," she said quietly. She seemed to have been waiting to say this to him since the night they met on the ship, trying to get it exactly right. "You play cards so that for a little while—a night, an hour, a hand—something seems to matter."

He didn't contradict her. Yet, for all her bluntness, she hesitated before she spoke again, in case she might offend him. But then there was nothing to lose either. "Besides," she said, "these mountains *are* yours. And one day you'll know it."

They were only a few feet apart, but in the silence that followed they studied one another as if from a distance—two different decks of the ship. He felt stupid, not to have understood till now that the revolutionary passion in her was real. But what really unnerved him was that she understood him better than he did her. His deep fixation on her hadn't even given him the edge. He felt as if he'd been playing with half a deck, without any face cards.

They smiled in the lamplight, making a provisional truce. They appeared relieved, both of them, to have let it all out, wherever it led. And he finally felt ready to touch her, if only in a glancing way, more like an ambiguous friend than any sort of lover. He reached out a hand and grazed her arm. She didn't pull back. Were they comrades now? Was it more than that? They needed the smile to go on a bit longer before they knew. Needed this velvet silence as the tropical night came down in waves of ultramarine.

Then the door shook with a crash, like a battering ram. They turned to look, and it smashed open. A handful of soldiers rushed into the room, guns leveled. Instinctively Jack grabbed Bobby and stepped in front of her, shielding her between him and the fireplace. The intruders sported ragtag bits of military gear, their motley uniforms more improvised than not. Rebels then, not Batistianos, but the guns were just as real.

The captain was barely out of his teens. He studied Jack and Bobby with a surly eye as his troops moved restlessly through the house. He wore frayed fatigues and a gringo cowboy hat pulled down over shoulder-length hair. He had learned the swagger of revolution, if nothing else. When his soldiers came back and shook their heads—nobody else in the house—he stepped up to Jack and Bobby, seeing them clearly at last in the lamplight.

Then he gasped and stuttered like a teenager. "Señora Duran . . . !" He made a half bow, showing how well his mother had brought him up, and extended a hand. Bobby moved out from behind the gambler and shook the captain's hand. "I'm sorry," he apologized effusively in Spanish. "We heard voices in English. We thought—"

"Something has happened," she declared urgently, cutting right to the quick. "SIM has the radio. They found it before it could be moved."

She was speaking in rapid Spanish, so Jack only caught the drift. But he knew what it meant when the captain glanced over at him suspiciously. All Americans were guilty until proven otherwise, since America was the main prop to Batista's bloody rule. "Amigo," he heard Bobby say, mollifying the captain.

"This is a friend," she assured him firmly. Then her voice quickened once more, so much to tell him and so little time. "They caught everyone—Ricardo, Tomas, Monica, Bufano." As the names rolled off her tongue Jack could see they had all been friends of the young captain, for he winced as if they were bullets. "The group is finished," Bobby declared. "Carlos . . . Arturo." The captain swung his eyes to meet hers, but he had no words. "You can't transmit," she told him. "Finished."

Just then a young rebel stepped into the room from the veranda. He crossed to the captain, crisply marching, exulting in his life as a soldier. "The radio is functional, Captain. It's time."

But the captain didn't appear to be listening. He still held Bobby's eyes, and he bowed again more deeply, formal as a grandee. "I'm so sorry, señora," he said mournfully. Then he leaned against the mantel, staring at the floor and figuring fast. A moment later he cocked his head toward her again, a decisive look in his eyes.

"Maybe one day we'll have time to grieve," he declared. "But right now . . . I think we must transmit anyway." And when Bobby's face creased in a puzzled frown, he added with bitter irony, "If Colonel Menocal is listening in Havana, then we should tell him something we want him to believe."

At that moment he seemed much older than his years, the adolescent jumpiness hardened by his shrewd resolve. He turned abruptly and left the house, the group scurrying to follow his lead. Suddenly Bobby and Jack were alone again. The gambler had more or less followed the drift of the talk, but there was something distinctly separate about him, more than the language he couldn't speak. He nodded mutely, almost apologetically, giving her leave to do what she had to. He didn't want her thinking he needed taking care of.

She reached out a hand and squeezed his arm, returning the gesture he'd made before the arrival of the rebels. Then without a word she turned and hurried out of the house. Jack stood by the fireplace for a minute, knowing he couldn't be part of what they were doing. He took the Pall Malls from his pocket, then realized the package was empty. He'd given Bobby the last one.

Restlessly he crossed to the window and pushed aside the finespun white linen curtain. Outside the dusk was blue, with a sliver of the Christmas moon rising over the jungle hills. In the overgrown yard beside the house, a wood-and-tarpaper lean-to marked the site of the outdoor kitchen, a firepit to one side and a well on the other. At the old slab worktable in the lean-to, the rebels were pulling a tarp off a radio transceiver. The radio was twin to the one Arturo's group had been using at the Academia Dance Hall—both of them built by Monica, their fallen comrade.

They were working by the muted light of a pair of shuttered lanterns, but close enough for Jack to see them clearly. The captain held the microphone in one hand, checking his watch with the other, timing it down to the second. Bobby stood beside him, the rest of the troops surrounding them in a semicircle, bristling with anticipation. At the precise moment, the captain spoke a couple of staccato commands into the microphone.

Then they all watched the transceiver, frozen with hope and dread. Even through the window Jack could feel how the whole group seemed to be holding its breath. Then a burst of static erupted from the unit, followed by a stream of excited Spanish. Once more the captain leaned into the microphone and rattled off a list of names, and then something that sounded like the coordinates of a street address in Havana. Immediately after, he switched the keys off, silencing the radio.

The group of rebels stood still for a moment, savoring their triumph. Then the captain turned and embraced Bobby. There was nothing erotic about it, just the clasp of comrades, and yet Jack could feel his own body tighten in response. As the rebels hurried to replace the tarp over the radio their sense of exhilaration was palpable. As Jack Weil let the curtain fall back across the window he seemed more solitary than usual—left out somehow, the way he used to feel about the penthouse games at the Lido.

He crossed back to the fireplace, wanting a cigarette more than ever. The lamplight fell on a table by the hearth on which there was a telephone. Automatically he reached to pick up the receiver, curious more than anything to see if the line was still open. He heard the reassuring high-pitched beep of the dial tone, proving to himself that he wasn't cut off at all, even out here on the dark side of the moon. And yet the sound of the dial tone seemed to mock him, too, for he had no one to call—no one urgently waiting to know his whereabouts. He let the receiver drop back in the cradle.

And then he was aware—was it the scent of her lily

perfume?—that she had come back into the room. The oil in the lamp was so low that the darkness was barely affected by the gold of the lamplight. He didn't turn around, but merely asked in a voice just above a whisper, "So, how'd it go?"

"I think it was all right," she replied, remarkably matter-of-fact. It was as if she felt no need to discuss it any further. The act was all that mattered. "You want something cool to drink?" she offered, and she could have been just another idle mistress of a *finca*, with no more responsibility than to please her guests.

She moved through the near darkness to a table near the windows, where a crockery pitcher was set on a tray with delicate fluted glasses—wedding crystal that would never survive a ransacking by government troops. One might as well use it now, her movements seemed to indicate. She poured serenely, then turned and brought him a glass.

He took it from her, and they toasted a silent *Salut* and drank.

"Listen, Bobby," he blurted out, as if his own time was growing shorter by the minute, "I don't know about a lot of things. I didn't go far in school. The things I know, I know from my gut. And so I keep out of the way of stuff I don't understand. Mostly."

She sat down lightly on the arm of the sofa, listening intently but giving him all the time he needed. It was a struggle for him to speak, but not because he didn't trust she'd understand. On the contrary, he seemed to be counting on her capacity to understand him better than he did. For he was speaking of things he'd never expressed before, even to himself. Especially to himself.

"All this . . ." he declared, with a vague sweep of his arm, taking in the plantation house and the scene he'd just witnessed in the kitchen yard. "It's like . . . living your life in the newspapers. As if you were *reading* what you're supposed to do." He made an impatient grunting sound, annoyed at himself for sounding so superior. Bobby waited, raising no word in her own defense, not needing to. "I

141

mean, the papers make too much of everything. Most of the time nothing's going on out there. Just . . . life.''

There were only a few feet separating them, she at the sofa, he by the mantel, but the light had dwindled so low that they saw one another mostly in silhouette. The darkness seemed to make it easier for him to talk about something as bald as life. For a man whose very existence was pegged to a world of the purest concreteness—deck of cards, pile of chips—the words he was speaking now were amazingly open-ended. Like a path out of a dark wood.

''A guy goes for a walk,'' Jack said, ''and maybe he sees the shadow of a cloud moving across a hill. Or maybe some sheep, if it's that kind of country. And that's all. You can't . . . live ideas.'' He struggled again, groping to give it a shape she could see in the dark. ''Most things that are alive don't even *have* ideas. What's *really* going on happens before ideas. Before talk. Before anybody says anything.'' Now he seemed almost afraid to go on, as if he'd come farther than he ever intended. ''Before . . . and maybe after,'' he added tentatively. ''In the quiet.''

She didn't reply right away, letting the silence build for a moment, as if to give him the respite of what he called ''the quiet.'' When at last she spoke, it was not to refute him. Instead she appeared to be building on the ground of his groping philosophy, as if she had always planned to construct a fortification there.

''It isn't an idea, really,'' she answered softly. ''It's more of a feeling. Like being part of something that stretches around the world, from the past into the future. Something more than yourself.'' Her voice was warm and earnest, taking pleasure in the words. Perhaps she was recalling them from the vanished tongue of her husband. In any case, it didn't sound false at all. ''Like a song,'' she added tenderly. ''A song people sing together, the living and the dead.''

He leaned forward, acutely listening. ''I guess I'm not in there singing, am I?''

No reply. It was his own moment of discovery, not for

her to try to shape. She seemed to know the exchange had left him more exposed than he wanted to be. She could almost feel him try to shake it off, but he couldn't.

"Something's happening," he declared uncertainly, as if someone had just changed the rules for five-card stud, right in the middle of a hand. "I bailed you out—what? Forty-eight hours ago? Seventy-two?" He shook his head in astonishment. Events had long since outpaced his capacity to process them. "I made you a sandwich," he continued, plucking the detail out of the whirlwind, turning it over like a stone in his hand. "Then I drove . . . I don't even know where this place is. . . ."

As his voice drifted off he stepped away from the mantel, seeking something more solid than words. He moved close to her where she sat on the sofa arm. Even so near, all he could see in the guttering light of the oil lamp was the flickering shine in her eyes. "You want to change the world?" he asked, his voice grown suddenly husky, even as it challenged her. "Change mine."

Utter stillness for a moment. Then he slipped the glass from her hand and set it down on the table next to the telephone. She shook the cascade of her hair in the last of the light as he moved to grip her shoulders. He lifted her from the sofa and engulfed her in his arms, burying his mouth against her throat. Drinking her in as he nuzzled her softly. Finally setting his lips to hers, so the burning could start in earnest.

Time didn't measure it, only fire, the aching intensity of their hungry mouths that had lived too long on words. They groaned and whimpered with passion, seized by the one kiss, as if they understood it could all be torn from them at any second, before they could go any farther. When she finally pulled her mouth from his, it was with a soft wrenching cry. They both gasped for air, and she breathed her question in lonely terror, clawing for purchase before she went under again, "What's going to happen to mine?"

He answered her with another kiss, not so urgent or desperate, but deeper because they were building on the last.

For the first time they truly looked like what they'd been from the very beginning—a couple of strangers who met on a ship and forgot their destination. He could feel the tears on her cheeks, could taste them. His longing to protect her was inextricable from the pitch of his desire, river and ocean meeting in a place of stillness like a tidal pool.

"If I go with you," she practically sobbed, clinging to him so she wouldn't drown, "what's going to happen to mine?"

The echo hung in the air and had no answer. And even if he could have responded, he would have been mute, for now she was drowning him with kisses of her own. Breathing each other like oxygen, holding on for dear life. They had to do this thing together once and for all, and then see what survived the fire and the flood, in the changed world that waited at the end of the night.

X

THE WHITE FRAME HOUSE was ghostly in the predawn light, seeming to hover on the mist that blanketed the sleeping meadow. A distant rumble like faraway thunder echoed off the mountains, but the sky was clear as a bell, ripe with the promise of morning gold. The last of Venus glimmered in the west as the boy ran up the driveway past the Cadillac, his scurrying feet soundless as a deer.

It was the same boy who'd led Jack here, the one who had ridden the hood of the car as if it was a stallion. When he reached the veranda, he didn't go up the steps, but moved around the side of the house toward the kitchen yard. He may have been the youngest rebel in Santa Clara, yet he made no move in the direction of the radio under the tarp. Instead he walked to the back of the house, where French doors covered with muslin curtains opened into the bedroom.

One door was a foot ajar. The boy stepped up to the gap but didn't put his head in. "Psst!" he whispered. "Señora Duran!"

A stirring inside, and the murmur of voices. The boy waited discreetly, and a moment later Bobby appeared at the half-open door, clutching a robe about her. She gave him a questioning look. The words came tumbling out of him, his voice rising excitedly. "Señora, they're coming—

the Batistianos! They've started a counterattack! You must go quickly!"

For all his breathless impatience, there was something graver and tougher about the boy today. He was ready to pick up a gun himself, and it seemed like the revolution was finally ready to let him. He couldn't have been more than ten years old. "Now!" he commanded the mistress of the *finca*. "The road to Santo Domingo is open! An hour from now the Batistianos will have it blocked!"

He gave her no chance to respond, but turned and sprinted away through the morning mist, running off to be a grown-up rebel.

Bobby closed the door and swiveled about to translate for him, but Jack was already out of bed and half-dressed. No explanations required. The call to evacuate transcended language. Bobby shrugged the robe from her shoulders, standing naked as it fell in a pool at her feet. She hurried to pick up her own clothes, and the gambler stopped buttoning his shirt, permitting himself just a moment to gaze at the milky softness of her body. The memory of the night had already transformed itself to an ache of longing for another and then another.

As she shrugged on the purple shift they could hear the gunfire sweeping closer over the hills, no longer like thunder or anything else but war. They bolted from the bedroom, leaving the swirl of sheets still warm with the heat of their passion. Jack ran out ahead to turn the car while she grabbed her purse and stuffed a few things in, mementos that meant nothing to anyone but her. Then she walked out with her head high, no looking back, and trotted down the drive to join him.

They rode in silence down the rutted lane through the trees, then turned onto the main road. The way was eerily deserted as they picked up speed, the boom of mortars echoing off to the right. Bobby stared straight ahead, even when he glanced at her sidelong, trying to read her feelings. It wasn't just the suddenness of their escape that had left them so quiet. It wasn't even the threat of government troops waiting around every bend in the road. No—this had to do with the two of them.

"It's gonna be okay, Bobby," he said at last, reaching a hand to touch her knee.

She glanced at him, her eyes stark in the morning light, then looked away. "Yes," she replied simply, but it was clear she wanted no further reassurances. Nothing was certain yet, and they both knew it. They had to cross a minefield first, before they could even begin to be free. And she wasn't the type to pretend, even for the sake of love—not after what she'd been through.

After a while they began to pass donkey carts in slow flight, goaded by frantic peasants. Then groups on foot, families straggling exhausted, bound for nowhere. At the top of a hill they had to inch their way around the smoldering carcass of an army truck. As they left it behind she seemed to brim over with haunted memories. "Were you in the war?" she asked him quietly.

He replied with an unexpected laugh. "Yeah, I ran the biggest card game in the South Pacific. By popular demand. Had the time of my life."

She smiled, admiring his resilience. "I'll bet you were a good soldier."

His lip curled sardonically. "All the good soldiers are dead," he retorted.

Again she looked away, mournfully gazing over the sea of green, taking it in for the last time. She seemed to be storing it up, in a heart already heavy with countries lost. She felt his hand clasp hers on the seat between them. She stared at the two hands intertwined, trying somehow to weigh it against the burden of her memories.

And then suddenly, over the ridge ahead, a B-26 bore down on them like a predatory bird. The dusty road exploded with strafing, the spray of bullets sweeping back and forth. Jack swerved the Caddy onto the shoulder, skidding into the cane brush as the plane zoomed over.

They lurched to a stop, and he scrambled out, dragging her after him. They were half stumbling, half falling down the slope of a ravine. The plane was almost out of sight, not bothering to turn around. But as he pulled Bobby in under the overhang of a downed tree two more B-26s flared over the ridge, strafing the road at random. The ground shook as one of them dropped a jelly bomb.

"I'm not doing this, it's somebody else!" Jack crowed defiantly, holding her close. "I'm out by the pool drinking Coca-Cola, catching some rays and reading *True* magazine!" As the bombing continued, slamming the earth all around them, he shook his fist at the sky. "I'm *reading* about some jerk driving a dame through a war!"

"What are they bombing?" Bobby demanded, dazed and incredulous. "There's nothing to bomb!"

The bombing of nothing continued about a minute longer, and then it was over as suddenly as it had begun. In the stunned quiet that followed—no birds, not even the zing of insects—he kept his arm about her, the closest they'd come to embracing since they were routed out of bed.

"You wouldn't happen to have a cigarette on you," he asked softly. She shook her head with a regretful smile. "Just remember," he said with a grin, "I came two hundred miles after you with one cigarette, and I let you have it. Now is that love, or what?"

They laughed, streaked with sweat and dirt, the tension broken. Then they made their way up the ravine, exhilarated to be doing something physical. By the time they climbed in the car and took off again, they looked rather more like guerrillas themselves, toughened by life in the open. They held one another's hands now with just the right pressure, neither too soft nor too hard, balanced on the knife edge of their intimacy.

They encountered no further enemy fire. They kept passing more and more refugees, but the road was never blocked, and they made good time because there was no other traffic. They stopped only once, in a large deserted village with a rusty phone booth beside a pharmacy. Jack got out and made a quick call, barking a couple of orders into the phone, looking to Bobby just like the young captain huddled over the radio.

They reached the outskirts of Havana in the middle of the afternoon. Jack turned off the main road and steered his way through a shantytown, heading for the water. When he reached the ruined boulevard by the seawall, he pulled up behind a beat-up Chevy station wagon parked at the curb. The Chevy was held together by wire and tape, looking as if it had been through a couple of strafe bombings itself.

Wordlessly Jack and Bobby got out of the Caddy and moved to the Chevy. Behind the wheel was La Polaca, coughing and wheezing and smoking at the same time. Bobby got in on the passenger's side and accepted the finespun shawl offered by the landlady. As she hooded the shawl over her copper hair La Polaca turned to Jack for instructions. The old woman's eyes were tough as a buzzard's, accustomed to surviving, not taking no for an answer from life.

"Take her in through the back way," Jack instructed her. "Keep her till I get upstairs. I'll tap the pipes if everything's okay."

The landlady nodded and started the car, the muffler roaring like a wind tunnel. As Jack stepped away Bobby murmured something to La Polaca. The old woman laughed and reached into her string bag, pulling out a package of cigarettes and handing it out the window to Jack. He grabbed it, grinning tightly, and the Chevy pulled away in a cloud of black exhaust—two peasant women minding their own business.

An hour later the colonial quarter baked in the merciless afternoon sun, weirdly still as a ghost town. No urchins on the street, no pushcart vendors, no cacophony of radios. The scraps and tatters of Christmas decorations in the shop windows looked like relics from another world, vanished like Pompeii. The Caddy was parked in its regular place in front of the baroque apartment building, but car and building alike seemed abandoned, as if the keys to every door had been confiscated.

Jack Weil stood at his window, tilting the blinds closed. Behind him the door to the apartment opened to the landlady's touch—God himself couldn't confiscate La Polaca's ring of keys. She hurried Bobby in and quickly yanked the door closed.

He turned from the window. "It's Sunday, I can't reach Willy till tomorrow. My guy with the boat." His tone was brooding and preoccupied. "So we can't get out of here till morning."

She nodded indifferently, as if nothing could surprise her anymore. "I've never heard it this quiet," she said, practically whispering. Any sound would carry, it seemed, across the lunar silence of the city.

"People don't know what's going on out there in the mountains. Everyone's waiting."

The phone rang on the center table. Neither of them moved, staring as it rang again. "Aren't you going to answer?" she asked, looking around awkwardly, as if she was in the way.

Instead of replying, he stepped around the table and gathered her in his arms, burying his face in the fragrance of her hair. The phone rang a third time—then silence. She cradled his head as he kissed her neck, and now she was laughing softly. "It's someone who knows how small the apartment is," she said.

He murmured a sound of protest, as if to swear it wasn't a girl. Then he was lifting her off her feet, carrying her into the bedroom. Ever since this morning, when they woke into the teeth of panic and flight, they'd known it deep in their bones that the chance to love might never be given again. Now it was like a delirious gift as he tumbled her onto the bed. They struggled to tear off their clothes without breaking the hungry kiss that fused them.

What was the hour now? As they faced each other, naked—hands everywhere, nothing untouched—they either had no time at all or all the time in the world. He was inside her almost immediately, and yet there was no urgency once the bond was sealed. They would ride like this forever, curved to each other like the sides of a ship, cutting the endless waves of the sea.

The afternoon passed into dusk, no words anymore, and finally no sounds. The silent cave of their loving was deeper than the silence of the city. Once, as the light faded, they were staring straight in each other's eyes, startled as deer. A second of pure surreality, where they didn't seem to know anymore who was who. And he felt her mouth with his fingers blindly, reading her lips like braille, and said with a kind of awe, "You."

When they came to themselves, drifting back to the world, it was night. She got up and went to the bathroom and let the water run hot in the tub. He came in to find her kneeling in the water enshrouded with steam, transparent as a nymph, almost a mirage. He knelt beside the tub and began to soap her back, rhythmic swirls of foam on the alabaster whiteness of her skin. Then he cupped and lathered each breast, tender and lavish, anointing her like a goddess.

She ran her hands up the cords and sinews of his arm, her fingers grazing the hard bump on his inner forearm. "What's this?" she asked with lazy curiosity.

"I don't know. Nothing." He shrugged. "A scar."

Now she looked at him, piqued by the evasion in his voice. "No, it isn't. Tell me."

"Why?"

She smiled. "Because you don't want to."

The corners of his mouth curled in a grin. He leaned forward and kissed her lightly on the lips, then moved to whisper it in her ear. "It's a diamond."

He reached a coffee can from the side of the tub and dipped it to rinse the water from her back. He pretended to ignore the stunned look on her face. It wasn't easy to throw her, and it seemed to please him mightily. *"What?"* she demanded, incredulous now.

"Yeah . . . I swallowed it."

She gripped his wrist to stop him pouring. "Please tell me," she said, at once seductive and petulant.

He struggled to find the words. It was such a long time ago, the impulse of a boy. "I knew this old hustler when I was a kid," he said at last. "What they call a mechanic—a crooked player. And he showed me how he had a diamond sewed into his arm. By a doctor." As he spoke she grazed her fingers across the spot, almost as if there was something erotic about it. He sighed. "So when I was in Yokohama I bought this diamond and had a Jap doctor do it. The idea was . . . no matter what they did to you or how bad it got, no matter what . . . you've got this last chance. You've always got the diamond."

He stopped speaking, stirred by too many memories, maybe even a little embarrassed. She bent her head and brushed the spot with her lips. "You still feel that way?" she asked him softly.

"Hey, I was in my twenties," he retorted, trying to shake the heaviness. Then he stroked the exquisite curve of her neck, feeling it arch against his hand, and he said almost in spite of himself, "Yeah, I do."

She sank low in the water, her body floating in a limpid calm, but her words were very precise, "Tell me about the boat."

"Our boat?" She nodded gently, rocking in the water. "All you have to know about it is, it'll take you anywhere you want to go." He leaned his elbows on the side of the tub, bent down and touched his tongue to her nipple where it surfaced out of the water. She gave a soft gasp. "Where do you want to go, pal? You want to go to California?"

She ran a slow hand through his hair. "Are you going with me, Jack Weil?"

"Sure, I haven't been there in ages." He grinned at her, suddenly alive with possibilities. "Where else?"

Her face was as peaceful as sleep, and she seemed to speak out of a dream. "Anywhere?"

He nodded eagerly. "Anywhere in the world, Bobby,"

he said. And she reached up her arms from the water, a siren beckoning. He leaned into her lush embrace, losing himself in the mist of the sea goddess. His mouth sought hers, and they drank each other again, drawn like restless sailors to the very rim of the world.

They were the desert island.

It was morning, and he was shaving, smiling at himself in the mirror, stupefied at the sight of his own happiness. He splashed hot water on his face, then groped for the towel, breathing in her smell as he patted himself dry. He grabbed a white shirt that hung from the doorknob and slipped it on. He winked at the guy in the mirror on his way out.

When he stepped into the bedroom, he expected to find her still in bed, asleep the way he'd left her, the gold of her hair spilled on the pillow. Instead she was standing at the window, wrapped in his robe with her back to him. "Hi," he tossed out cheerfully.

She didn't turn. Now he saw how her shoulders seemed to huddle inside the robe. He knew there was something wrong, so he tried to keep it easy, willing it all to be the same. "Almost noon," he said with studied casualness. "I gotta get moving. Don't answer the phone. If it's me, I'll let it ring once, hang up, and call again."

He turned to go without touching her, afraid she might jump like a cat. He was already through the doorway when she turned. "I can't . . ." she said helplessly. "I can't do this."

He stopped. He waited. He didn't dare look in her eyes. She pressed a hand to her forehead and stumbled on. "I feel . . . I don't know, as if I've been drugged or asleep." A throb of laughter broke from her throat, dusky and heartsick. "But that doesn't make sense. Because I laid there for hours, staring at the ceiling, wide awake. So maybe I've just been dreaming. You don't have to be asleep to dream, do you?"

"You're awake now," he replied carefully. The only evidence of the tension in him was the flexing of his hands.

She sat down heavily on the bed. "I'm a partisan," she said, almost defiantly. "I was never neutral, even when my country was. I'd see the Nazis in uniform in Stockholm, when my girlfriends and I went to dances at the Summergarden. We treated them like tourists." Her voice was suddenly raw with contempt. "Why? So they wouldn't do to us what they did to everyone else in Europe. It was like a gentlemen's agreement. Good for us, good for the Nazis. Bad for the soul." Her mouth was tight, sneering with disgust.

"What do you want to do, Bobby?" There wasn't the slightest threat in his voice, or even the hint of a wound.

"Two things at once," she replied, rueful and ironic. She took a deep breath. "You said that most of the time nothing is going on. Just the days passing and people going about with their little lives. Well, then I guess I live for the other times. When things matter. When they're difficult." She stood up again, stronger now. She tossed her hair. "Being neutral is just an excuse for not doing something. Or not feeling something."

"Then what happened in Santa Clara, Bobby?" Still that eerie objectiveness, as if he was only here to take down the facts. But his hands still flexed at his sides.

She moved to him in the doorway and reached to take his hands in hers. Her grip was firm, and her gaze was steady. "You moved me," she said with feeling. "You came all that way . . . through the fighting. You didn't even think how bad it might be. I was very moved by that. You'll never know." Now she looked away, caught by a sudden wave that filled her eyes. She swallowed with difficulty, then looked at him, her voice unbearably gentle. "But . . . who are you, Jack Weil? You're a guy I met on a boat. You took care of me when I felt like dying, but what would we have? What *could* we have? What's the best it could be?"

One edge of his mouth crinkled, the ghost of a melancholy smile. "How about fun?" he asked quietly. Then he shrugged and winked like he did in the mirror. "You've heard of fun, haven't you?" His tone was tender and mocking, but now it deepened as he returned the grip. "Listen, I don't let anyone down. I bluff sometimes, but I don't cheat." He seemed prepared to reveal every secret to convince her.

He turned and led her into the living room, suddenly looking around at his shabby digs with a critical eye. "We'd live well when I'm winning," he declared wryly, "and not bad the rest of the time. It'd be a good change for you, Bobby. Not so serious. Politics, you said once, is a kind of hope—"

"Arturo said that," she interjected softly.

His face blanched with apology. "Yeah," he replied awkwardly. "Well, I never met a card player who wasn't full of hope. He's gotta be, see, 'cause he's always waiting for the cards to fill a straight. And to raise . . . hey, that's pure hope if I ever saw it." When he smiled at her now, there was something almost childlike about him, a sort of innocence she'd never seen before. "That's what I'm doing now," he said. "I'm raising."

He looked away, too exposed again, but willing himself to stay that way. He spoke slowly, groping for purchase. "Maybe I can learn to think about . . . what you think about. I'd try." He was gripping her hand so hard now it must have hurt, but she raised no protest. "One day at a time, Bobby," he said, not afraid to plead now. "We can take it one day at a time. You don't have to say yes. Just don't say no."

His eyes searched her face. He touched her lips with his fingers again, the way he had in the throes of their loving, but now it was much more tentative. He didn't dare kiss her, as if that alone would be probing for an answer she wasn't ready to give yet. He let her hand go and moved heavily toward the door, then turned back with his hand on the knob, not brave enough to leave without a sign.

She folded her arms and tilted her head. "Anywhere in the world?" she asked, echoing back the words of the dream.

He looked as if he was going to cry for joy. The words

came with difficulty, fighting to be stark naked. "You're
. . . I don't know, like my fucking right arm. How did that
happen?" His eyes were full of astonishment. The next
words rang like a contract written in blood. "Anywhere in
the world," he repeated. "We're the ticket. You just name
it."

And then he hurried out, pulling the door behind him
quickly, as if anything further would be a demand. She
heard him go thundering down the stairs, then crossed to the
window and peered through a slat in the blind, watching as
he got into the Caddy and sped away. Then she yawned
luxuriously and bent to the radio on the table beside the
sofa. She snapped it on and fiddled the station dial. Jo
Stafford's foggy voice shimmered in the room. "You Belong to Me."

As Bobby listened to the bittersweet lyrics, she moved to
the center table and picked up her bag. She rooted inside
and pulled out a hairbrush. Rhythmically she began to stroke
her copper mane, running it through her fingers and brushing out the tangles.

She crossed again and flicked the dial, worrying it up and
down the band till she stopped by a kind of instinct. A rebel
broadcast barked through the static, a truculent voice reel-
ing off a list of demands. Bobby moved back to the center
table and sat down, listening intently as she brushed her
hair.

Then she noticed something in the chipped ceramic bowl
on the table: the paper umbrella from the Lido. She picked
it up and opened it, twirling it between two fingers. Then
she set it down in front of her and studied it while she
brushed her hair, listening to the voice of the revolution.

The marina was frantic. All the charter shacks were
jammed, people spilling in lines outside, everyone trying to
get out. No panic yet, but the tension was very very high.
The green Cadillac was parked at the foot of the pier, families streaming around it carrying children and luggage, the

middle-class version of the peasants on the road from Santa Clara.

Jack Weil stepped out of a tin-roofed office halfway up the dock, shaking hands with the grizzled Willy. Both men shook their heads in wonder at the stream of people lining up to fill the fishing boats and commercial yachts, an exodus that seemed to be growing by the hour. The gulls dipped and wheeled above the crowd of exiles, protesting shrilly that there were no fish to scavenge today.

As Jack moved to get in his car a cream-colored Rolls pulled up just ahead of him. The rear doors opened, discharging a middle-aged man and woman dressed for yachting. They bolted across the dock to a line that was filing onto a seventy-footer, followed by their chauffeur lugging a heap of Vuitton luggage. As they forced their way to the head of the line a fight broke out—pushing and shoving, everyone screaming just like the gulls.

Jack wheeled the Caddy in a U-turn and took the first narrow side street to get away from the melee of the marina. He twisted and turned his circuitous way through the crumbling warehouses, coming out at last onto a strangely deserted boulevard. He headed west, back to the colonial quarter, practically the only car on the road. Then his eyes were drawn to the line of high-rise casinos along the Malecon, just a half mile away. He found himself veering left and heading in that direction, as if he knew a secret shortcut, though in fact it was out of his way.

He came through a tunnel of royal palms and entered the strip that ran along the gold coast. Here the good old days of Havana seemed to thrive unabated as taxis and limos let off their stylish passengers, ready as always for another go at the tables. Jack studied them in their carelessness as he drove along slowly, these people who lived for the next spin of the roulette wheel. He smiled grimly at so much evidence of hope.

And then there was a moment of decision, a fleck of gold that flashed in his eyes as he passed the Lido. He swung the

Caddy in under the portico, pulling up in front of the liveried doorman, who opened his door and greeted him with the usual sunshine smile. The gambler sauntered into the lobby, hands in his pockets and looking around with a cool detachment, as if he couldn't quite believe it was all still standing.

The casino floor was eerier still. The combo, dressed in silver tuxedos, was playing its sexy samba rhythm from the stage. Only a few people worked the slots, and their luggage sat at their feet—as if they were in a terminal, which in a way they were. As Jack passed the center roulette table, a tall woman in a lamé gown calmly took off a cocktail ring the size of a robin's egg and placed it on Number 12. Jack didn't wait to see if she won.

In Joe Volpi's outer office people were scurrying about and packing files. They ignored the gambler as he walked across and entered the inner sanctum. Joe was behind his desk, cramming papers into a briefcase, wastebaskets on either side of him overflowing with trash.

"Moving day?" Jack asked dryly.

"Nah," Volpi growled. "I been meaning to get this place organized since '33."

"You call me yesterday?"

"Yeah, and the day before." The casino manager shot him a look. "Where were you?"

"Out of town." The gambler shrugged, lighting a Pall Mall. "So when's the game?"

Volpi stopped packing. This was more important. "Forbes and his guys are in," he said. "Tomorrow."

Jack squinted as he blew out smoke. "What time tomorrow?"

Volpi sneered. "You got a schedule problem, Jack? What's goin' on with you?"

Jack laughed. "What're you talking about? I'm right here, aren't I?"

Joe Volpi's eyes narrowed into slits. "Is this about a broad?" he asked with icy suspicion. "Is this about *that* broad?"

Jack's expression hardened like stone. "This is about a card game, Joe." He made it clear the discussion was closed in every other direction.

Volpi shrugged and nodded. "Two-thirty tomorrow. Meyer's suite." Then, as if the mention of Big himself gave Volpi another shot of toughness, he added with caustic precision, "These guys are always on time, Jack."

The gambler nodded curtly in return, heading out of the office without another word. He didn't look very excited as he retraced his steps through the end-game crowd in the casino. In fact he seemed almost irritated by the prospect of the game he'd been waiting for all his life. He drove away from the Lido, making his way back to the colonial quarter, and his face was rigid as a mask, except for a tic in the corner of one eye. A religious man would have called it the face of guilt, as if the gambler had just ducked into hell for a quickie.

He parked around the corner from the apartment, not quite trusting his usual space, though he couldn't have said why. He locked the car and began to walk down the deserted sidewalk, missing the urchins and street noise. He'd just reached the corner when he caught a flash of movement to his left. And suddenly they were on him, shoving him against the wall.

A blur of pushing and punching, accompanied by a stream of vitriolic Spanish. There were two of them, but they were young and angry and fought like five. "Wait a minute! Hey!" Jack cried, fighting back. He managed a kick that knocked one of them to the ground, and the next moment the other one pinned him to the wall, an arm at his windpipe. They both breathed sharply, hissing with rage.

"What *is* this?" croaked the gambler.

His assailant snarled, the accent thick. "You are with his wife. . . ."

"Huh?" Jack stopped fighting, scrambling instead to understand. "Arturo Duran is dead! He's—" Then he saw a glint of something in the young man's eyes, and neither of them was fighting anymore. Jack felt the choke in his throat, but this time it was his own heart. "What?" he demanded, as if the young rebel had spoken. "What do you mean?"

But the rebel released him mutely and turned away. The two of them took off between parked cars and disappeared down an alley, leaving the gambler breathing hard, rubbing the pain in his shoulder. He stared after the thugs in a kind of horror, and at last he looked like a man who'd been touched by war.

BOBBY WAS DROWSING on the sofa, listening to jazz on the radio, when Jack walked in. She sat up, startled. Then her face went pale at the sight of his torn shirt and the bruises on his jaw and cheekbone. She leaped up and rushed to him, her heart hammering with anxiety. "What happened?" she gasped.

He gave a dry laugh. "Baby, you have no idea how irritable people can get over a little boat. . . ."

Her face was a breath away, examining the scrapes. He cradled an arm around her waist, needing to anchor himself. "Tell me what happened," she demanded again, in a voice that wanted to fight back.

"Really," Jack replied easily, playing it down. "Everyone's trying to get out down there. It's a friggin' circus."

"You have some antiseptic?"

"Soap's fine," he declared curtly, moving past her to the window, peering out through the blind. The street below was dead quiet. At her beckoning insistence he followed her into the bathroom. As she ran hot water in the sink he embroidered the story more, as if he couldn't let it alone. "I tried to buck the line," he said. "Boy, have people got short fuses. I thought this lady was gonna shoot me. . . ."

She dabbed a steaming facecloth on his jawline, frowning as she worked. "You had to fight for a boat?"

"Yeah, sixty-footer. No problem. We're in with Willy. Tomorrow sometime."

She pulled back, fretful and troubled, as if it was all happening very fast. "All my things . . . at the house . . ."

"No," he declared bluntly. "You can't go there."

"I know," she answered softly, forcing herself to resume her swabbing, a concrete task to keep her in the present.

"I have to get Willy paid today," he said, his mind racing to work it out step by step. "Friend of mine, Joe Volpi, he's holding some cash for me. At the Lido. I gotta go try to catch him." His eyes flickered nervously, as if he was torn in two directions. "It may take some time," he added haltingly. "Will you be all right here?"

"Of course," she assured him with a smile, dabbing the last of the scrapes. "I feel at home here."

He turned and checked himself out in the mirror. All cleaned up. "You're very good at this," he complimented her wryly as she moved to unbutton the torn shirt.

"I like taking the hurt away," she said in her husky faraway voice.

"Maybe you should go with a prizefighter." He laughed, pulling another shirt out of a bureau drawer. He let her slip the other one off his shoulders, then happened to glance in the mirror and saw the cloud on her face—as if she was locked in a cell again. He gripped her shoulders and said, "Tell me."

She nodded, knowing it was better to get it out. "Once Arturo brought home"—an involuntary shiver ran up her back, and she winced at the memory, but still struggled on—"a young man who was so badly wounded . . . that I could barely look. But then I felt so good when I was able to—"

She stopped abruptly, threw her arms around his neck, and buried her face against his throat. He waited, watching his own blank face in the mirror. "I feel so terrible," she whispered, fighting back tears, "about something . . . so crazy."

Now he pulled her face back so he could look in her eyes. "About what?" he coaxed her gently.

"About the thought of . . . being happy." She ducked her head, as if she couldn't bear the tenderness of his gaze. "It's because . . . I wouldn't be here with you if Arturo . . ."

He clamped a hand against her mouth. "Don't," he said. "Don't. Don't." He released her mouth and drew her more tightly into his embrace. They could feel the throb of each other's hearts, tidal as the sea sounding in a shell. "Please, Bobby—don't feel that way."

She nodded against his neck, calmer now. Then drew back and smiled to show she'd recovered, knowing he had to go. She helped him put on the shirt and buttoned it up. Now it was he who seemed uncertain as he said, "I'll be back as soon as I can. Remember about the phone."

"Yes sir," she replied with a mock salute. "One ring, and if it rings again, it's you."

She leaned up to kiss him lightly, permitting herself a moment of the happiness she feared, as if she would have to immunize herself in small doses. As he gave her a final embrace he caught a last glimpse of himself in the mirror, which luckily she couldn't see. Because he looked hunted and haunted and lost, not the sort of man who believed in happiness at all.

Jack moved rapidly along the downtown sidewalk, where men still walked two abreast in tropical business suits, the last gasp of business-as-usual. The gambler turned in at the entrance to the *Havana News,* waiting as a stream of workers emerged through the revolving door, carrying boxes of files. Behind them came Ramos, lugging a typewriter with a dictaphone perched precariously on top.

"Hey Ramos," Jack cried, "where's the story?"

The journalist gave him a baleful look as he crossed the sidewalk to a Volkswagen parked at the curb. The assistants were already loading the boxes of files into the backseat, and Ramos set the typewriter down on the roof with a groan that sounded like he had a hernia. He turned to Jack and wiped a sleeve across his sweaty forehead.

"What the hell's going on?" asked the gambler.

"The government just closed the paper," Ramos replied bitterly. "The editor's in jail. There *is* no press anymore." He turned back to the car and loaded the typewriter and dictaphone into the passenger's seat. Then he hurried around to the driver's side, not a moment to waste. He seemed to forget that Jack was even there.

"Hey, pal, slow down," Jack bawled, leaning across the car's roof. "Where are you going?"

Ramos looked drained and wired at the same time, like a junkie drying out. "I was on my way to Oriente to join Fidel," he said. "But then I hear you have to bring your own gun, which isn't exactly what I signed up for. So I'm going to Miami Beach."

He slung himself into the car, and Jack had to scramble around to stop him before he took off. The gambler grabbed his shirt through the window. "Hey Ramos . . . could Arturo Duran be alive?"

The journalist laughed in his face. *"Sí, amigo,"* he mocked. "Also Hitler and Amelia Earhart. Don't you get it, my friend? It's all rumors now. The facts are dead."

Jack shook his shoulder urgently. "I want you to help me," he hissed through gritted teeth.

"Help you what?"

"Find him. Find out if he's alive." It was beyond desperation. It was like a holy mission. "Would Menocal have him? *Where?"*

"Man, you are crazy." The broken journalist sneered. "I'm unemployed, but not *that* unemployed."

A flash of stunned innocence suffused the gambler's face. "But I thought you loved this guy. I thought you'd do anything for him."

Ramos grinned like a death mask. Beneath the stress and the exhaustion was a horrible pathos, a man who'd somehow misplaced his soul. "Ah, my friend," he retorted, "but don't you see, that's the tragedy of the Cuban middle class. We're paralyzed by self-doubt and intellectuality."

Jack gave him a knock to the head, which wasn't entirely

without affection. "Cut the shit, Ramos, will ya? Gimme a hand. I don't even know where to start looking."

The journalist looked back at him from a terrible distance, pain in his eyes, as if he could see the yawning gulf of his own cowardice. He swallowed, and his voice changed. "I'll tell you this, Jack," he said. "If he *is* alive he's not in a public jail."

"Where then?" pleaded the gambler. "Come on, you're supposed to have *sources*."

Ramos sighed deeply as he started the rattling engine. He looked over at the mute typewriter on the seat beside him. Then he stared at Jack and spoke precisely. "You know how many Edsels there are in Havana? Just one."

And with that he shoved the Beetle into gear and pulled away from the curb in a smutty cloud of fumes, heading for a life that meant nothing at all. Ramos's story was over.

The maroon and charcoal Edsel was parked on a sloping street in the garden quarter, its front wheels turned to the curb. The graceful apartment buildings here were sleek with deco stone and brass, the window boxes rife with gaudy winter flowers. There wasn't a scrap of litter on the street— nor the usual mix of daylight strollers. An eerie silence reigned, as if the chic residents of Frontera Street were all taking afternoon naps at the same time.

Marion Chigwell emerged from a building whose facade was a checkerboard of black and white tile. The WASP correspondent sported his best Brooks Brothers seersucker, slightly rumpled around the edges as always, but definitely in the club. He carried a prissy briefcase in one hand, descending the steps to the curb where the Edsel was parked.

He opened the door and got in, settling himself with a whining grunt on the sun-warmed leather of the seat. He patted the pockets of the seersucker for his keys—just as Jack Weil erupted out of the backseat and flung a viselike arm about his neck. The gourmet dandy squirmed and squawked, but the gambler had him pinned tight. Chigwell gaped in the rearview mirror to see who his assailant was.

"Don't—Jack," croaked the correspondent. "I can have you hurt. Break your face." The threat sounded painfully mealymouthed.

Jack made a clucking sound of disapproval. "Now is that any way for a Yale man to talk?" he teased. Then his voice dropped. "Is Arturo Duran alive?"

"What do you care?" Chigwell sneered, flapping his arms ineffectually, his patrician face turning blue as his blood. "You're fucking his wife, aren't you?"

"So he *is* alive," the gambler whispered, trying to hide the catch in his own throat. He released his grip so the other could breathe, fearful of killing the messenger.

"Wait a day," Chigwell gasped. "You'll have her all to yourself."

"Where is he?"

"How would I know?" the WASP drawled in utter contempt, irritably flinging Jack's arm off and leaning to fix the knot of his rep tie in the mirror.

"How would *you* know, Marion?" Jack replied dryly. "Because you're a spy, that's why. Hey, it's the talk of the town."

Chigwell's eyes narrowed in the mirror, staring back at his tormentor. He raised his hands and began to applaud dispiritedly. "Hooray, you win the prize," he said in a deadpan voice. "And let me tell you, Jack, it's a brilliant operation. 'Cause you'd have to be some kinda genius to screw up like this." The self-loathing made him manic, a lifetime of anger that never said boo. "Did you hear, the ambassador thinks Castro's a communist. You think he's a communist, Jack? 'Cause I don't—"

"Where's Duran?" interjected Jack.

"—but I think if we keep fucking up all the time, he'll *go* that way. As of this afternoon, we've managed to make enemies of every faction in Cuba. Right, left, center." He was slumped against the door, spewing this acidic harangue as if he were running for office. He was stone-cold sober and sounded poison drunk. "What the hell, they all hate us anyway."

"Goddamn it, where *is* he?" Jack barked, shooting a hand out and grabbing the tidy little Windsor knot on Chigwell's tie.

"Whatever you want to know," replied the overdressed informant, "I don't give a damn. None of it matters anymore. Haven't you read *Pogo* lately? The enemy is us." And then Jack wrenched the knot hard, and the mocking tone evaporated in a strangled curse. Chigwell waved his arms, pleading to be released, then gasped as the pressure came off. "Menocal's got a place . . . in El Lagito."

"Okay. And what's it gonna take for him to give Duran up? Dollars?"

Chigwell bobbed his head. "*Lots* of 'em. Plus he's gonna want asylum."

Jack frowned, releasing his grip on the other's neck. "What kind of asylum?" he asked impatiently, annoyed to find himself out of his depth.

"Just tell him you're with the Agency."

"What agency?"

Chigwell laughed deliciously, as if he'd just heard the best one-liner he'd heard in years. "Jesus Christ, Jack," he retorted merrily, clapping the gambler on the shoulder, intimate as two old sports at a very exclusive club. "You really *are* an innocent, aren't you? Just say it the way I told you. *He*'ll know what agency."

Jack's eyes squinted, not sure who was holding the aces here. "Will he believe me?"

Chigwell nodded, ever the eager outsider who wanted so hard to be liked he could taste it. "Say that Wilson okayed a safe place for him," the fawning WASP declared. "Him and his whole family. In Virginia."

"Is he going to buy that?" Jack asked suspiciously.

"Why not?" Chigwell laughed dryly. "It's probably true. We've okayed all the scum in the world to relocate in the Land of the Free. We're becoming a fucking retirement community for ex-torturers. Hell, if he takes a few lessons, he can play golf with Ike himself. . . ."

Jack swung the back door open and climbed out of the

Edsel. He'd had more than enough of Marion's bitter self-hatred. As he walked back to the Caddie he could still hear the empty sound of Chigwell's laughter, shrill and slightly frantic, like a parrot let loose in the jungle who wanted his cage back.

It was nearing dusk as the green Cadillac made its way to the northern suburbs of the city. Here there was no memory at all of the colonial past, no stucco villas or manor houses with deep verandas. Instead they had bulldozed the cane fields and erected a postwar subdivision, so they could just as easily have been living in Miami. This was the Cuba that looked more American than America: red-blooded modern ranch houses, split-level with three-car garages.

The yards were Texas size, big enough to keep horses, and surrounded by chain-link fences that you wouldn't want to touch with a wet finger. Jack drove slowly, checking numbers on the gates against a scribbled slip of paper on the seat beside him. He seemed surprised, when he came to the colonel's property, to find the gates wide open and un-guarded. He turned into the gravel drive, balling the paper into his fist, and still no plan in his head about how exactly he would proceed.

First law of poker: If you didn't know how to improvise, you'd better go find yourself another game.

As he came around a mammoth hedge of oleander he saw the sprawling ranch house set back on a razor-cut lawn of Bermuda grass. The firepower that was missing at the gates was more than made up for here. A half-dozen goons in cheap suits patrolled the yard with machine guns, looking as if they'd been put out to pasture. The Caddy crept forward, parking next to an olive-drab Oldsmobile 88, on the door of which was lettered SERVICIO DE INTELIGENCIA MILITAR.

As Jack stepped out of his car—slowly, no sudden movements—two of the goons lumbered in his direction, tilting their guns so they pointed right at his heart. Jack resisted the temptation to raise his hands and said with sharp impatience, "Jack Weil. I have information for Colonel Menocal."

The goons' faces registered nothing, but they stepped aside and indicated that Jack should walk between them. The door to the house was opened by one of the dimwit bodyguards who'd covered the colonel the night they'd played cards in the Lido penthouse. The bodyguard carried no gun at all, though he looked as if he could break bones with his little finger.

He led Jack through the living room and dining room of the ranch house, the decor so banal and ugly it could have been the lobby of a cheap hotel. The bodyguard pushed open a swing door, and Jack stepped into a brightly lit kitchen, chockablock with all the latest appliances. Menocal was sitting alone at a garish Formica table, eating what looked like rice and beans, a peasant at heart. He wore a Yankees baseball cap, a baby-blue polo shirt, and pistachio-colored Bermuda shorts—ready for a twilight double header. Behind him against the wall were stacked cases and cases of soda pop, as if he was storing up for a long hibernation.

The colonel smiled at the gambler. "Something to report, Jack?" he asked pleasantly. "About the wife, perhaps?"

"No," Jack replied curtly. "Nothing to report."

The colonel, still smiling fixedly, stood up and went to the refrigerator, where he pulled out a bottle of orange soda. He grabbed a church key from the counter and flipped off the cap. Then he handed the drink to Jack, as suavely as if he'd just mixed a batch of martinis. "Then why do you come?" he asked, barely interested.

Suddenly there was a bloodcurdling shriek from the pantry, and something low and grotesque came hurtling into the room. Jack recoiled in shock as the colonel laughed. The manic creature was a monkey—hulking, scruffy, and mean. It ricocheted around the kitchen, bouncing off the cabinets, then stopped to squat and shit in the middle of the floor. Menocal continued to watch the gambler's jarred reaction with amusement as the monkey bolted and scuttled out through the swing door.

"Why do you come?" the colonel repeated, stepping around the monkey turds and taking his place at the table again. The goons would clean up the mess.

"I work for some people," the gambler replied carefully, sitting on the edge of a chair opposite the colonel.

"What people would that be?"

"Let's just say you've done business with us," said Jack. It surely was a poker game now, nothing missing but the deck of cards.

Menocal scoffed. "This is a joke, no? I work for El Presidente. That is all the 'business' I do, my friend." He resumed eating the rice and beans, haughty as if it was caviar.

Jack ignored the denial. "They want Arturo Duran," he announced. "Alive. Well. COD."

"*Qué lástima.*" The Colonel shrugged mournfully. "The man is dead. I'm a good Catholic, señor, but I can't bring the dead back to life."

"Hold it, hold it," Jack hissed, leaning forward on his elbows so his face was barely a foot from the colonel's. "Let's not fuck around, huh? Nobody's interested in details. They want what they want. So you better get a little miracle going."

"Mmm," the colonel replied indifferently, taking a long swig from his own bottle of soda. Then he smacked his lips and smiled playfully at Jack. "And do 'they' know that Duran's wife is in your apartment? Right now?"

Jack hadn't even heard the door swing open, but now he was aware that two of the bodyguards had moved in front of the refrigerator, one of them cradling his machine gun like a baby. Jack's eyes flicked toward them, then back to the colonel. "Sure," he said with self-confidence. "That's why they sent me to Santa Clara. To bring her back."

Menocal stared at him for a long moment, unblinking. Jack thought about all the people the man had tortured, how they must have had to endure that pitiless, unblinking gaze.

Menocal reached for a folder beside his plate and slipped a photograph from it. "Do you wonder how I knew?" he asked archly. Then placed the photograph on the table between him and the gambler, as if he were laying down an ace.

It was grainy and taken with a long lens, but the image was clear enough: Jack and Bobby embracing near the window in his apartment. The moment wasn't especially erotic, but the sense of violation was no less dislocating. Coolly Menocal watched the brief flare of pain and anger in the gambler's face.

The colonel sighed. "You're right, it doesn't really do her justice," he said, lingering on the final word as if even he appreciated the irony. "Doesn't do *either* of you justice." He smiled, then shook his head and clucked. "Terrible, isn't it? Just the kind of thing that happens when things are falling apart in a country . . . especially a little country. Your poor landlady was afraid. She was afraid it might become Budapest again."

He tapped his finger on the image thoughtfully, smudging it with his fingerprint. "It was a good idea," he continued with a meditative frown. "But unfortunately it didn't work."

"What was it supposed to get you?" Jack asked, sneering contemptuously.

"Ah, who knows what kind of *información* a man like Duran might have? One always hopes for a jackpot. You know? Like the slot machines—everything clicks, and the money pours like a faucet." Menocal chuckled with satisfaction at his own vivid image, then frowned again at the picture of Bobby and Jack. "But he spit on it. See right there? Spit." And he nudged his finger at the corner of the snapshot, precise as a forensics expert.

Jack said nothing. His face was the mask of a man who was playing a very dicey hand. He concentrated on looking directly at the colonel.

And Menocal said with a small dismissive shrug, "You're not with them."

Jack shot back, "Look, we don't have time to bullshit, Colonel. Chigwell's laid it all out."

Menocal's eyebrows lifted about a millimeter. "I can call him, amigo."

"Call him," barked the gambler. The final bluff on the final card.

The colonel suddenly flared and slammed a fist on the table. "What the hell is going on?" he bellowed. "You people pay me to keep the communists under control. Now you come and say let this one go, we need him! For what?" He growled and spat out a stream of invective in Spanish, pulling off his baseball cap and dashing it to the floor. It landed perilously close to the monkey shit. "You're crazy," he snarled at the Yankee gambler. "You Americans are like . . . I don't know, pregnant women. Everything is a whim!"

"I just do what they tell me," Jack Weil said, in a tone of impeccable indifference.

"And what happens to me?" the colonel shrilled, the veins in his temples pulsing now with outrage. "I'm your Cuban trash collector, but when I go to the embassy for a visa, you treat me like shit!"

Jack nodded sympathetically. He lobbed the next card on the table. "Asylum," he declared with judicial calm. "Wilson is prepared to offer you asylum."

"Asylum from what?" The colonel seethed with disdain as he rose from the table. His two goons took a step aside to give him room to thunder. "Don't you listen to the radio, Jack? We're beating the shit out of those guerrillas! They'll never take Havana!" He stood by the refrigerator with his arm raised, shaking his fist like a sword, the full macho melodrama.

"Well, then"—Jack grinned lazily—"you've got nothing to worry about, have you, Colonel?" The silence that followed was brief but unusually deafening. Then the gambler added, almost as an afterthought, "Where is he?"

"And I live on what?" the colonel barked in reply, ignoring for now the hostage part of the deal. Like all men with the wrong kind of power, his voice was always veering towards a whine—sulky as an adolescent, never enough respect.

"Twenty-five thousand," said Jack. "And a job."

"Another joke!" Menocal took two strides to the table, standing over the gambler. "You see how I live, señor. I support a family. And a monkey."

"Of course," said Jack carefully, stroking his fingers along his forearm. "I mean *fifty* thousand. Cash. Ameri-can."

Menocal bent to the table and lifted the lid of a humidor. He drew out a ten-inch cigar and shut the lid, not even considering offering one to Jack. It was the small petty insults that kept the colonel going. He turned and hissed at the bodyguards, dismissing them like dogs. Then he sauntered across the kitchen to the back door, and though he'd offered no invitation, Jack followed.

As they came outside the evening was cool with a breeze from the mountains, the air sharp with the smell of orange blossoms. The large backyard extended over an acre, most of it planted in fruit trees. Menocal walked slightly ahead of Jack, a clipped quality to his stride, almost like a goose step. Suddenly in the silence of the orchard Jack wasn't sure exactly where the poker game was going—as if it was too dark out here to see the cards.

"Where is he?" he demanded brusquely.

"I haven't said yes or no," the colonel replied, stiff with arrogance.

Jack stopped walking on the gravel path. "Yeah? And who says you can deliver the goods at all?"

Menocal turned to face him, hands on his hips. They were a pair of duelists in the falling night. "I'll show you photographs," the colonel offered.

Jack shook his head. "Touch," he replied bluntly. "Feel. Talk to."

The curl of Menocal's sneer would have been palpable in pitch darkness. "They're going to make him part of the new government, aren't they?" he asked, sounding more bitter than Ramos and Chigwell together. Then he laughed hollowly as he flared a match and lit the cigar. His face was demonic in the sudden burst of sulfur. "Christ, they're fools! You're all fools!"

Jack waited till the colonel had taken a first deep puff of the glowing cigar. "Maybe they're just going to make him disappear," he offered quietly.

"Ha! *I* can make him disappear," the colonel retorted haughtily.

The gambler shrugged. "Well, you didn't do such a hot job of it last time."

Menocal bristled with wounded pride. "Why don't I give them his body? Is that 'disappeared' enough for you?"

"They want him alive!" Jack blurted out, too eager, too quick. He forced his voice to be casual. "They want to talk to him."

Menocal nodded slowly, as if he understood better than anyone the need for getting a prisoner to talk. Indeed, it was what he lived for. He blew cigar smoke into the trees above his head, tainting the orange blossoms. Then he laughed in an easy way, man to man. "He's a real Cubano, that one," said the colonel with wry appreciation. "*Cojones!* You won't get a fucking thing out of him."

"Then what do *you* want him for?" Jack asked, genuinely fascinated by the intricate shell game of the colonel's mind.

"Insurance." The colonel shrugged. "In case it goes the other way. If the rebels win . . . well, at least I have something to bargain with."

"*We're* the insurance, Colonel," Jack replied decisively, playing his final card in the dark.

Menocal nodded philosophically, then turned and led the way through the trees once more. About forty feet farther on, they came out of the orchard into an open space. Across the twilit grass was a tin-roofed garden shed. In front of it sat two plainclothes goons on spindly chairs, their machine guns across their laps. As soon as they saw their colonel they leaped to their feet and stood at parade rest.

"Let him in," Menocal called to the guards, gesturing at

Jack with his cigar. Then he turned abruptly and headed back through the trees, completely uninterested in having a further look at the prisoner himself.

Jack could feel the sweat beading on his own forehead as he crossed to the garden shed. His throat constricted in a sort of terror, as if he was about to be interrogated. The padlock came off the door, and the guard swung the door open. Jack took a deep breath before he entered, one small part of his mind still full of dread and uncertainty. For all he knew the door would close, and he'd never come out again.

═══════ XII ═══════

THE SHED WAS small and stiflingly hot, about the size of a dungeon cell. The door slammed shut behind him, causing the single candle that burned in a niche in the wall to gutter. The stucco was whitewashed, so the place wasn't grimly dark, but it had no windows, no way to know if it was day or night. A seatless portable toilet was set beneath the candle niche like some kind of grotesque altar, and the smell was rank as a barn.

The man seemed very small as well, almost shrunken, as he lay curled on the cot, knees drawn up and facing the wall. A table and stool cluttered the space beside the cot, where the interrogator would sit. Jack took a tentative step, opened his mouth and tried to speak, but his throat was closed with emotion. He moved closer, hunkering down beside the cot, wanting to touch the man but fearful of hurting him. He felt suddenly ashamed, as if he was somehow responsible for Arturo Duran's incarceration.

"Arturo?" he asked softly, bending close to the hunched form.

Duran slumped over on his back and stared up at Jack. His face was streaked with sweat but otherwise unmarked. That was the skill of a master like Menocal, knowing how to keep the bruises and scars away from the face. But something worse than physical blows was visible in the visage of the proud aristocrat. There were blows to the mind and the soul, echoing worse than screams. The eyes of the rebel leader were glazed with the desolation of every imprisoned belief, the whole world over. In the blank gaze of Arturo Duran was the proof that hope could die.

When he looked at Jack, he was puzzled at first, vaguely recognizing but not connecting. Everything in his life before two days ago was a million miles away. His punishment in this little room had erased the outer landscape, the lazy flowering of tropical days, the Cuban people he loved so much. Who was this blond Yankee?, his troubled eyes seemed to wonder.

Then a shocked moment of recognition, and the haunted looked congealed into rage. His lips pulled back over bloodied and broken teeth as he hissed like a snake. The voice was cracked and hoarse, hardly a whisper, and yet the whisper boiled with venom. "Bastard!" he seethed. "Get out of here! How dare you come to me!" Then with all his strength he hammered a fist against the wall. "Get him out of here!"

The door swung open, and one of the guards began to enter. Jack held up a firm hand, gesturing that everything was fine. The guard slipped out again, and in that moment Arturo Duran struggled up on one elbow, gasping at the pains that racked his body. Fury made his voice stronger. "Why are you still in Cuba, you scum?" he demanded. "Don't look at me and say to me she's still here. Don't!" There was a terrible pleading at the end, as if Jack was about to take away the last shred of his dignity.

Jack stammered. "Listen—I'm going to get you—"

"You think I can take any more?" choked the beaten man. "If she's caught again, that's the end of me, too! Are you stupid? No, you're a monster!" And his head fell back to the cot again with a groan of despair. He turned back to the wall, making a low keening sound.

Jack leaned over and gripped his shoulder, forcing him to listen. Arturo tried to spit in his face, but his mouth was too dry. Then the choking desperation once again. "Where is she?" he begged. "This minute!"

Jack's answer was strong and calm. "She's having tea at the American embassy," he said.

Arturo appraised him coldly, the sharpness cutting through the veils of pain. He frowned with suspicion, but there was a flicker in one eye, an edge of the old irony. Something in him decided to trust the gambler. He started to cough, but only to cover the urgency of what he had to say. "Closer," he said between coughs. "Listen to me. You can't do it."

"Yeah, I can," Jack murmured in reply. "He thinks I'm with the CIA. Good name to drop these days."

Arturo Duran laughed savagely through his hacking cough, sounding as if he would split a gut. "Fool," he panted, mocking the gambler just as the colonel had. "They've been swindling the CIA for years! Why the hell do you have to be so ignorant?"

He struggled to sit up again, his eyes darting to the door. The two guards were watching suspiciously, straining to hear. "Quick," Arturo whispered, "pretend to examine me for bruises. Open my shirt. Look in my mouth. Hurry!"

Shakily Jack did as he was told, unbuttoning the sweaty shirt. He winced and didn't want to look, for the flesh of the chest was purple with welts, the nipples crusted with scabs. He gaped at the wounds in horror, seeming to understand at last how deep was the cave he had entered.

"He's trying to figure out how to fuck you," Arturo murmured urgently. "That's all he's thinking, I promise you." Then he opened his mouth wide, showing where the teeth had been pulled. Jack shut his eyes, and the aristocrat continued, "But I want to thank you for seducing my wife."

Jack blinked, his head hunching into his shoulders. He looked a bit tortured himself, all of a sudden. Duran gripped his shirt and spoke with passionate sincerity. "I mean it," he said. "It's like water—or the blackest coffee. All that anger kept me going. Sometimes when it was bad"—he fell back exhausted against the cot, gasping, and yet there was a smile on his face, unbelievably cold and vindictive—"the only way to keep from losing my mind was to concentrate on the ways to kill you!''

Jack Weil stared at Arturo Duran, accepting the savage disdain of the man he had unwittingly cuckolded. And he saw something in Duran's eyes that went beyond the broken rebel, the tortured aristocrat clinging to life with the last shreds of his pride. Worn down as he was, with no road out of the war zone, it was as if Arturo was begging Jack to feed a dying fire.

Jack smiled like a poker player with kings over jacks. ''Yeah, she's a hell of a lay,'' he declared softly. Of course they both knew it was a game—humiliating to the brutalized figure on the cot, painful to the interrogator, but necessary all the same. Where every card was a matter of life and death, winner take all. ''And you know something, amigo? I hope you don't make it. 'Cause then she's mine, free and clear. *Comprende?*''

Duran's eyes flared with hatred. A fleck of foam appeared at the corners of his lips, the spit he couldn't summon up a minute before. But instead of spitting, he choked out a question. ''Does she—does she know I'm alive?''

Jack laughed, a dry one-note laugh of vast superiority. ''She buried you, man,'' he retorted, turning on his heel so he wouldn't have to witness the flinch of the other's pain.

He strode from the shed, looking neither right nor left at the guards, but making his swift way back through the colonel's orchard. The sky was still shot with the last pearl of twilight, stars winking on like Christmas lights in the branches. As Jack emerged from the trees he saw the tall and elegant figure of the colonel, waiting in the courtyard outside the kitchen.

The yellow glow of the kitchen lights illuminated his costume change. Now he was crisp in his dress uniform, fussing at the ribbons on his tunic. He began to speak as soon as the gambler came into view. ''Make it fast, Jack,'' he said briskly. ''He's like meat going bad, that one. He won't keep.''

Jack nodded curtly. ''Have him at his house, Colonel.

That means cleaned up and nicely dressed." He lifted his wrist and made a show of studying his watch. "At midnight, shall we say? Don't worry, the money will be there. But I'll need till then to get it together."

The colonel seemed positively eager. "And the visa?" he asked impatiently.

"You'll go to the American embassy tomorrow morning," Jack replied sternly. "Just ask for Chigwell. He'll have it all ready."

He walked away from the colonel without so much as a good-bye, hoping it didn't show that the only card in his hand was the joker, wild as ever.

At the presidential palace the glow of Christmas wouldn't go away. A stream of limousines and European town cars crowded the circular drive, inching toward the glittering portico, where footmen waited to lead the guests in. The Christmas tree was ablaze as ever in the garden before the palace as the guests alighted from their cars. The women were dressed in long gowns, usually black or white, depending on the jewels they favored for the evening. Rubies and emeralds were very popular for the holidays, though diamonds were never wrong in Havana. And of course there couldn't have been a safer place to wear them, with half of Batista's army stationed on the grounds.

Many of the Cuban men who escorted them were in full-dress army and navy uniforms, all their ribbons and medals on view, red sashes across their hearts. These strutting military men seemed to make it a point not to glance at the sandbagged terraces at every corner of the palace. They refused to look up at the parapets, where the shadowy outlines of soldiers crouching with their rifles ready could be seen. They left their limos and Rollses to the care of their chauffeurs, ignoring the armored trucks stationed at the palace gates.

A party was a party, after all. The New Year beckoned with good champagne and caviar, and here at least the reigning powers of Cuba could be permitted the nice illusion that the party would go on forever.

The night was alive with revelers, in fact—as if the whole city had been hiding too long behind closed blinds. Bobby Duran could hear them in the street below Jack's apartment, careening through the colonial quarter in open cars, singing and passing bottles. She sat on the sofa tensely, waiting, too distracted to listen to the radio. Suddenly the telephone rang, and she jumped, staring at it as the first ring ended, praying there would be no second ring.

But there was: it rang and rang, mocking her till she wanted to scream. And when it stopped, she put her face in her hands and began to weep with frustration. The New Year's shouting in the street below was no distraction at all. There were no more parties left for her in Cuba. She sat there like a wallflower, as if no one would ever ask her to dance again.

Down at the marina, the man called Willy stood on the dock staring at his watch, counting the minutes to midnight. A young man in boating whites stood by him, silent and attentive. In the slip beside them was a sleek motor yacht, sixty feet with its engines idling. With its running lights ablaze, it seemed to hover on the water like a ghostly lantern. It wasn't at all clear what sort of party was going on here as shadowy figures scuttled about with their luggage, making their way to a night passage.

But then, everyone had his own way of marking the end of time. Some blew horns, and some got drunk. There was no right way of doing it. The last tropical night was alive with possibilities. Some had guns in their pockets, and some had guns in their mouths. The only thing to figure was how to go out with a bang. At midnight the churches would do what they always did, ring out the old and ring in the new. A man still had to make his own separate peace.

There was no telling what Jack Weil was doing in Chinatown. A few short streets of garish neon, paper-dragon kites arching over the intersections—all sorts of intricate games were played here, but not poker. And yet the green

Cadillac sat at the curb, Jack sitting pensively behind the wheel, watching the street dancers cavorting like exiles from the Peking Opera.

Even over the tooting of New Year's horns, he could hear the distant rumble of explosions, a different sort of revelry entirely. He reached into the glove compartment and pulled out a pearl-handled penknife. He tossed it up and caught it, then slipped it into his pocket as he got out of the car. He moved swiftly up the street, weaving his way through the Asian crowd, no more alien here in this ghetto than he was in all the rest of the foreign ports of Havana. As a gambler, he made it a point to be a man without a country.

At the corner of the street ablaze with paper lanterns, an elderly Chinese man smiled at the night, his arms tucked in his sleeves like an ancient sage. For him the night of revelry would usher in the Year of the Dog, and he seemed to be filled with contentment, pure as a monk who lived on grain and water. When he saw the gambler approach, he bowed with deep respect, catching Jack off guard. The gambler nodded his head in return.

The old man smiled his most Buddhist-like smile and said, "You like very young girl, Charlie? Some enchanted evening? For you very cheap, and she go all night."

Jack shook his head no and kept on walking, smiling grimly in silent prayer for all the sages and philosophers of Havana. He was looking for something very special, though he couldn't read one character from the next in the squiggles of neon Mandarin. He glanced in the windows of dirty cafés and fortune-tellers, shops full of worthless junk. He'd know the place when he found it, though, because he'd been there once before—on the other side of the world.

It was an hour closer to midnight when the Caddy glided to rest at the curb in front of the apartment building. As Jack stepped out of the car he seemed a little slow, almost punchy. He moved heavily across the sidewalk and through the archway into the inner courtyard. As he turned toward his staircase he caught sight of La Polaca, rolling a battered garbage can across the tiled court in the direction of the alley. He would have gladly slipped upstairs without a confrontation, but suddenly she saw him.

She stopped in a stunned silence, letting the garbage can tip over on the ground. It was hard to say which was more intense, her terror or her shame. She raised her arms in a helpless shrug, then seemed to huddle in fear of a beating as Jack moved toward her. She covered her face with her hands and whimpered.

Jack reached out and embraced her quaking shoulders, making a hushing sound as she gasped to keep from sobbing. "It's okay, it's okay," he whispered, like a son comforting a war-weary mother, without any judgment of her betrayal. They were all doing the best they could, and what was done was done. The landlady bit her lip and held her tears, pushing him away, knowing how precious his time was.

He turned and trotted up the stairs, one hand holding the wall to steady him. As he clicked the key in the lock to open the door, he felt a corresponding click in his heart, only there a door was shutting.

He'd barely entered, and Bobby was in his arms, gathering him close. She was breathless with relief as her mouth sought his, kissing blindly and trying to talk between the kisses. "What happened? I was so worried. The telephone kept ringing and I—"

"It's all right," he whispered, swallowing hard, still shaking the daze from his head.

"We have a boat?" she asked, anxiously searching his face.

"Yes—no problem." He tried to smile, but his jaw felt numb and rubbery, as if he'd just come from the dentist. "Everything's fine."

She laughed nervously, standing away from him and pointing to her blouse, the same white silk she'd worn the night they met on the boat. "I washed this and dried it in the oven!" she declared, mocking herself. She was manic from being so long alone. "Well, *almost* dry," she corrected. "But you don't have an iron, do you?" She leaned up and kissed him again, as delirious as a schoolgirl. "It's so wrinkled!"

"It looks . . . fine," he replied soberly, unable to match her giddy mood. "No, I don't have an iron," he said with a shake of his head. "I . . . never had an iron."

"Oh well," she scoffed, tossing her hair, "I can get new things in Miami." He nodded, his eye catching sight of the paper umbrella on the table. "When are we going?" she asked, aching with suspense.

"Uh . . . there's one more thing to do."

"Then do it," she pleaded impatiently. "Do it."

He gazed into her eyes for the first time. "I will," he said in a tone that was both tender and wounded, as if something hadn't quite healed yet.

She saw it in his face, but wouldn't admit what she saw. "Is it a big boat?" she asked cheerfully. "*Ocean*-going?"

"Uh—no, I don't think so. No, it's not exactly ocean-going." And to cover the queer flutter in his voice, the awkwardness of his clumsy hands, he slipped them around her waist and tried to return her kisses with an urgency equal to hers.

But now she needed to know more. She pulled her mouth from his, the crease of a frown between her eyes. "Well, at least we can take it to Miami, right? And then where?"

"Listen, Bobby—"

"It doesn't matter." She laughed, as if her heart were beating as rapidly as a hummingbird's wings. "Maybe from Miami we can take a train." He didn't know how to stop the rush of her heartbroken words, her yearning for something she'd already lost, any more than he knew how to tell the truth. "Yes—a long train trip," she continued breathlessly. "In a compartment, very, very private. Not even worry about where we get off." She laughed again. "Maybe never!"

"I used to like trains," he declared softly, but even the gentleness couldn't mask the tone that shivered her blood, the lonely cry of fate. He started again, gripping her shoulders: "Listen, kiddo—"

She buried her face in his chest, stubborn as a child. "People don't say that anymore," she said, pouting.

"Listen, will you!"

"It's from the twenties—I never heard anyone say it before." She was crying and didn't know why. He pulled her roughly against him, as if he would smother the talking out of her. Of course she knew better, but she said it anyway, grasping at straws: "Are we going to bed?"

"No."

She nodded against his breastbone, surrendering at last. "That's right—you have something to do. I guess you'd better go do it. There isn't much time. . . ." She could speak no more. The silence that lay like a desert between them could only fill up with the truth now.

"You know," he said tenderly, stroking her hair, "if I'd never met you, I'd have lived my life . . ." And he shrugged, helpless to put into words the piece that would have been missing. Instead he gritted his teeth and spoke his own sentence, sure as a firing squad. "He's alive."

She lifted her head from his chest and looked at him, utterly expressionless, just as she looked the morning she left the prison, when the torture was finally over.

"Arturo is alive," Jack repeated. And when she said nothing in reply, he blundered on. "I just saw him. Ten minutes ago. At your house. They just brought him there."

She put a hand to her forehead, as if she was dizzy. His hand about her waist was the only thing holding her up, so he left it there, but the embrace was mute and passionless now, deliberately so. He was trying to allow her as much distance as he could.

Then suddenly the hand at her forehead lashed out and stung his cheek. And again, slapping so hard that the trace of her fingers was printed on his flesh. As she swung a third time he snatched her hand and stopped her, drawing her close in a real embrace, for the distance didn't work.

"There's nothing to say, Bobby." His voice was a hollow murmur, like the sound of somebody trapped in a cave with the air all used up.

185

She straightened and stood away from him, one hand touching the wall to steady herself. "For a moment," she declared flatly, gazing toward the window. "For one . . . moment I was lost. In a sweet place . . . but lost." She almost smiled, except the muscles didn't quite work. "Thanks," she added curtly, averting her eyes, then turned and started carefully toward the door.

"Wait," he whispered. She stopped, but didn't dare look back at him. "I'll take you there."

Now she looked, and shook her head slowly. "No." A moment of helpless silence, and then she repeated it. "No. Nowhere."

The ship had finally docked, the passage only a memory. They looked at each other as the gangplank rolled into place, ready to be strangers again. The gambler smiled, the bravest thing he could think of. "So long, pal," he said.

She turned abruptly, still unsteady on her feet, as if she couldn't get used to the feel of dry land, too solid. She pulled the door open and slipped out, shutting it ever so softly behind her, not wanting to wake the dead.

And Jack Weil stood alone at the brink of his destination, not sure why he had taken the journey at all. Instinctively, like a nervous twitch, he reached to the table for his deck of cards, prepared to deal himself a new hand. His fingers grazed the paper umbrella, frail as a butterfly's wing. He watched it rock softly, going nowhere, hypnotized by its brief flutter of motion, back and forth. Watched it till it was still again.

And didn't touch the cards.

══════ XIII ══════

THE BALLROOM OF the palace was lit by a thousand candles, and over the long banquet tables a snowfall of sequins glittered, a field of dazzle. On the apron stage a giant conga line twisted and furled like a sea dragon. The moment was now as the president's expensive guests began to shout "Happy New Year!" The white-tailed orchestra, imported tonight from the Lido, swung into "Auld Lang Syne" with a samba beat.

A captain in dress blues darted in from the foyer, making his way among the tables, not joining in with the singing. As he reached Colonel Menocal, the chief of torture was raising a glass of champagne, ready to rhapsodize about the dawn of the year. He looked irritably at the rattled captain, ready to torture his own men if they made a wrong move.

"He's fled!" blurted the captain. "Batista has fled!" Heads at nearby tables turned. The singing began to die. "The president is gone!" cried the captain, not caring anymore who heard.

Menocal stood with his glass still raised, a look of utter bewilderment on his face. But the crowd had already started to move in a wave, sweeping from the tables and pushing toward the doors. The band still played, because they were being paid to, but it was only a matter of seconds before the whole room was herding in panic, as if someone had just shouted "Fire!"

They poured out onto the palace steps, terrified and defenseless in their ballgowns and tuxedos. They shouted for their cars, but nobody seemed to be in charge anymore. All the footmen had vanished. A white-haired planter and his new young wife rushed across the driveway to their black Mercedes limo, only to have the chauffeur slam the door in their faces and pull away. Another millionaire, with enough land in the west of the island to call it his own country, discovered his Rolls filling up with strangers. He shouted indignantly, but to no avail, and his bodyguard was nowhere to be seen. The Rolls lurched off into the night.

The night was chaos everywhere now, as if the flight of the president was the final straw. The streets were full of crushing mobs, the old year dead and the new one already a nightmare. There was no more public transportation, no more taxis. The people dressed for parties mixed with the people dressed for revolution, but none of them seemed to know where to go or how to get there.

Bobby pushed her way through the madness of the streets, dazed still from her last encounter with Jack, and somehow comforted by the upheaval all around her. She stopped on a corner, huddling against a street lamp as the crowd poured around her, and watched across the street as a group of young men and women trashed a small casino. One by one they brought out the slot machines, smashing them into the gutter. Bobby tried to remember what the revolution was for and where it was all going to take them. But it was too noisy to think.

Several streets away, Jack Weil was pushing his way against the tide of another mob. He was totally self-contained, isolated and lonely but somehow in control. The masses in the street didn't frighten him at all or deter him from his mission as he headed for the Lido. Trucks roared by with hand-painted banners, proclaiming a victory nobody understood yet. Loudspeakers commanded in Spanish for the crowd to be calm, but nobody listened.

As Jack crossed a wide intersection toward the boulevard of hotels, students were directing the traffic, but playfully, like clowns. Along the curb the parking meters were being ripped out of the concrete and smashed against the pavement, spilling their pennies. The revelers scrambled for coins like urchins.

Big cars sped by on the boulevard, crammed with major and minor Batistianos, still in their New Year's finery. News of the president's flight had spread like a lethal virus. All the bureaucrats and functionaries had raced home from their parties to grab their portable safes, the already-packed suitcases, the furs and holy statues. Now they were all bound for the marina, honking and shrieking to clear the crowds from the streets.

To Jack as he walked up the sidewalk toward the Lido, the Batistianos in their fancy cars looked just like the fleeing peasants from Santa Clara, all their worldly goods perched on donkeys. The same desperation to cut their losses. And the gambler could only imagine the pandemonium at the marina; too many fat cats and too few boats. He looked at his watch and knew that Willy would wait no longer. Even now the last lines were being cast off, and the yacht was slipping away. So good-bye to that dream.

The Lido doorman was gone. Inside, the lobby was practically empty, except for a half-drunk couple screaming at each other beside the parrot cage. It seemed a little late to be arguing about whose fault it all was, but maybe it just felt good to scream. There was no one behind the reception desk, and Jack could see the unmanned switchboard in the glassed-in booth beyond, blinking like a Christmas tree, nobody getting through.

As he walked through the portal into the casino the floor men and dealers were feverishly trying to haul away the slot machines and roulette wheels. A few people still wandered around looking to lose a little money, but the place had ceased to be open for business. Jack watched the desperate activity of the floor men, packing up the show to take it on the road. Then he lifted his eyes to the landing at the top of the double-curved staircase—

And there was Joe Volpi, surveying it all as usual, the captain on the bridge. He wore his Midwest accountant's suit and his black-rim glasses, colorless to a fault. Jack strolled over to the foot of the stairs and looked up at the casino manager. He gave Volpi a mock salute.

"I been calling you," said Joe, not sore about it or holding a grudge. "Would you believe it, Jack? These guys are playing. Right now." He pointed a finger at the ceiling, meaning the penthouse. "So I guess it's not too late."

"Yeah, it is," drawled the gambler, mounting the steps to Volpi's level. "It's 1959, Joe. As late as it's ever gonna get."

Volpi nodded slowly. "Where's the lady?"

Jack shrugged. "With her husband. Where else?"

"Ah, nobility. I always said you're a noble guy, Jack. A regular prince." Volpi slipped his fingers under his glasses, rubbing his eyes. As far as Jack knew, Volpi had never slept in all his life. "We're nothing but cocks—right, Jack? Leading our brains around. Just like the nuns used to warn us."

Suddenly below them there was a terrific crash. They turned to look, just in time to see the mob pouring through the plate-glass windows of the casino. They came like a tidal wave, pouring in to wreck the place. Stripping the sconces from the walls, jumping to pull down the chandeliers. The floor men had managed to remove perhaps a third of the tables and equipment, but now the rest of it was abandoned to the frenzy of the revolution. The mob smashed the orchestra stage and heaved over the bar, passing the bottles around to fuel its drunken glee.

Volpi wore the most curious expression, as if he was wholly separated from the mayhem. He studied it like a scholar, peering through his glasses, then turned to Jack with the old sour smile. "Looks like fun," he observed dryly, then made a motion as if to doff an invisible hat. "Time to leave, Jack."

Yet neither one moved for a moment more, watching it all with fascination. Some of the pillagers were students, and some were workers. They were hauling everything out through the gaping holes of the broken windows, smashing the slots on the boulevard. The street was littered with chips and coins, the pot of gold at the end of the rainbow. The first time anyone had beaten the house at the Lido in years.

Jack Weil and Joe Volpi looked at each other one last time, nodding and winking like a couple of boulevardiers. Time to leave, indeed. Volpi turned on his heel and headed back to his office, to pick up the worst of the evidence before he disappeared. Jack trotted down the steps and skirted the edge of the wrecked casino, heading for the lobby doors.

Neither man required a souvenir of the place or so much as a backward glance. For the place was never the point. Wherever they landed next—prison or exile, feast or famine—the cards would come out, and the whole thing would start all over again. Both of them knew it, and so did the rest of their kind. Havana and the Lido had always been temporary quarters. The game was the thing, and it stayed alive by being a moving target.

In the gilded morning light of the new year, the plaza that fronted the Malecon seawall was weirdly peaceful, as if all of the night's revelers were hung over and still in bed. The café-bars along the front were open but mostly deserted. The green Caddy was practically the only car for several blocks.

As Jack walked up to the outdoor tables the waiter was swabbing the sidewalk with a string mop. He grinned at the gambler in recognition, or perhaps he was just glad to have a customer. He hissed and scooted a sleeping cat from one of the tables, then gestured for Jack to sit down. It was the very same table where he'd sat with Bobby, the morning he'd sprung her from jail. Perhaps it was just another co-incidence, the waiter choosing at random. Jack didn't ask. He sat down quietly and looked at the sea, its vast indifferent beauty squandered in foam on the tropical shore.

A liberated military truck raced along the plaza, the bed of it filled with kids wildly waving a homemade banner. A loudspeaker mounted on the truck's roof exhorted all within earshot to honor the general strike. Cuba, Jack thought sardonically, had been having a general strike for as long as he'd lived here. He smiled as the waiter placed a bowl of milky coffee in front of him. Then noticed another man having a drink at a table across the café: Chigwell.

The fey correspondent was reading a book as he sipped his hair-of-the-dog. He was sporting his regulation blazer and button-down shirt, ready for lunch at the club—any club would do. Jack neither ignored him nor waved to get his attention, for the meeting was fated either way. The gambler drank his coffee, and a minute later Marion was standing beside his table, scooping the shock of hair out of his eyes, a dithering smile on his face.

"Things went well, Jack?"

"Yeah, just great," Jack replied, squinting into the sun behind Chigwell's head. "And you, pal? You win or lose?"

Chigwell laughed dryly. "It's never over. So we never lose."

"Then you never win either."

"Like poker, I guess," the correspondent mocked, the first time Jack had ever heard him sound superior, or anything else but fawning.

"Oh, by the way," Jack said lightly, "Menocal's probably looking for you at the embassy right about now. And where *you* off to?"

Chigwell's grin was bright with promise. "Far East," he retorted, thrilled as a schoolboy spinning a globe. "I'm going to start a new book. *The Cuisine of Indo-China.*"

Jack frowned. "Where's Indo-China? I mean, I know but I don't know. . . ."

"Long way away, Jack," Chigwell assured him, making a vague gesture out to the sparkling blue of the sea. "Maybe I'll see you there someday. So long, Jack."

"See you, Marion." Jack nodded as the other strolled away. Then he pulled out a deck of cards from his jacket pocket and spread them face down on the table, as if he was about to do a card trick. A shadow fell on the table, and he spoke without looking up. "Pick a card," he said cheerfully, mocking himself.

Then he did look up—at the flashing gold of the sun, and Bobby Duran standing in its radiance. One or the other nearly blinded him, but he didn't flinch or look away. It was only a beat of silence, but the moment seemed to hang, suspended, the way it always did with them. "How come you're not celebrating?" she said at last.

He shrugged. "Wasn't my fight." The glare was so bright behind her that he couldn't quite see her beauty in all its unbearable detail. He preferred it this way. "Where is he?" he asked casually.

She moved a step closer, away from the sun, and now her features were vivid and sharp. She glanced across the plaza, up the hill toward the crowded pulsing center of the city. "With them," she replied simply. She wore the same white silk blouse, but someone had ironed it for her.

"How come *you're* not with them?" He couldn't keep the bristle of a challenge out of his voice.

"Oh, I'll join them later," she said, and then something in her eyes shivered with memory. "But I . . . knew you'd be here."

He laughed his one-note laugh. "Funny, *I* didn't know it till twenty minutes ago."

She looked down at the half-empty bowl of coffee. She smiled. "Were you waiting for me?"

"All my life," he answered softly.

The silence that followed was no refuge. It seemed as if one or the other would have to bolt, chalking the final meeting up to an error of fate. She clutched her bag and shifted her feet. Jack reached up as if he would caress her hair—then snapped his fingers next to her ear and opened his palm before her eyes, revealing a coin.

"That old trick," she scoffed with a curl of ironic disdain, refusing to be impressed.

"Uh-uh," he replied, shaking his head. "Used to be a quarter. This is a half." He flipped the fifty-cent piece up in the air, caught it, and slapped it on the back of his other hand. He nodded for her to call it.

She looked away, as if his games were only making the

whole thing harder. "Where are you going, Jack?"

"Don't know." He shrugged, lifting his hand to look at the coin. It was tails. "California, maybe."

She nodded distantly, gazing at the diamond sheen of light on the sea. There was something inexpressibly sad about it, like a ship had disappeared over the horizon while she wasn't looking. "How did you get Menocal to let him go?"

"I bluffed," he replied succinctly, his fingertips grazing the fan of cards on the table. He knew she wanted all the details, and then she was going to thank him. The gratitude would have been the worst, like wishing a gambler too much luck. The next words came out of nowhere, a freak roll of the dice. "Come with me now," he said.

"I can't." The response was instantaneous, as if she knew it by heart, waiting for just that dare. Her eyes never left the horizon, refusing it as much as him. "I can't," she repeated, and this time it sounded far less certain, or perhaps she was answering a question of her own.

But her next gesture was very decisive. She tore her gaze from the ocean and stared at his arm on the table. Then reached down and gripped his wrist in one hand and pushed up his sleeve with the other. A length of white gauze was wrapped about the forearm, right where the diamond used to be. He was watching her face the whole time, so he saw how completely she wasn't surprised. She stroked her fingers lightly along the bandage, a woman who'd learned how to fight by binding wounds.

"You don't quite believe what you know," she declared with the tenderest irony. "Do you, Jack Weil?"

His smile was no less open for being tinged with resignation and regret. "Oh yes, I do," he replied emphatically, without the ghost of a hedge or a bluff. "I love you, Bobby. And I also know that a butterfly can beat its wings over a flower in China—and cause a hurricane in the Caribbean. I *believe* that, Bobby. I've been in this game long enough to know they can even calculate the odds." His eyes were locked on hers, and neither of them wavered. "It just isn't likely," he continued softly. The pain was unmistakable, the aching dryness of his blue gaze worse than tears. "And it takes so long."

She was still cradling his arm, and the hand on his wrist appeared to be taking his pulse. He stood up from the table, flashing a sudden grin, shaking off the melancholy reverie. He seemed determined to make their farewell something ineffably casual, even jaunty. "Hey, you know how to find me, huh?"

Bobby nodded, her careful impish smile the mirror of his. "Walk into any casino," she said, precise as if reciting a lesson. "Look for a high-stakes poker player, and ask him, 'Where's Weil?' "

"Right." He winked and gave her a brief embrace and let her go, all so quick she barely had time to register it. He was trotting across the boulevard to the green Cadillac parked by the seawall. She could feel he'd put something in her hand, but didn't look at it yet. She watched him get into the convertible and swing it in a wide U-turn, heading toward the ferry slip. He tossed her an easy wave, and she returned it, as careless as he.

Then she looked down and opened her hand, where he'd slipped her a single card: the jack of hearts. She lifted her eyes to the water, looking more than ever like a solitary figure on a pier, watching the last of her dreams sail off. Then she tossed her hair and turned inland, walking uphill with a resolute stride, back over the border into the new world—the country of incalculable hope.

The *Suzi*'s engines were running at a deep throb as she churned in her slip, as if impatient to go. The straggle of cars on the dock entered the portal of the auto deck, and the very last one was the green Caddy. The customs crew was at skeleton strength, detaining no one. It was all unspoken as the lines uncoiled from the pilings that this was the final journey along the sea lane between Havana and Key West. The last scheduled departure, for today all the schedules were being rewritten.

The ferry lounge was filling up with the odds and ends of exile as the ship's horn blew its double blast. There were Cuban officers in civilian clothes who'd paid a life's savings for the twelve-dollar fare. Various American businessmen, looking cranky and cheated as they sat brooding over their sample cases. And several motley tourists, the ones too dumb to get out last week, because the hotel bill was all prepaid.

The morning drinkers moved right to the boomerang bar, ordering up their first rum fizzes and vodka tonics. A few moved like magnets to the round table by the wheelhouse door, sniffing out a poker game. With a few brief grunts and nods, there were four of them sitting and ready—a salesman in sharkskin, a lounge singer from one of the big hotels, an American sailor, and a too-tanned tourist.

Jack Weil stepped in through the double doors off the main deck, and the tourist caught his eye. "Care to play some cards?" he asked the gambler, a bit too eagerly.

"I don't know," Jack replied with a vague, indifferent smile. "What're you playing?"

"Deuces and one-eyed jacks wild," came the cocky answer. Bronx by way of Miami.

Jack's eyebrows perked a little. "And what's the ante?"

"Quarter," the sailor replied curtly, pouring a handful of change on the table.

"Pretty steep." Jack grinned, grabbing a chair. If he was laughing at anything, it was himself.

"Listen, pal," drawled the salesman, "we're all just damn lucky to be outta this pisshole. . . ."

There was a jerk as the *Suzi* nudged out of her slip, and then the throbbing began to fade as the engines moved her forward. A deck of blue Bicycle cards appeared on the table, and they were cut for the deal. Jack cut the ace of spades. Now he began to shuffle, his hands growing supple, as if the blood had come back into them. The ship's horn blew a last mournful good-bye to the glittering chaos of Havana, and the gambler started to deal.

Epilogue: 1963

THE BEACH AT the butt end of Key West was silent by the time dusk fell. Even the terminal romantics had gone home once the sunset show was over. Besides, it wasn't exactly a picture-postcard place, with the rotting timbers poking out of the tidal eddy and the sand strewn with the detritus of rubber-tire bumpers and rusty winches. Three years ago it was a ferry slip, the jumping-off point for the ninety-mile trip to Havana. Now it was just another casualty of war, too dangerous for swimming or walking barefoot.

The distant headlights of a car swept over the dunes, approaching along the crumbling road. The sand and saw grass had more or less covered the site of the old parking lot, but the slowly moving car seemed to know where it was going. A black-and-white '63 T-Bird, all muscle and confidence. It pulled to the lip of the pavement and stopped, dousing its lights. And out of it stepped Jack Weil, looking as prosperous in his white linen suit as the car he was driving these days. He walked out onto the ghost of the ferry slip, careful as an archaeologist, straight across the sand as if he was walking down a pier.

I do this sometimes—drive down from Miami. It's not that I expect her. The ferry hasn't run in years. Not since the revolution . . . .

He looked south over the dying pewter gleam of the sea, toward Havana. Suddenly his head swiveled a quarter turn, caught by the flash of a ship's lights, miles offshore to the south/southeast. He grinned as if he'd just drawn a pair of queens.

But it happens sometimes. I see a boat offshore, and something . . . goes faster in me. Hope, I suppose. And then I wonder if she keeps me to herself. . . .

The evening breeze had sprung up out of the Gulf, rustling his blond hair. He flipped up his collar and shoved his hands in his pockets, riding the tail wind of memory.

Somebody came out of Havana—told me Baby Hernandez was the big winner that night. Lives in New Jersey now. And I got a postcard from Volpi. Picture of the Sistine Chapel but postmarked Santo Domingo. So I guess he's still in the game—running things for Meyer. You never really know who's gonna survive. . . .

The ship's lights fluttered and vanished, dipping over the horizon—going, not coming. The gambler threw back his shoulders and squinted to see the first star in the sky, but he didn't know what it was called. He definitely looked like a survivor himself, but a solitary one. Then he turned on his heel and headed back to the T-Bird, pushed by an inner clock that told him the night games were about to start.

I'm doing real well these days—way ahead. But hell, why not, it's a whole new decade. We got our own revolution going up here. And I always sit with my back to the wall so I can watch who comes in. You never know from one day to the next. Somebody looking for a little luck . . . somebody blown off course . . . .

He climbed into the T-Bird and swung it in a wide U-turn on the sand-blown asphalt. In a moment its taillights were already winking and fading in the gathering twilight, homing north to Miami.

You never know what your chances are till you start to play. Anything could happen. After all, this is hurricane country. . . .